WHEN IN ROME . . .

"Believe it or not, we are throwing a party for you," Scipio said as the ship rose into the sky.

"For me?"

"For the most important crosstime traveler ever to visit Rome. Don't look so surprised. What we are celebrating is the glorious day on which you saved the Roman Republic, Mr. Strang, by assassinating Gaius Julius Caesar!"

Books by John Barnes

The Man Who Pulled Down the Sky
Sin of Origin
Orbital Resonance
A Million Open Doors
Mother of Storms
Kaleidoscope Century
One for the Morning Glory

The Timeline Wars series:

Patton's Spaceship*
Washington's Dirigible*
Caesar's Bicycle*

By Buzz Aldrin and John Barnes

Encounter with Tiber

*Published by HarperPrism

Caesar's Bicycle

TIMELINE WARS #3

JOHN BARNES

HarperPrism
A Division of HarperCollinsPublishers

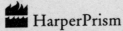
HarperPrism
A Division of HarperCollins*Publishers*
10 East 53rd Street, New York, N.Y. 10022-5299

ISBN 0-06-105661-8

Cover illustration by Vincent DiFate

First printing: October 1997

Printed in the United States of America

Visit HarperPrism on the World Wide Web at
http://www.harpercollins.com

❖ 10 9 8 7 6 5 4 3 2 1

*This one's for Ashley Grayson—
my agent,
my friend
the guy Calvin probably grew up to be.
With a sense of relief that he will probably never
get his hands on any such hardware
as is contained in this book.*

1

Chrysamen was looking sad, and since she has huge dark eyes, she's good at looking sad. Though we were running just a little late if we wanted to get to the Met without rushing, I knew, after some years of marriage, that it was better to talk about whatever it was than to try to brush it off until there was time to talk about it, so I sat down next to her, and said, "Is something the matter?"

"Not a lot, just a minor case of frustration." She tossed her dark curls with her hands and shook her head, as if working out a kink in her neck.

"Anything you want to talk about?"

"Oh, just realizing I'm probably never going to lose back the three pounds I put on after we had Perry, and that even if I'm physically a lot younger, I'm almost fifty."

I shook my head. "On the same scale, I'm fifty-three. That's what a lot of time travel will do for you. And in this timeline we're both still under forty, legally; heck, in *this* timeline you're minus seven hundred something. Figure that if the life-extension drugs work as well on us as they do on Ariadne Lao—"

Mistake to mention our boss. Ariadne is a charming, pleasant, usually polite person, but there was once a slight spark of interest between us—long before I met Chrys, mind you—and Ariadne *is* pretty stunning, thanks to the long-life drugs, even though she must be past eighty. Consequently "Ariadne Lao" is an extremely bad thing to mention when Chrys is feeling unattractive.

A few years of marriage gives you enough experience to recognize that you've said something stupid, when it's only a *little* bit too late. I put an arm around Chrys, and said, "Look, we're actually only about a fifth of the way through our life spans. I mean, through what our life spans would be if we were in a normal line of work. We both might be shot dead next week, of course."

"You certainly know how to cheer a girl up."

"Well, damn it, it's hard to work up sympathy for you when half the women on the planet would kill to look like you."

"That's more like it," she said, smiling, and stood up and stretched. That was a view I enjoyed a lot; she had on all the lingerie but hadn't yet put on her dress (one of those little black things that seem to be part of the dress code for women at the opera). She has a mass of dark curly hair, high cheekbones and a full mouth, very light brown skin, and an athlete's body that I know, in several different ways, is all hard muscle, no matter how well shaped it is.

"And as far as self-confidence is concerned, Mark, that leer from you is all I needed."

"I am not leering."

"You're right. It's more like the way a lion looks at a gazelle."

"Rrrrr."

"Not now, dear, but hold the thought. You look pretty terrific in the tux, yourself." She slipped into the dress and turned to be zipped up, and I figured we'd gotten past this little attack of the blues with no harm done, but then she said, "I was just thinking . . . well, it may be silly."

"If it bothers you, it's not silly," I said, pulling up her zipper.

"Well, it's just . . . you and I are doing our part, certainly, in the war against the Closers. And ATN seems to be doing pretty well in the fight, though with millions of fronts it's hard to tell. But even if we're really clobbering them, as far as I can see, we'll still be fighting them a thousand years from now. You and I will grow old and die—or get shot or blown up—and so will Porter and Perry . . . and the war will go on, and more people will be born and grow old and die, and the war will go on, and maybe we'll be as far in the past as the time of Christ before the war is won."

"You can't let yourself think like that," I said. "We have a lot to do, and we're just two Crux Ops; ATN has thousands like us, and we just do our parts and hope for the best. I'm sure somewhere there are generals or field marshals or something who are paid to worry about that, but it's not our lookout."

She sighed. "Oh, I don't mean I think it's being badly run, and I know as well as you do that it's the fight in front of us, and the *next* one, not the last one, we have to worry about. All I mean is . . . well, why haven't they sent back word about who wins? Does the war just go on forever?"

"Maybe they're afraid of changing the result by letting us know," I said. "We need to get moving if we're going to get to the opera in time for me to show you off to the other guys."

We had imposed a firm rule ages ago. Since this timeline is not aware of the war that rages across a million timelines, we don't discuss ATN business anywhere where we might be overheard. If you think waiters and cabbies are nosy about your marriage or your job, imagine what they'd be like about the fate of whole universes. So we went to the opera, chatted mostly about my ward Porter Brunreich's career (at eighteen she was having a very successful European tour, and nowadays she was mostly performing her own compositions for organ and piano), our three-year-old son Perry (we both agree he's a genius, and handsome, too), and that sort of thing. We were pleased to note that the cab driver agreed with us.

Placido Domingo was wonderful as always, *Rigoletto* was terrific (the director and designers stuck to the story), and for that matter the coffee and cheesecake afterward were great. (Sure, Lindy's is a cliché, but they got to be a cliché by being worth going back to.)

Chrys came from a timeline where opera had never developed—it was good that the special language chip behind the ear allowed her to speak English without an accent, because if anyone had asked her nationality, "Arabo-Polynesian" would undoubtedly have raised a lot of questions. Three days after she came here to marry me, she was idly playing with the radio when she hit WQED in Pittsburgh, the local classical station—and that was it. Hopeless addiction. There aren't a lot of Pittsburghers with season tickets at the Met—that's a lot of airplane tickets in addition—but we're two of them.

As Dad said to me, if you find you're married to a junkie, your choices are to try for a cure, which rarely works, or to take up the needle yourself. At least it was only opera she'd gotten hooked on. It could have been heavy metal.

I thought she'd forgotten all about her early case of the blues. But that evening, as I closed the door on our hotel room again, she said, "It's such a beautiful world, Mark. Yours, and the one I came from, and all the millions of others. And if there weren't Closers, we could open the gates between them and let more people see them all. I'm sure we'll win. I just wish we could win during my lifetime, or our children's. I'd like to be around to enjoy it."

"Me too," I said, surprising myself a little. I'd always been the much more eager killer of the two of us— Chrys came from a timeline that had been conquered by the Closers, and then liberated a couple of generations later by ATN forces, and you'd think she'd have more hate for them. But Chrys's people were largely pacifists when they were conquered, and the bitter war of liberation afterward had sickened them so much that there were only a few aberrant ones, like Chrys, who could bear fighting at all.

Me? I'd lost half my family, including my first wife, to them, and a lot of friends along the way, and there had been a time in my life when nothing gave me a rush of pleasure like pulling the trigger on a Closer bastard. When ATN agents—including Ariadne, the first Crux Op I'd ever met—had turned up and recruited me, shown me who was behind the terrorist group I was after, and armed me to hit back at them, I'd become a kind of killing machine for a while.

But that had been before Chrys, before the birth of our son . . . before a certain bitter fight on a blazing airship, when I had faced a version of myself from another timeline, a version that had gone to work for the Closers—and seen that hatred was *their* weapon, not ours, and that when you got down to the last moment of choice and the last ounce of will, it wasn't a match for plain, ordinary courage. I had seen the kind of broken, poisoned thing I could become, and turned away.

Mostly. The old feelings came back now and then, and if I occasionally found myself enjoying a battle with the Closers a bit more than was good for me, well, so it goes. Nobody changes overnight.

So I was more than a little surprised to realize that Chrys's ideas had gotten into me to that extent. I, too, could imagine a future where you could visit the thousands of beautiful things and places that exist across the many parallel timelines. There were timelines out there where Beethoven didn't go deaf, where Marlowe didn't die young and lived to be Shakespeare's great rival, where the great library at Alexandria was never burned.

There were dozens of different Parises, Athenses, New Yorks, Saigons—all beautiful in their different ways. There were timelines where there had never been human beings, where you could still find herds of buffalo that stretched farther than the eye could see, great herds of elephant and rhino in Africa, flocks of moas and dodoes. Worlds where elegant white cities shone in the wilderness, where you could walk from the equivalent of the Met right out into the equivalent of Yellowstone.

All of that was out there, just a quick flip of the time machines away—but every time a traveler crosses, the pulse can be registered in many other universes. Cross often enough, and the Closers get a fix on that timeline—and then suddenly they're there, vast armies pouring in out of nowhere, and another world falls beneath their iron heel, only to be won back at a cost of millions of lives and vast destruction. So travel between timelines is restricted, as much as we can, to timelines that they already know the location of, and those timelines are defended as heavily as can be managed.

Of all those wonderful doors, only a few can be opened . . . and only for emergency military purposes.

I knew how she felt; so much wonder, hardly any time for it. We could go anywhere and anywhen, but we had to spend all our time jumping into places where rude strangers shot at us.

"Well," I said, though the joke was feeble, "we'll just have to hurry up and win the war."

"Yeah, right." One great advantage of the ear gadgets is that you only have to move toward speaking the language gradually, but you don't make any mistakes on the way. Chrys's English was now as good as her Arabic and Attikan—and mine were equally good—and she said, "Yeah, right," with the true Pittsburgh spirit, the way that lets the world know that no one is going to fool *you*.

I stepped into the bathroom for a second, and when I came out she was removing the little black dress very slowly, which pretty much killed discussion for that night. Ever had a fantasy about sleeping with a beautiful female agent? I do every night—though there was a period of sharing responsibility for two o'clock feedings in there as well. The job's risky, but there are fringe benefits.

On a New York weekend, you're always running out of cash, which is probably why New York is so fond of tourists. So after breakfast in the Wellington's coffee shop, we went around the corner to a bank to get more. It was a pretty typical Saturday morning—everyone looking bored and a lot of huge-haired tellers with bright blue eye shadow desperately trying to pretend that they had a date for Saturday night, in order to keep away the guys who might figure the girl at the bank was the last possible chance. The security guards were a couple of bush-league rent-a-cops rather than off-duty NYPD, so the bank could save a few bucks on a time when there weren't likely to be many robbers.

I wondered about that idly. In our line of work, jumping into all sorts of violence all the time, you get such a habit of casing the joint that it's easier to do it than not to.

Maybe they figured all the robbers would be at home watching cartoons or something, because this place was really pretty wide-open. There was one amiable guard, a very young-looking man with a big nose, pasty white skin, and black hair, who was trying to talk to the rightmost teller, a girl whose hair was dyed platinum blond and piled into a huge meringue. The other guard was middle-aged, a black man with gray hair and mustache, and a distinct gut; the way he stood and shifted his weight suggested he also had a bad back, but at least his eyes were on the door and the customers. As I scanned him, he yawned. I noted also that I'd been looking at him for a while and he hadn't looked back or noticed he was being scanned.

This was one of those modern, friendly banks that have a lot of low tables and just a counter for the tellers, not one of the old 1920s ones that looked like a tough prison or maybe a fort, or one of the more recent ones that looked like a biolab where they expected every customer to be infected with something deadly.

"You're really checking the place out," Chrys muttered to me as we stood in line.

"It's something to do."

"Have you checked the four that just came in?" she muttered. "I know you see everything in New York, but it looks like a new flavor of everything."

What was coming in was one woman with thick butt-length red hair and the kind of body that men turn and stare at, wearing a tiny little sprayed-on white dress and heels halfway up to the sky, and with her were three dignified older guys in three-piece suits.

"Ha. They threw a party with the little lady last night and came up short on cash; now they're going to get some additional so they can pay her, probably so nobody comes around to threaten them. No big thing—"

As I said it, the girl turned from the men and clattered over toward the younger security guard and the teller he was trying to pick up. The teller had a clearly displayed CLOSED sign in front of her window and had been counting bills very slowly.

That was the first warning bell that went off in my head. If this was a high-priced good-time girl collecting from a bunch of johns, the last thing she was going to do was move away from them, until they paid her. Nobody heads for an obviously closed teller, not when the line is already long. And besides, she took two big clacking steps and deliberately shook her shoulders before she started out.

Which, aside from letting everyone in the room know she wasn't wearing a bra, also got almost everyone to stare at her, the women because most women stare at someone who is really overdoing it, the men because . . . well, you can imagine.

Anyway, she made enough noise for a cavalry troop

on a tap-dance floor as she crossed over to the guard and the teller. The teller looked up in obvious relief, clearly glad to have anything get the guy away from her, and the guy was busy staring holes in the woman's little white dress.

"Hand on your NIF?" I muttered to Chrys.

"Always. Ready when you are."

It so happens Chrys and I were both the kind of nasty kids for whom magicians hate to work birthday parties. You know how stage magic always works by getting people to look in one place while you do something somewhere else? Well, we were always the kids who were saying, "He's really putting it in his sleeve," "He moved it while he was waving the flowers," or "That's not the one you started with." And this woman's little routine was screaming, "Hey, look over here!" so naturally we were looking everywhere else, as unobviously as we could.

What I saw was one of the guys in the three-pieces stopping to tie his shoe by a potted plant—and getting into a perfect position to draw a pistol from an ankle holster and blow the younger guard away.

On the other side, she told me later, Chrys was seeing one of them heading over toward the manager's desk, and number three approaching the other guard as if to ask him a question, but also reaching into his jacket.

"Excuse me," their woman accomplice said, with that loud, cutting New York accent that goes right through crowd noise, "but I really need sex right now." The corner of my eye showed me that she had whipped the dress off and was now naked except for the heels. "Would anyone like to—" It was quite a list, but I was too busy to listen.

I put a NIF round into the wrist of the one I was

looking at before he quite got the pistol out of the ankle holster. Chrys nailed the guy with his hand in his jacket, and he hit the floor with an extrahard double thud—his head and the pistol. Then she got the one approaching the manager (who had just gotten up to deal with the disturbance, and appeared to be pretty perturbed by it, at least to judge from the way she strode toward the naked young woman) with a clean shot in the back of the neck, and he fell over, but he'd actually had time to draw his pistol.

NIF stands for Neural Induction Fléchette, which is the projectile it fires. The fléchette is a self-guiding dart, so small that on a sheet of white paper it looks like a dust grain or a gnat, that homes on body heat and flies at just below supersonic speeds. When it connects, it finds its way to a nerve, and does whatever it's programmed to do. Chrys and I usually set ours to knock the person unconscious for a few hours and then let him wake up slowly with the mother of all hangovers, but a NIF could do anything from making you itch all over to stopping your heart right then to giving you strong enough convulsions to break every bone in your body.

The projectile itself would dissolve in a few minutes, leaving no evidence that a doctor in our timeline would recognize. This was going to make *News of the Weird* for sure.

There was a long pause; the robbers' distraction had been so good that no one was noticing three unconscious men with guns just yet, because everyone was still gaping at the naked woman. She really wasn't all that pretty, I decided, just big in the chest and very made-up, and from the way the hair had slipped, I knew it was a wig.

I considered whacking her with the NIF, too, just for

tidiness and that aesthetically important sense of completion, but I figured it was too amusing to see what
she'd do now.

The NIF is almost silent—it makes a noise like an electric drill, but just for the instant that the tiny fléchette it
fires is going out the barrel, and only about half the volume. Since we'd fired just three single shots, very fast, and
gotten them back under cover, no one had noticed the
three brief squeaks, or even the three men going over.

"Miss, you're, uh, going to have to leave the bank,"
the manager said, still unaware of the man, collapsed
and motionless, on the floor behind her, a gun still
held in his limp fingers.

"That's not a bad idea," Chrys said to me. "We could
go up the street to a bank-card machine. Might be a lot
faster than hanging around here—there are going to be
cops all over the place soon."

"Yep," I said. We turned and went, doing our best to
look like any middle-class couple whose day has been
mildly disrupted by something that they will talk about
for weeks afterward—but that fundamentally doesn't
matter.

Just as our cash came out of the automatic teller
machine, the screen began to flash at us. Abruptly, it
glowed with three words of Attikan that were the current password, and a PRESS ENTER in English below that.
With a sigh, I did.

The screen lit up like a full-fledged video screen, and
a grainy image of Ariadne Lao said, "Please acknowledge. Report to the mid-Manhattan gateway immediately. Please acknowledge."

There wasn't any microphone on the automatic
teller machine, so I figured she couldn't hear us; I nodded my head at the security camera and pressed the
ENTER/YES button.

"She doesn't look happy," I said.

"We aren't supposed to use ATN ordnance on local events," Chrys pointed out. "So I guess we compromised security. Probably we're just going to get chewed out."

"Very likely." It was the kind of thing that could spoil a day but not more than that; and at least we would be returned to the same time and place we had departed from. That was in our contract.

We were almost there when my beeper went off. "Damn. Just a minute, Chrys, it's probably nothing much—"

I found a working public phone—always a small miracle in Manhattan, and it took me about five minutes—dialed the private line to my bodyguard agency, and waited a long second for the connection to Pittsburgh.

Mark Strang Bodyguards is a real agency—it was my real business before I started working for ATN, even if it was never a particularly lucrative one. Nowadays it was actually making much more money than it used to, but I didn't do much work in it; it served as a cover for the large payments that came in from my real employers, and, to maintain the fiction, my two assistants, Robbie and Paula, now ran the place. They'd built the above-ground part into quite a respectable business. It helps to be obviously affluent and have a reputation for being exclusive. People think you must be guarding a lot of celebrities, and they're willing to pay accordingly.

Paula answered the phone, as I expected. "Boss, it's Porter. She was attacked after her Oslo concert. She wasn't hurt, but Robbie was—it wasn't serious, but they've got her in the hospital for observation, in case it's a concussion. I've made sure your Dad and Carrie are covered, and I'm going over there as soon as I can."

My gut sank like I'd swallowed a frozen brick. "Right," I said. "What's the situation on coverage for Porter?"

"Three reliable backups are on it, and as soon as she's over into Germany we have full police security. She got on the chartered plane because Robbie insisted, so she's in the air right now."

Not great but better than nothing. "Okay," I said, thinking furiously. "Tell Robbie to get better fast, or she'll have to answer to me. Do you know what the injuries were?"

"Just a bad beating, it sounded like. No kidney damage, one cracked rib for sure. They want to hold her for observation. I think she'll be okay." Paula and Robbie have been the closest of partners since I've known them, and that's some years now. Paula must have been frantic, but she didn't let it show in her voice.

"Well, get over there and make sure," I said, completely unnecessarily. "And you be careful, too, you hear? I want both of you up and well."

"Probably you should know, too, boss," she said, very slowly and carefully, "that Porter is why Robbie is alive. She, uh, made use of that .38 you trained her with. Took down two of them while they were busy beating Robbie."

"Is Porter okay?" I asked.

"As okay as you can be, I guess." I could hear the resignation in Paula's voice. "She's not one of those people that enjoys killing, boss, I suppose you'd say. And she didn't damage her hand either. She's planning to play tonight. If I can get Robbie transferred or released, I'll cover Porter at that concert myself."

"Don't hesitate to wave agency money around if it helps," I told Paula, "but it's a shame we're dealing with this in Norway—too many honest civil servants, and they're too well paid."

"Yeah, one more complication. I've got to get on a flight, boss, I'm most of the way out the Parkway West to the airport right now, and if I get the commuter flight to Kennedy, I can make a Concorde if that's okay."

"Of course it is! Use whatever money you have to. We can always get more."

That was one difference between them; Robbie is a small woman, very strong for her size but mostly just fast as a whip, and when there's action of any kind, she moves too fast to worry about what the rules are. Paula's nearly my size and probably stronger, and if it were up to her, we'd have a manual of procedures for everything. ("Terrorist attack: 1. Agency personnel are to avoid getting shot . . .")

"Thanks, boss. We'll get it under control." It was more from the gratitude in Paula's voice than from anything else that I understood how worried she was. "Got to run—just turning off the Parkway now."

"Take care of yourself. Bye."

I hung up the phone and turned to Chrysamen. "Bad news, and I think we better get to the gate right away." I summarized it quickly as we rounded two corners and entered one of many midtown office buildings.

"Shit," Chrys said. "What did Al Capone say? 'Once is happenstance, twice is coincidence—'"

"'Three times is enemy action,'" I said. "But I'd bet on it already. Two of those robbers were in great positions to whack us—I think we'd each have taken the round after the guard did."

"Good thing you're not the ogling kind," she said, with a little smile.

"I'm a speed ogler. Got her all ogled before I had to do any shooting. Not that there was much to ogle—all packaging and no product. Anyway, here we are."

It's one of those anonymous midtown buildings with offices on the lower floors and apartments above, the kind of place where you always wonder if you saw it in a movie sometime, and you never did. There's an automatic elevator that goes up a few floors and dumps you into a space where you are facing a glass door with a bunch of names in white on it that looks vaguely like an architect's partnership, a brokerage, or a law firm. No lights are ever on, so you wonder if it's closed.

The door unlocks only when an ATN agent, like Chrys or me, or the Special Agent for our timeline, approaches it; just where the gadget that recognizes us is, I've never figured out. I never know how any of this stuff works, I just use it. Think of me as a caveman with a VCR; I like the show, but that's all I can say.

The door clicked open as we stood in front of it, and the lights came on as we opened the door. We closed and locked the door behind us and went down the hallway where, in a normal set of offices, the private offices and the conference room would be. Instead, there was just a blank wall, which turned gray and faded as we approached it, like a perfectly smooth, backlit fog. We walked into it.

It was dark as a deep cave, we were as weightless as you are in orbit, and there was no sound at all, not even the ringing of ears or nervous system. For a time I couldn't define I couldn't feel that my body was there.

Even, dim gray light came in from all directions, brightening, swimming into focus first as dark patches and then as lines and shadows, color adding suddenly.

At the same time a low rumble, an octave below a sixty-cycle hum, swelled in my ears, and then cut off abruptly when the colors came back.

The world around us turned into the early-twenty-ninth-century Athenian timeline, in a perfectly ordinary reception room for a gate.

Ariadne Lao was waiting for us. She looked grim, and worried—and not at all like we were about to get reprimanded.

"We're under some kind of Closer attack," she said, "and whatever it is, it's put all our connections to our own future into flux. I'm getting the senior Crux Ops together to try to formulate a plan of action, and it's a relief every time any of you comes through the gate. There've been attacks on Crux Ops in almost every timeline so far."

"Ours too," I said. "We think on us, and for sure on Porter Brunreich."

She nodded grimly. "We've lost nineteen Crux Ops that I know of, dead, injured, or seized. Six critical people have died in timelines we were watching. *And* we can't contact our own future much beyond the next few weeks. Whatever it is that's happening, it's big."

2

There were more than a thousand Crux Ops in the auditorium for the meeting, and security around us was amazing. Instead of the usual meeting place, the giant space station Hyper Athens, which hangs over the equator on the same line of longitude as the city of Athens, we were on the back side of the moon at the Earth System Defense base. The whole moon was under guard—heavily armed warships orbited it in a complex dance, every ship on red alert, waiting for trouble. The base itself was ringed with robot and human defenses, and the building the auditorium was in was crawling with crack security forces.

And then again, the strongest security of all was what was in the auditorium itself. Crux Ops are deadly in a fight, and there was no nonsense about checking arms at the door—first of all, most Crux Ops would rather check their pants, or kilts or togas or whatever. Secondly, if we weren't capable of making faster and more accurate decisions about what to shoot and when than anybody else, we wouldn't be Crux Ops. So if anyone, particularly any Closers, were stupid enough to come in shooting with ground forces, there was going to be a hell of a fight, and they were going to lose.

On the other hand, if they knew our exact location, a gate might pop open and a tactical nuke might take care of the whole thing. Closers have a horror of nuclear weapons in any system they might occupy, but in purely enemy territory that position tends to be flexible.

A few of the Crux Ops filing in were old comrades, people Chrys and I had worked with on one mission or another, but mostly they were strangers. ATN operates across millions of timelines, and for most of them it can only spare the once-in-a-decade or so visit of a Time Scout; an important one might have a Special Agent assigned to it permanently. Crux Ops normally go in only when the regular forces are put out of action, like when expected transmissions from a Special Agent fail to show up. So the half million Time Scouts and fifty thousand Special Agents are backed up by fewer than ten thousand Crux Ops, and since it's an occupation in which people tend to die, living long enough to get to be a senior Crux Op is rare.

Generally we operate alone or in pairs—Chrys and I had been lucky enough to be assigned as a permanent pair, partly because it seemed like a good idea to Ariadne Lao and mainly because they had owed us a whole lot of favors, and we'd insisted on it.

Even though few of us knew many of the others, all of us knew a few, and the room was buzzing with conversation and little, happy noises as people greeted each other. There were four people there from our class at COTA, the Crux Op training camp, but they were all talking to other people. Over on one side was Roger

Buckley, a guy about my age who happened to be from a timeline descended from the very first timeline in which I had intervened, a guy who had at first approached me about the same way I would approach George Washington.

In fact, George Washington was there, from a timeline where we'd recruited him because there was no United States to need a president, and the Empire was at peace, so King George didn't need a general. I knew him slightly—I waved to him, and he nodded in his usual formal, correct way. He looked to be a bit past fifty, but with ATN's advanced medicine, he had all his teeth and was as strong and healthy as anyone. Scuttlebutt among the Crux Ops was that now that he wasn't the father of his country in his own timeline, he'd been fathering a lot of other countries in other timelines, and from the way Chrys muttered, "God, he looks *great*," I was inclined to believe rumor.

Over to one side, unsmiling, grim as death (but that was usual), and looking just a little worried (which was new), was General Malecela, Ariadne Lao's boss whenever he wasn't personally supervising training, who most of us held in awe.

There was the usual array of social stuff—several hundred flavors of tea, coffee, chicory, maté, chocolate, and tisane, a dozen different kinds of breads, and, for those who wanted them, more kinds of beers and wines than you'd ever have imagined possible. For Chrys and me it was still early morning—we discovered they had grabbed everyone we talked to from sometime shortly after breakfast—so we weren't particularly inclined to get alcohol, but I noticed that even people from timelines where booze at breakfast is normal were passing it up. People wanted to be alert; this was an unprecedented event.

We found seats. "It's been a long while since we've been back here," Chrys said. "At least we know they're not bringing us in here for a chewing-out."

Another hour went by as people trickled in, but none of the additions were people we knew. I realized after a while that no one was going to ask anything— "Whatever happened to X" or "Surely Y must be a senior agent by now"—because the likely answer was grim.

That got my mind turning back to the things Chrys had said, either last night or eight hundred plus years ago or however many years that was sideways, depending on how you counted. Look around the room, and you could figure that though there were a few hundred of us here, very few would die peacefully. Most of us would be blown up, burned to death, shot, skewered, poisoned . . . it was a room full of targets-to-be. Hell, I had killed a version of myself that had gone over to the Closers, stamped on his fingers as he clung to a ladder until the bones broke, and he fell to his death.

Or should I have thought, Until I fell to my death?

It's the nature of people who face danger regularly that they're convinced that bad luck is something that always happens to everyone else. They can look at statistics that say that every single person in their line of work dies by violence sooner or later, and shrug and say that after all, *I'm* still alive, *I'm* not dead yet, many times I've been places where I could have been killed, I could have died a lot of times and I haven't, and so on and so forth. After all, they're fighters and adventurers, not insurance actuaries, not statisticians. . . .

And the thought that came to me then was that I had been thinking "They." When more accurately it should have been "We."

I was like that myself, and so was Chrys. If we were

rational, we'd have known that the way we lived was more dangerous than skateboarding on freeways. As it was, we both figured that the life-extension drugs would give us our full two hundred–plus years, instead of figuring the obvious thing—that ATN gave us the drugs because that way we could be young, fast, strong, and sharp for as long as we lasted—and that still would be a matter of a decade or two at most.

Most of us senior Crux Ops were like the old people you sometimes run into, heavy smokers and drinkers who are pushing ninety and therefore figure they're never going to die. The fact is that if you put enough people through a process that only kills most of them, there will be a few that last a long time, just as, if you roll dice long enough, you will come up with any roll you like as many times in a row as you want. You just can't say when it will happen or how long it will all take, and you certainly can't say which it will be. But the lucky dice are not the especially virtuous or smart or strong dice—they're just lucky.

And the three-pack-a-day man who makes it to ninety-two is just the last one of his group to die, because everyone dies eventually, and his group died early. In a normal group the last guy to die would have been over a hundred.

So a senior Crux Op . . . I decided I didn't like the trend of thought, and told myself to give it up.

Now, none of us was a volunteer "for the duration"—at least half the people in the room had enough time in to resign or retire if we wanted to. Chrys and I did, for that matter. But the war with the Closers is a total war, about as total as it gets, and neither side recognizes retirement. You can decide to go off somewhere, even to go across time to some timeline the other side has never discovered—and chances are still pretty good that one day your car blows up, or in your luxury suite on your spaceliner bound for Mars someone barges in and shoots you, or the stirrup cup some groom hands up to you is poisoned.

It doesn't matter to them that we retire. Why should it? It doesn't matter to us. If I had known that the other Mark Strang, who worked for the other side, had retired to grow roses and learn the harpsichord, I'd still have been perfectly happy to cut his throat.

The only difference retirement or resignation makes is that nobody is looking out for you. They no longer check to see if you're okay, and when the inevitable happens there's no revenge for you, no investigation . . .

You're going to die the same way regardless, so you might as well get a few licks in.

Chrys saw an old friend from COTA that I didn't know very well, and we went over to talk with her. I stood beside them, alone with my thoughts, occasionally distracted by the animated way Chrys was talking and gesturing with Xiao Chu.

My wife was very beautiful. In the time since I had known her, she'd had an eye and two limbs regrown by the advanced ATN medical technology; I'd had the same done for three limbs and a large part of my liver. She was very full of life. In our line of work it was really just a question of time before one or the other of us was blown apart so badly that they couldn't do anything for us, because although they can practically regrow you from your head and the stump of your neck if they have to, once the enemy bags your brain you're gone. And sooner or later they get your brain.

She was the mother of my child, and like a second mother to my ward, and chances were excellent that we would never see Porter's college graduation, or even see Perry enter school. Chances were also that one of us would live out some lonely years as a widow or widower—crazed and living only for revenge. I had done that before, and I didn't like the thought of doing it again, or of having Chrys do it.

The Closers had made me a widower once before, long before I ever heard of ATN or the Closers. They had killed my wife Marie, brother Jerry, and mother in the same car-bomb blast that had cost my sister both legs and one arm . . . and very nearly cost me my sanity.

There had been a long time during which I lived only for revenge and pleasure of killing Closers. It had been a time when life seemed pretty simple, if ugly.

Things had changed, a lot. I had a few other interests now . . . and most of them demanded living longer.

I did not want to see Chrysamen die and have to go on without her, and, for that matter, I did not want to die myself and miss so much of life together.

And as Chrys had pointed out, the war was nowhere near over, hadn't even reached a point where we could say which side was winning. In all probability there would be many thousands of years more of fighting, and long after I was buried and forgotten in some timeline or other, probably far from home, the fighting would go on. Perry's grandchildren, for all I knew, might end up as Crux Ops.

It wasn't putting me in a very good frame of mind.

The last of us filed in, and after a decent interval so they could get refreshments and find seats, the people up front started to shuffle papers, adjust lighting, and generally do all the things that are the same wherever or whenever you go—hinting strongly that it would be a good idea if we all took our seats.

Chrys slid back into her seat next to me, and I took

her hand. She seemed agitated and nervous; a second later she whispered in my ear, "At least half the people I talked to just survived an assassination attempt or a major fight. Everyone is getting pulled in out of very heavy action. A couple of them were badly shot up and just got here from treatment."

"We already knew that whatever this is, it's big," I whispered, and then the room got too quiet to keep talking.

The first person to address us was General Malecela. "Crux Ops," he began, "I have no doubt that all of you will have figured out six things that this meeting might be about, and rejected all of them as implausible. I won't keep you in the dark any longer; you are here because we've lost touch with a very large number of futures, and because we think we know why and we're going to need all of you to do something about it."

There wasn't a sound from the room. As yet he had not said anything that required any response, and we all wanted to hear what he said next.

Malecela nodded to us, as if he took our silence as a courtesy, and said, "Citizen-teacher Zouck will explain matters further; then Citizen-senator Thebenides will discuss our plan of action. After which there will be time for lunch and questions. But to allay whatever concerns you may have—you have been summoned here, I know, and you have been attacked in many cases, I'm fairly sure, because the news is *good*. They are hitting back as hard as they can because they are being hit very hard indeed. We have an opportunity to alter the balance of power tremendously, and with a bit of luck, that is just what we shall do."

"Citizen-teacher" isn't exactly a title like "Doctor" or "Professor." The Athenians don't see much connection between research and teaching, so the title implies only a lot of familiarity with the subject and an ability to explain it clearly. It's a highly honored title, and the little implants behind everyone's right ear explained this to us in the quick, abrupt way they usually did— *Stand up and bow your head.*

I'm used to doing what the implanted gadget tells me; they're carefully programmed to talk only when they know more than you do, and then only when it's urgent or you ask a question. Everyone else's is pretty much the same way, so we all stood as one and bowed our heads.

"Return to your seats, please," said a soft, gentle, woman's voice.

We all sat again—with almost no sound, for Crux Ops are all athletes of a high order, and we don't waste motion. The woman facing us at the podium was just slightly gray at the temples of her crew cut and had small, wide-set eyes and high cheekbones; her smile seemed warm and kind. I figured that she never had very much trouble keeping a class of students in line.

"I am honored that you honor me," she said; it was a polite phrase used between experts in different fields. "Let me try to take as little of your time as possible.

"You know, better than any of us who merely teach, what a crux is. Timelines don't naturally divide, or at least not often; whenever they can, they close back up with each other, leaving, perhaps, a few anomalies in the record. You all know a case or two of such things, I suppose—the couple who cannot agree on what evening they first danced together, the police files in which the same person appears to have died in an accident and to have committed a series of crimes afterward, the mysteriously scrambled records that drive historians half-mad trying to find out if a given ship was at a given battle or what rank an officer held, with clear evidence on more than one side.

"Those are cruxes that closed, places where things could have gone two or more different ways, and because finally it didn't matter, the diverging timelines sealed back together.

"But if the timelines are pushed farther apart—if one of our agents, or one of theirs, intervenes, or a time traveler comes back to force a change—then the crux widens until the two timelines will no longer reconcile, and at that point a new timeline forms. Such a timeline is always unstable in the great scheme of things, for whatever formed it at the crux can always be altered further, making it disappear, or reconverge, or go somewhere else entirely.

"Now, at first, when we found ourselves at war with the Closers, we were playing catch-up. They had found out how to travel across timelines and forward and backward along timelines. We had not. They had been operating for a long time. We had to invent things quickly.

"But we've come to realize that they tripped over their own idea of superiority. It never occurred to them that they might encounter serious resistance, so during the fifty years or so of head start, they didn't put nearly the effort they needed into developing other timelines to be allies.

"In fact their very nature may have precluded it. We have pretty good evidence that the Closers all come from just one timeline, that the only relation they will tolerate with any other timeline is complete control and subjection. As you all well know, when the Closers take over a timeline, a few hundred of them move there, and the native population is kept as slaves of one kind or another. Thus, as you all have seen, though

Closer forces are often well trained. If their officers are killed or they get beyond supervision, they fall apart quickly. Once we realized this, we began to capture them in large numbers, and we've learned steadily more about the Closers themselves.

"The biggest revelation is that the Closers proper—the ones who call themselves 'Masters'—are universally trained from birth as fighters and officers; by the time he's twenty a typical Closer male has commanded a full division somewhere. Apparently there are many positions for which they won't use even their most trusted slaves. Thus the war is taking more of a toll on them than on us, even though they began with many more timelines, for they simply can't mobilize as many forces as we can. That's part of why we've been gaining steadily in strength relative to them.

"Our other big advantage has been in our diversity; because we don't make every timeline alike and run it from the top down, we discover more things. Thus ever so slowly, due to the cross-fertilization of so many different ideas, we have been pulling abreast of them, and in a few areas we are now definitely ahead."

She paused and nodded at all of us. "Now, no doubt some of you are impatiently waiting for the status report to be over so that you can hear the news. But I'll have to explain one more part of what we've been doing first.

"When a crux is embattled—when there are Closer and ATN agents fighting there—quite often all the timelines from which it is descended become inaccessible. Our signals and cargo won't travel crosstime to them because it's not settled whether they exist or not. Eventually, the embattled timelines open up again, or they vanish forever. Sometimes they're just somewhere else in time, somewhere that we can't find because there are so many or somewhere that is simply inaccessible because the volume of paradox we'd have to tolerate to contact it is just too high. Either things settle down, and we can then reach that timeline, or they don't.

"Well, for the last eighteen months, everywhere in the ATN more than twenty years in the future has been out of reach in just that way. And, in fact, the distance into the future we could reach has been steadily shrinking. We are down to being able to contact our own timelines only about fifty days into the future."

A buzz ran through the room, but when Citizen-teacher Zouck raised her hand, we fell silent again.

"This might be taken as bad news, but instead, what we are finding is that the opposing timelines seem to be in a very different state. Everywhere, where we know the addresses of the Closer timelines, our agents have been able to penetrate with little difficulty, and universally we've found that those timelines are up in rebellion. In many of them the Closers have already been slaughtered and—because they tend to keep time travel and cross-timeline technologies only in their own hands—the gates are closed. The armies left in those timelines have generally mutinied and shot their Closer officers. Sometimes democratic revolutions are under way, sometimes civil wars, sometimes the army is taking over and trying to keep things going without the Closers, sometimes you have 'warlordism'—all the military units fighting each other for control. Nowhere did we find an intact Closer society.

"So, tentatively, our conclusion is this—whatever is about to happen apparently involves destroying the Closers entirely, but it also involves changing the societies of the ATN so completely that we are unable to reach them from where we stand. And just to complicate matters, way out at the fringe of what we can detect, we seem to be seeing many, many more timelines than have ever arrived before—we have probes under way to a few of them even as we speak, but the effort and expense in locating and landing in them are enormous. We don't even know if those are ours, theirs, some third force's, or what.

"But still and all—I believe I bring you good news. The overthrow of the Closers, at least in the hundred thousand or so of their timelines we know about, is right around the corner. I cannot believe a great victory of that kind is causing anything bad to happen to us, however strange it may be."

There was a round of applause when she sat, though it was sort of strange applause since only about half of us were from cultures that applauded speakers, and maybe half the ones who applauded clapped their hands—there was also whistling, barking like dogs, shouts that sounded like "Oh—wah!", and people making the "bibibibi" sound with fingers on lips. I was pretty sure we all approved anyway. Citizen-teacher Zouck nodded politely, acknowledging our approval, and sat down.

General Malecela stepped back to the podium and gestured for quiet. As the room fell silent, he said, "To complete your background information, here is Citizen-senator Thebenides."

Thebenides was a small, dark-haired man with light brown skin—which is what just about half of humanity looks like across all the timelines, palefaces like me being fairly scarce—who seemed just a little nervous, as if he wasn't quite sure he should be up there. I suppose standing in front of a room filled with the most lethal people in millions of universes will do that to a guy.

"Well," he began, "Citizen-teacher Zouck's news, as

you might guess, has caused quite a stir in government circles. We, too, find it very hopeful that the Closer timelines seem to be disrupted and destroyed by whatever is just ahead of us in the future, but naturally, to us these concerns are something more than just academic."

I did not like the way he said "*just academic.*" Now, I knew I was a bit sensitive on the point, because way, way back, when I had no idea that I would ever end up as a professional killer, when the world was a happy playground for people like me and my first wife Marie, I had been headed into the academic life as an art historian, which is about the most unemployable thing you can be outside of academia. So the notion that professors and academic issues are somehow less important than "the real world" always irritates me a little in the first place.

But in the second place, it sounded like he had just patted the previous speaker on the head and told the silly little dear that now that she was done, the government man was going to straighten matters out for everybody. The lack of respect shown for someone with considerable knowledge bothered me, especially coming from a politician. She was trained to think; he was trained to smile. I knew who *I* trusted more.

And then, too . . . something about the way he did it. When people paint their opponents as theoretical dreamers, and themselves as hardheaded realists . . . well, at least, whenever I had done that, it was because I was about to do something brutal. And brutality is something governments tend to do, especially when they're nervous and don't know what's going on. I had a deep, deep feeling that whatever he was about to propose wasn't going to be anything I would feel good about.

Somehow all of that crystallized into feeling that this guy was whiny and devious and not to be trusted. That at least activated my Crux Op instincts—I leaned forward to listen and watch more carefully.

While I had been thinking, he had been blathering on in vague generalities, about how he was so glad to be among practical people of action who could take the necessary steps. It was a real bad sign as far as I was concerned, and utterly unnecessary—none of us could vote, so we had nothing to give him; we already knew what it was to be the best fighters there are, so he had nothing to give us.

By the time he got down to the meat of his speech, I wanted to frisk him for small arms and toss his room for child pornography. Chrys noticed how I was reacting and glanced at me with a little puzzlement, then turned back to continue watching Thebenides.

"There are several possibilities about what is going on," Thebenides was saying, "and with all respect to my esteemed academic colleague, she has presented only the most hopeful of them. It is possible that the new timelines coming in are bringing with them some superweapon, some new way of organizing ATN that brings about a swift and sure victory, and we must be open to that possibility. But it is also possible that what they indicate is the appearance of some catastrophe that spans all the timelines we know, including those of the Closers.

"I need hardly remind you that if, for example, there were a rogue planet out there about to smash through the solar system, none of our known timelines would be capable of dealing with it, and so it would arrive in millions of timelines at the same time, and the chaos it caused could well produce these effects. Against such a situation there is naturally little we can do except try to ensure that the methods exist for getting our high-tech resources back on line as quickly as possible."

It occurred to me that what he meant by that was probably something like "getting the time machines and the crosstime equipment running again," but the way he had said it would justify almost anything the government might want to do. Zouck might have been academic, but she had managed to talk plain language to people who spoke it; "high-tech resources back on line" was a collection of weasel words to justify any old thing.

He went on. "Another possibility is that the impinging timelines do in fact represent a third force, one that is hostile both to us and to the Closers, and that we have been hit even harder than they have. In such a case, a certain kind of flexibility might be warranted, and toward that end we must explore—"

"Horseshit," I muttered. People turned and looked at me; Chrys looked embarrassed.

Whatever words he used for what we were supposed to be exploring was lost to me in the little stir around me, but I knew damn well what he was hinting at.

"And still another possibility," he added, "is that although those timelines are hostile to the Closers and friendly to us, they are in effect so advanced and so alien to us that their advent is like the arrival of a high-technology industrial society into a Stone Age backwater, as has happened in many timelines. It will do us little good to be free of the Closer menace only to end up permanently as the 'little brother' in a paternal relationship."

In the first place, you have a paternal relationship with something that looks like your father, not your big brother, and at least an academic wouldn't have abused language quite that far. In the second place, while I could see that it would be bad news (as in having to do something useful for a living) for Thebenides and the other citizen-senators, the Citizen-archon, and a whole lot of citizen-bureaucrats, I didn't exactly see having people who knew what they were doing take over the show as a complete disaster. There were parts of my own timeline where arriving American armed forces had found people in the Stone Age and left them operating airports, universities, hospitals, and all the rest. Even if they came to dislike the Americans, I never heard of any of them saying, "What a relief! Now that the Americans are gone, we can go back to washing clothes by pounding them on a rock, letting every other kid die before the age of five, and worshiping the chief as a god!"

"Thus," Thebenides was finishing, "we must be aware of the wide range of possible dangers and opportunities and be ready to move in any direction."

I was a little disgusted that my fellow Crux Ops seemed to applaud him more than they had Citizen-teacher Zouck, but maybe they were just more psychologically ready for it.

"What was that all about?" Chrys whispered to me.

"What was *what* all about? That speech? Hell if I know except—"

"I'm talking about the way you behaved. People noticed."

I blinked, hard, and realized my wife was angry at me, and obviously I had embarrassed her. "What did—"

General Malecela was back at the podium, and he was doing the usual things, thanking everybody and assuring us all that we had just heard things we really needed to hear. I did my best to pay polite attention to that, gesturing to Chrys that we would talk in a minute. I figured there would be assignments announced, and if I'd already embarrassed myself somehow, I didn't want to compound the problem by not knowing where I was supposed to be.

Malecela finished the platitudes and handed things over to Ariadne Lao, who gestured at a large screen that appeared behind her. "As you can see—"

At that moment the screen blew into bits, and a fusillade of projectiles roared into the room. I could see bodies falling over; something or someone was firing on us, and even in this heavily guarded room, we were under attack.

I was firing back at whatever was coming through the space where the screen had been before I even had time to note that so was everyone else; the big auditorium rang with the fire of a thousand weapons.

3

Where the screen had been there was the blank grayness of a gate, and a dozen figures in black uniforms, masked and goggled, each firing a long, spidery gadget that looked more like a broken-off television antenna folded into a child's idea of an Uzi than anything else. My NIF was aimed and firing before I thought it in words, but I recognized the weapon—Closer standard issue, a gadget something like our own SHAKK—and I sprayed the lot of them with neural induction fléchettes in less than a heartbeat.

So had a lot of other people, I realized, before my finger was entirely off the trigger, and as my eyes probed desperately into the grayness of the gate, watching for whatever might come in next.

Each of those initial dozen raiders must have been hit by at least a hundred rounds from SHAKKs alone. I could hear the deep bass whoosh from a vast chorus of them—all of those rounds had homed in at Mach 10, found the bodies of the Closers, entered them (with more than enough speed and force to kill with the internal shock wave alone, even if they entered a hand or foot) and then spiraled to a stop within the body. The Closers had simply, instantly, turned into bags of red jam.

There were probably a hundred-plus NIF rounds in all of them, too, but none of them had enough nervous system left to feel them with, and it takes twelve times as long for a NIF round to get there—probably the set of fléchettes arrived an entire eyeblink late.

My thumb found the selector on my NIF—I was still set for temporary unconsciousness, as I had been in New York—and naturally flipped toward instant death before a better thought struck me, and I flipped it to severe convulsion.

Holding the trigger down on full auto, I sprayed a deadly stream of the tiny, gnatlike projectiles directly into the grayness of the gate. Gates are two-way, and if there was any unprotected human flesh on the other side, the fléchettes would find it and burrow in.

I pictured what would happen to the Closer then. The muscles of the body would lock against each other with sudden, brutal force, hard enough to shatter the bones and tear them out through the flesh, the jaw smashing the teeth to red ruins and driving them up into the sinuses, the scalp muscles crushing the skull, arm, and leg bones ripping out through flesh and clothing in great, sharp splinters, hands and feet bursting into shredded meat, all in an instant before the heart locked down and burst from internal pressure, and the chest muscles collapsed the rib cage. The ripping, dissolving figures would emit one unbearable scream as the air and blood from the chest was pushed with enormous force through slammed-shut vocal cords and crushed jaws.

It was a horrible noise and a terrible sight, which is why I was trying to cause it over on the other side. If that starts to happen around you, even the toughest fighters tend to suffer a loss of morale. And if they began to hesitate—

There was a scream from the screen that cut right through everything else—one of the Closers coming through must have stopped one of my rounds, and airfoamed blood sprayed everywhere for an instant before everyone else's SHAKK rounds tore him apart.

The second rank had managed to arrive in a body, stepping out all at once and diving and scattering, so they returned some of our fire, but now that their surprise was gone, the advantage was all with us—we could see them coming out before they could see to shoot, and they were only coming through one narrow aperture.

They got off a few stray rounds, and because both sides have homing hypersonic ammunition, some of their rounds found targets. Perhaps a dozen more of us died, torn to bloody rags around us. The man in front of me, a tall guy with Oriental features who had been pumping SHAKK rounds at the screen in a steady rhythm, suddenly burst apart backward, his heart and lungs driven out through his rib cage and coat to spray Chrys and me.

I wiped my face, but I kept sending fléchettes into the hole where the screen had been.

Still, even though they scored on us a few times, and much as I was sorry anytime one of us died (or one of them didn't!), they lasted for only a few seconds before they, too, were mowed down; they looked more like criminals trying to make a break from in front of a firing squad than a body of organized troops. Their bodies flopped around and sprayed blood, and they were still.

Whatever the third rank was supposed to do, all they did was die. I don't think many of them even made it out of the gate—there was a storm of SHAKK and NIF rounds pouring in there by then, and what it must have been like on the other side is hard to guess.

I saw General Malecela rise cautiously from the deck up there and toss two things through the gate before he fell down, hugging the dirt again.

A moment later, the surface of the gate—with shadowy figures still half-falling through it—glowed red, and then there was only blank wall where it had been. There was a long moment while we all checked to make sure that all the Closers who had come through were dead; then another burst of activity as people grabbed their fallen comrades, hoping—though with the weapons of that future, it's hopeless—that someone had somehow survived a hit.

I suppose I should give the Closers some kind of credit—obviously it was a suicide mission, which takes guts, and they certainly kept coming. But after the initial explosion into the room, and the first hail of deadly projectiles that killed sixty of us, they barely managed to get forty fighters through the gate they had opened, and our total deaths were under a hundred. I call that amateurish and sloppy, and since I wasn't used to seeing either from the Closers, it told me in part how desperate they must be.

Within a minute or so, the ATN staff were back in action and had opened an emergency gate. We all filed through it in quick, silent order; they were popping us to a concealed base deep inside an asteroid in an uninhabited timeline, one of many sanctuaries that ATN maintained for times when absolute security was imperative.

As I stepped through the gate, I glanced back and

saw that a detail was taking the bodies out; there were several bodies lying in the aisles or in seats with living Crux Ops kneeling or sitting beside them. I thought of how I might have felt had Chrys died in the attack, and realized I'd have been doing the same thing—saying good-bye, getting it into my brain that she was gone. As we went through the gate, I shuddered.

It got gray, weightless, and soundless; as always, light came back first, color last. At the end of the process we were walking on a seemingly endless steel walkway that curled around over our heads; the asteroid was spinning to provide artificial gravity, and the walkway ran around the outer edge.

The assembly hall here wasn't nearly so comfortable. There were no refreshments, but I doubt that anyone was hungry or thirsty.

We milled around for a moment, and then General Malecela came in. When he took the podium, everyone fell silent.

"Let me begin," he said, "by asking you all to take a moment to reflect on your fallen comrades, to ask any deity in which you believe to take care of them, and to calm yourselves and get ready for the next step."

The room was plunged into excruciating silence for a long time; finally Malecela spoke again. "First of all, I want you all to know that I'm proud to be one of you. Collectively your quick reflexes and speed in maneuver held our casualties far lower than they might have otherwise been, and, moreover, the returned fire was very intelligently executed—some of you may have noted that I tossed two PRAMIACS through that gate. I had set one for ten megatons, to go off whenever the gate closed, and the other for a couple of tons of explosive in hopes of destroying the generator. I discovered that the rest of you had already tossed in at least forty

PRAMIACS set for the maximum, to blow off when the gate closed, and, moreover, several of you tossed various charges and fired various programmed rounds in there that collectively must have ensured that the gate generator would fail. In other words, we couldn't have done that better if we had planned it.

"Another detail is more significant, if you think about it. There has been no further attack on the base on the back side of the moon, and our probes into the immediate future show none as far as we can trace. Yet, having lost the battle, why did they not toss a bomb through at us? It would have taken almost nothing at all, compared with their known resources, to open another gate from a military facility somewhere, push through a nuclear bomb or a large mass of antimatter, and switch off the gate.

"The answer to that can only be one thing. They didn't do it on the first shot because they wanted to capture at least some of us—several of the bodies had stun weapons among their equipment. They know by now that we don't negotiate for hostages, so they were looking for someone to interrogate—and they chose to try to get prisoners from the most dangerous possible time and location they could have picked. That means that, from the standpoint of whoever planned this thing, the prisoners *had* to be taken from that meeting—probably the only place they could identify where the information they needed could be found.

"Moreover, there's only one reason we can think of that the Closers would mount such an inept expedition, and then not even follow up with a bomb . . . we think that it's because they *couldn't*. What we were attacked by was something thrown together at the last moment, a last-ditch effort by some isolated Closer base. Which, thanks to you all, just received about four hundred megatons in return."

There was a very long, stunned silence.

"Yes, you are thinking accurately," Malecela said, repeating himself, then looking up and grinning at us. "That attack was from the last Closer base capable of mounting an attack. The evidence is that sometime very soon—and god knows we don't know how just yet—we are about to win this war."

The place broke into the wildest applause I've ever seen in my life; even people whose faces were still streaked with tears for their dead were cheering. It took a long time before there was enough quiet for Malecela to be heard again.

"Now," he said, "we've managed to get enough staff and personnel into this base to get some sort of quarters ready for all of you. We'll give you a couple of hours to settle in and clean up—which also gives us a little time to do some planning and arranging—and then, after that, we'll be meeting with you individually and in small groups. Right now I don't have the foggiest idea of what you will be doing, but I do know that given the number of timelines we must investigate at once, there won't be enough of you.

"That's all for now. If you'll file out to my left and place your thumbs on the reader, you'll receive directions to your rooms."

There wasn't much to say, but everyone was saying it loudly and rapidly. Chrys and I could barely hear each other and gave up trying, figuring it would be easier to talk once we got to our room.

The thumbprint reader told us that we were on Level 8, Wing 4, Room 80; before we had time to ask where that might be, we saw a bank of escalators, labeled with "Level 2" up through "Level 8."

"They put us in the penthouse," I said.

"Not much of a view here," Chrysamen pointed out. "That means eight levels up from the outer edge of the spinning asteroid. We're deeper inside than anyone else."

"People get penthouses either for the view or for the privacy," I pointed out.

"You're incorrigible."

The escalator ride was a strange sensation because when you use centrifugal force for artificial gravity, the gravity falls off very rapidly as you move in toward the center, and at the same time the apparent Coriolis force gets more noticeable. The total effect was that if you shut your eyes, it felt like the escalator was twisting upward to the left, about to curl right over and dump you off. We both hung on, though Chrys seemed to be getting a kick out of shutting her eyes and letting go momentarily.

But then she enjoys parachute drops and roller coasters. Chrys is close, but nobody's perfect.

"You really ought to try this," she said, grinning at me.

"No thanks. I prefer only to be scared to death when there's actually something to be scared of."

She shrugged. "Think of it as staying in practice."

At the top of the escalator, there were moving sidewalks like the things they have in airports, fanning out from the escalator head, and one of them was clearly marked for "Wing 4." It was enough to make me wonder if all this had been sitting here waiting for centuries (it might well have been) or if they had suddenly realized they would need it, dropped a construction team back five years in time, and then built it right after the attack on the back side of the moon. In principle the only way to tell would be by asking.

The room was in that gray range between hospital, barracks, and hotel, clearly not a place intended as anyone's home but not entirely devoid of comfort either. They had provided us with some simple tunic-and-pants uniforms, since we had no bags—those were "still" back at the Wellington in New York in my home timeline, god knows how many years crosstime but at least 850 years back. Supposedly after this mission we'd be returned to that time and place—where Paula was on her way to cover Porter, where Robbie was in a hospital bed in Oslo, where with Paula gone, the second team would have to cover my son, father, and sister.

Time travel costs a lot of money; probably if it hadn't been for the Closers, it would have been millennia after it was discovered before anyone did it regularly. *In principle* they could have sent back a probe to see how it all came out and let me know whether my family and friends were all right. *In principle*, if it's before noon, you could be in Paris tomorrow morning from almost anywhere in the United States. It would merely cost you so much that you wouldn't think of doing it. In the same way, unless there was a remarkably good reason other than the nerves of two senior Crux Ops, they weren't going to do that. And being able to know is not at all the same thing as actually knowing.

I was about to work my way up into a fine fret, since there was nothing else to do until they called us, and I don't respond well to having a lot on my mind and nothing I can do. So I took a shower and changed, as Chrys did, and *then* I started to work on developing a fine fret.

Maybe because she recognized the warning signs, Chrysamen abruptly asked, "So, just before the meeting was extremely rudely interrupted"—the funny twist in her mouth told me the joke was supposed to make me a little more relaxed and easy to talk to—"you were acting like there was a snake in your pants leg. And you were focusing a lot of your strange squirmy energy, my dear husband, on Citizen-senator Thebenides. So I think you didn't like what you were hearing, but unfortunately I think you made that very clear to everyone else."

"Hmmm." I sat down on the bed, kicked off my shoes, and stretched out. She did the same and lay in my arms. After a couple long breaths and a false start, I began, "So I suppose that if I start out by admitting that it's just a funny feeling, even if it's a very intense funny feeling, you're not going to be pleased?"

She made a face, twisting her mouth a little sideways, and then said, "Mark, you know I know you, and you know I love you, and by now I know you don't act up in public without a good reason. And you were really acting up, and I really couldn't see the reason. So if it's purely a gut feeling, I assume it's a very strong gut feeling, and if it's something more than that, it's probably important, but anyway—what I want to know is, *what did you see that bothered you so much?* You and I stay alive on our hunches and our feel for evidence, sweetheart. If there's something the matter, share it. I trust you."

I hunched up onto one shoulder so I could look at her face more closely, which also gave me an excuse to push some of her dark curls back from her face a little. She was so beautiful, even now . . . after all those years, after all the usual marital hassles . . . and, of course, after more than a dozen dangerous missions together. We'd seen each other shot and bleeding, fought side by side in worlds you can't imagine, and all I had to do was explain to her that Thebenides gave me the creeps.

How complicated could that be? As she said, if I couldn't trust her . . .

"Look," I began, "I think part of it is a matter of where and when I grew up. In my time and timeline, we weren't great trusters of politicians. I know that nobody is, but us particularly. We knew a little too well that when someone starts talking about how principles are all very well, but you've got to be practical, he means that he's going to do something he thinks you won't approve of, and he wants to head off your argument. Nobody ever says, 'Look, let's just get practical here' if he's talking about feeding or housing people, or about giving good jobs to vets or something. The 'I'm just a practical guy—let's all be practical together and not pay too much attention to those pointy-headed intellectuals' dodge usually only comes along when a politician is cooking up something so disgusting that it can't be justified in the normal way. It's the way Truman talked about dropping the bomb, the way Johnson talked about getting into Vietnam, the way Nixon talked about law and order, and the way Bush and Clinton talked all the time."

"And boy, did they talk all the time," Chrysamen said, grinning. "Okay, lover, I can buy that explanation. You think he's trying to put a fast one over on us, morally speaking, right?"

"I don't so much think that as I know it in my bones. And look at what he's saying, too, Chrys. 'Oh, sure, maybe we've won, and that's swell, but what if we didn't beat the Closers in a way that we would approve of.' Meaning, what if he doesn't approve of the way the ATN would have to change to win. But the only reason ATN exists is to fight back against the Closers. ATN never meddles in the affairs of a member timeline, or at least that's what they always tell all of us. Don't you see how peculiar that is? If I had to make a guess, it's that the Athenian timeline has a big bureaucracy, by now, with quite a bit invested in keeping the war going. I would guess the timelines war is big business for a lot of our good, generous, civilized Athenians."

She looked more than a bit startled. "Mark, you can't be serious. Your timeline and mine both owe everything to the Athenians. If they hadn't fought back, and developed the time machines themselves, and then organized and helped everyone else, we'd all be under the Closer heel. We even named our son after Perikles!"

I nodded. "You see how uncomfortable it is? But let's face facts, wars involve a lot of money, and the money flows through a central point somewhere. The central point always gets its hands on a lot of the money. That all makes common sense, doesn't it? So somewhere in the Athenian timeline, there are people with jobs or property who are going to lose out when the war ends. Since that wasn't supposed to happen for thousands of years, nobody thought about what to do when it was over. Now there's the scary prospect of peace real soon. And nobody is ready for it.

"But our boy Thebenides knows a voter's interest— or maybe a campaign donor's? I don't know how they finance their elections—he knows what they have at stake. Any good political hack does. And he's not going to let them get hurt. That's the first given. And the second given—well, so whatever timelines are now drawing close to our own, they seem to just possibly have it in for the Closers. That strikes me as just fine and a high personal recommendation.

"But good old Thebenides sees it differently. He's afraid that whatever is out there might not like ATN either. Which is quite possible. And considering we have member timelines that are absolute monarchies, and Communist dictatorships, and hell, there's even a couple of reformed Nazi timelines that joined up . . . well, maybe we just don't look all that good to the Intertemporal Good Guys. Maybe all the other little compromises that Thebenides and his crew have made would make us look not different enough from the Closers . . .

"Or maybe the new timelines are actually really bad guys, even worse than Closers."

I sighed and shrugged, holding Chrys tight. "Don't you see how much of a mess this is, at least potentially?"

"Maybe," she said. "Do you mean you're afraid Thebenides wants to make an alliance with the Closers?"

"I'm afraid he wants to leave the door open to it, anyway, and I don't like that one bit. I'm also afraid that he may have worse than that in mind. Like he wants to bargain out some balance-of-power deal. Like he suggests that if the new guys do turn out to be friendly, we keep the Closers around 'just in case' or 'for the balance of power.' You see the kind of thing I mean?"

"Maybe."

"Well, jeez. It's not easy to put into words. The whole idea of having a principle is that it's something to guide your actions, isn't it? And if at the first sign of things getting complicated or difficult, you decide to throw the principle over the side, there's only two reasons—either it was always a bad principle, or you've decided to do a bad thing. I don't think he wants to do anything consciously evil, but I think he's like politicians in my timeline—he wants to have the option. He doesn't care enough about right and wrong to let them get in the way of anything he wants to do."

"Well, it *is* practical politics, Mark." She looked straight into my eyes. "I mean, I come from a very impractical timeline. We were completely pacifist. We were taken over, exploited, slaughtered, wrecked, and we never varied from our principles until we finally made one huge massacre. And if we hadn't been willing to do that when ATN showed up and armed us . . . well, you can imagine. I'd probably have never been born—we'd have died out a generation or more before I was born. You can't be completely principled about these things."

"You can't be completely unprincipled, either," I said. "Look, it probably is just the experience of history. When I think about the deals my nation made to win World War II—deals with Russia that gave millions of refugees back to Stalin, deals with France that eventually got us into Vietnam, deals with Britain that got the USA into the business of preserving a colonial empire . . . well. During my lifetime we were so practical that we backed any murdering dictator who said he wasn't a Communist, and turned a blind eye to torture, murder, and repression anywhere that they'd let McDonald's sell a hamburger or Disney put on a movie. That's what 'practical' got us."

She nodded, and her face looked serious and far away. "I understand the problem, I guess. You think he talked like one of your politicians, and you don't trust them at all."

"You don't know 'em like I do," I pointed out, "and there's a certain analogy about the whole thing, too. In my timeline, we had just won a huge war, and we were sitting on top of the world, and then the wealthy and powerful grabbed the whole show for themselves and managed to make us roundly hated everywhere within a generation. Nobody was more liked and respected in

1945, and thanks to a few thousand dorks in suits whose only interest was in making money, nobody was more hated by 1965. I'd hate to think that after the war is over ATN would do anything except hunt down whatever Closer bases are still hidden, and then dissolve."

"Hmm. And Thebenides set off all those feelings in you?"

"Yeah, all those and more. See, the other problem is, the son of a bitch just comes across as a greasy liar."

At that, she finally laughed a little, which I found encouraging. I put an arm around her waist, and we kissed, long and slow. It occurred to me that there was at least one good way to kill an hour or so in a room alone with Chrysamen. Gently, I stroked her skirt up her thigh; she kissed me more firmly.

We were both most of the way naked and beginning to get to the intense parts when the little loudspeaker in the room said, "Agents Strang and ja N'wook, please acknowledge."

"Here," we said, together.

"Report in ten minutes to Conference Level 2, Wing 3, Conference Room 7," the voice said.

Oh, well, getting dressed in a hurry always gives me more energy for a long boring meeting. We caught the escalators back down and discovered that they deposited us right by the door of the conference room; we were even about half a minute early.

In the conference room were Ariadne Lao, Citizen-senator Thebenides, and General Malecela. I figured my confidence in whatever was to follow was at just under 67 percent.

They were polite, but they got down to business right away. I had already realized that if three people that senior were explaining the mission to us, it must be unusually important even for senior Crux Ops.

Without preface, Ariadne Lao said, "The new time-lines that are going to assist us in this war—"

Thebenides cleared his throat and Malecela glared at him.

Ariadne Lao began again. "It seems to be clear that our new allies will contact us through timelines which are derived from the ones in which Porter Brunreich becomes a figure of major importance. I therefore must apologize for assigning you to your own time, but it's become abundantly clear why they are targeting Porter Brunreich—the timelines that are our bridge to our new allies all spring from her."

"And let me underline and highlight that," Malecela added. "She must not only survive, but she must survive as the sort of person whose legacy will include trust rather than suspicion.

"Therefore—and I know it's not as interesting or exciting an assignment as it could be, but it's certainly the most vital—both of you are assigned at once to return to your own timeline and organize around-the-clock in-depth protection for Porter Brunreich."

"She's had that since she was thirteen," I pointed out, "but we can step that up several levels. And don't worry, it's the job we'd rather be doing. How soon can we leave?"

"We thought you might like a decent meal and a night's rest," Malecela said, "but you can go right after breakfast tomorrow if you like. We've sent one of our on-the-spot fronts to get your things from your hotel and get them shipped over to Europe; we can have you meet her in Weimar, just before her concert there. We've arranged, via your bodyguard agency, for her to get to Weimar by helicopter—you'll go by ground transport, but you'll get there a bit before her."

"Good," Chrys said, and since there wasn't anything more to add, we both got up to go.

But Citizen-senator Thebenides still had something to add. "And do your best to recall that not only are the Porter Brunreich timelines vital to our defense and to our contact with, er, the other new timelines, but since so often the culture of a given timeline is simply one person's prejudices writ large, I would hope that when you talk to Citizen Brunreich you will keep in mind the values of ATN and of Attika generally, and—"

"We usually suggest that she ought to do what's right," I said, without much trace of patience.

We were all the way back to the room, and beginning to mess around where we had left off, when Chrysamen whispered into my ear, "Okay, I see your point about Thebenides. Still, it's obvious that Ariadne Lao, and for that matter General Malecela, despise the man. I don't know how much harm he can do in the circumstances."

"Ever hear of civilian control of the military? He's the boss."

"He's one of a lot of bosses, Mark. Not necessarily the most important one, either. I agree, if he were really in charge, I'd be worried silly. He's slippery and greasy, and that's his most attractive feature. But right now we have a lot more to worry about."

"Funny," I said, "but it's easier to worry about Thebenides, who is merely an asshole, than about Porter and the future of all those timelines."

"I wasn't going to worry about Porter either. We'll be there to meet her plane, and if the Closers can't get a bomb to a Crux Op meeting, when they know the location and time, and when it would only be across time—they aren't going to get anything that can shoot down an airplane all the way back to a couple of critical hours in the twentieth century. We've got other things to worry about." She kissed me, then, very firmly.

"Such as what?" I knew she was right—Thebenides was minor, Porter was important but not anything we could do anything about—but now I didn't know what she thought we *should* be worrying about.

"Such as that a few weeks ago Perry wanted to know why he was an only child and suggested we get working on it." Now she slipped her arms around me and pressed her body to mine.

"Should've named that kid Aristotle," I muttered. "His major interest seems to be biology."

4

The next morning breakfast was what it usually is in that timeline—dense, heavy bread served warm, big chunks of feta cheese, olive paste, and coffee so strong it etches your teeth. We ate quickly and reviewed instructions; they would be putting us in through the usual channels, our bags were already in place, our briefcases and passports waiting on the airliner. They had appropriate clothing waiting for us as well.

"Will you look at this?" I said to Chrysamen. "I look like a yuppie instead of a goon. I think they set me up with Brooks Brothers Number Four, Corporate Boring."

She grinned at me. "My feeling exactly. How are they going to tell me from the flight attendant?" She gestured at the blue suit with its simple skirt, silk blouse, and string tie. "They must have gotten this out of a costume handbook or something. Though I have to concede I'm at least going to be inconspicuous. I'll look like every other female biz nerd on the flight. All the ones that everyone suspects are being exploited by their bosses."

A few minutes later we made the crossover. A gate opened in front of us, and the ATN couriers stepped through, handing each of us our ticket and passport. I noted with amusement that the male courier was about four inches shorter than I was and that the female courier was about three shades lighter than Chrysamen in skin tone—and had her hair tied up tightly in a scarf, which probably meant she didn't wear it anything like Chrys did. Well, supposedly this was a short commuter flight from Frankfurt to Leipzig; probably everyone would be reading, and no one would look closely at us.

We stepped into the gate. The world faded to gray, weightless silence; there was a timeless interval when we didn't exist; then light came back, and sound, and weight, and finally color—though there was little enough of that in an airliner bathroom.

We came out of the bathroom and everyone was staring at us; it then suddenly occurred to me that they had noticed a man and a woman going into an airliner bathroom, staying there several minutes, and emerging out of breath.

It was a very long walk back to our seats; fortunately our opposite numbers had left English-language newspapers for us there, though we felt more like hiding under them than reading them.

By the time the plane landed, people had mostly stopped staring at us, or at least stopped being quite so overt about it. Almost you might have imagined we were any other passengers—though a lot of the men on board certainly stared holes in Chrys's clothing on our way out.

Leipzig Airport is one of the world's uglier airports,

thanks to a remarkably uninspired set of Communist architects, and it's extremely busy all the time. That's a bad combination because one thing a Communist architect never figured on was heavy traffic. They do all seem to have figured that people would be standing in line a lot and would want some nice blank gray walls to stare at, and wouldn't want to wonder about where the seats were, so they didn't put too many of those in . . .

As always, the ATN couriers had been much too efficient, and gotten our bags on the airliner in Frankfurt first, so of course they were last getting off. While they were getting off I surreptitiously checked our passports and determined that we had officially been stamped through the day before. Once again those guys had thought of everything.

Which made me suspect that the trick of having us both come out of the same bathroom after a delay was a function of their sense of humor rather than their carelessness. "You know," I muttered to Chrys, "I won't have time to write a report on those guys for days and days, and by that time, I'll probably think it was funny."

"Then you'd better let me write the report."

"Absolutely. Is that your suitcase?"

It wasn't; just the third one like it on that flight. But the next one was hers, and then there was mine, and at last we were on our way.

The Fodor's people say that rail service in what used to be East Germany still has "one foot in the steam age." Every time we take a train through that area—and Chrys and I do often, because if you have money and an opera-crazed spouse, there's nowhere more attractive on Earth than that area where what used to be East Germany borders what used to be Czechoslovakia—I wonder just what age the other foot is in. Possibly the Late Stone Age.

The trip to Weimar was mercifully brief, all the same, and the fact that it was Weimar was a compensation. That little city is so small compared to its importance in art, theatre, and music that if you know any of its history, it's a constant shock to realize how close together everything happened . . . Goethe and Schiller didn't just live here at the same time, their families probably borrowed sugar from each other.

Porter was playing at the National Theater; we had been there a few times. The place has a strange effect on the visitor; the building is beautiful, and about as good a smaller auditorium as you're apt to find for opera, concert, or theatre—then suddenly you realize just how much of European intellectual history happened there. There's a statue of Goethe with his hand on Schiller's shoulder out front, and that reminds you . . . but you still have to think for a moment to realize that Franz Liszt and Carl Maria von Weber lived and made music here, both Cranachs painted there, Wagner's *Lohengrin* opened there, Gropius came up with the designs that half the modern world is built to—it goes on and on. All that in a little town smaller than Great Falls, Montana, and a lot of it right there in the National Theater.

The cab from the railway station carried us on past, and I finally looked down at the note they had given me to show the driver. "Upscale all the way this time," I told Chrys. "They're putting us up in the Elephant."

We had always figured sometime when we came here for a concert or opera, we'd stay there, but only as an indulgence—the place is expensive. What do you expect for a three-hundred-year-old hotel that can claim, "Hitler always stayed here when he was in town?"

It was about two hours till Porter was due, so we got checked in and had the fun of playing dumb tourist, checking out the appointments in the room, for a while before we got down to business.

Naturally the NIF in my coat pocket and the SHAKK in its special holster between my shoulder blades didn't require a permit—or rather they would have if anyone had known what they were, but since they wouldn't be invented for centuries in my home timeline, they weren't exactly against the rules. Not exactly within them, either.

Oddly enough, as part of my cover, I had to go to the bother of having a permit to carry my old Colt Model 1911A1, the basic "Army .45 automatic" you see in too many old movies. Sure enough, both the pistol and the permit were there in my bags, the pistol carefully disassembled and labeled in six different ways to get it through European customs. I carefully reassembled it, checked it out, and slipped it into my shoulder holster.

"Pretty silly," I grumbled, "when I'm better armed by far with stuff they wouldn't even notice, to have to call attention to myself with this."

"You're a bodyguard," Chrys pointed out, being practical. "And someone took a shot at your ward. It's what people will expect."

"Yeah, yeah." Actually it felt good to have the old overweight piece of iron back on, and at least in my home timeline it does have an advantage that the NIF and SHAKK don't. If you look at a NIF, you think, "cordless drill" or maybe "kid's ray gun"; if you look at a SHAKK you think, "super squirt gun sprayed with aluminum paint." Never mind that the former can knock out an infantry platoon with a burst and the latter, in a pinch, can blast its way into a bank vault or bring down a bomber. (I know, I've done both with it.) They don't look like real weapons, and you have to *use* them to convince people, and a lot of times you don't want to use it, you just want to convince them.

If you look at a Colt .45, however, you think, "This will blow big holes in people." Which can mean you don't have to pull the trigger.

There was a knock at the door. I moved to one side of it and asked, "Who is it?" in English.

"A friend from Athens."

That wasn't the password. It also wasn't *not* the password; it was the kind of thing a field agent might improvise, and also the kind of thing that a Closer agent might try.

Chrys drew her NIF and covered the door. I gingerly reached out and flipped the dead bolt.

"Come in very slowly," I said, holding the .45 level at head height.

Something was wrong the instant the door opened. Just what was wrong didn't register, but it was enough to know we were in a fight, and I pulled the trigger.

A .45 makes a deafening roar in an enclosed space like a hotel room, and that added to the confusion. The door swung wide, and I saw that the body falling onto the carpet was in a short black dress; Chrys's NIF whined, and something fell backward in the hall. She fired twice more, hitting nothing, though I could hear her rounds wailing off like tiny bees down the halls, looking for other targets. I hoped they were set on stun, so she wouldn't kill—

Oh, hell, a maid. Whoever was barging in had pushed a maid in front of him, and I had shot her—

There was no sound from the hall, and I crept forward to look at the body of the maid. She was middle-aged, gray hair dyed blond, face blue-black, the garrote

still embedded in her neck—she had been dead before
he ever knocked, before I fired—

"Mark! That package!"

I turned and saw that, beside the unconscious man,
there was a small cardboard box that could be a shirt,
or some pastry, or—

There was a great flash and roar, and the world got
very dark and quiet.

I woke up very slowly. As I did, I began to take stock . . .
my nightmares begin with the idea of being captured by
the Closers and waking up in one of their hospitals.
They wouldn't save my life because they liked me or out
of any humanitarian purpose, and I know too well what
advanced technology can do to the nervous system. If I
was waking up slowly, and in Closer hands, it just might
be possible I wasn't in restraints, and in that case I could
kill one or more of them—or kill myself before they got
to work on me. The kind of torture they can do, no one
stands up to for even a moment; it's not so much pain
that you can't bear, but the fact that they just strip-mine
your mind till there's nothing left, and you can feel the
whole process. Your consent doesn't really matter.

Nightmare number two is waking up in a modern
twentieth-century hospital. They mean well, but the
buildings themselves are nests of germs, most of the
available drugs are poisons—and, most of all, our doctors can't really *heal*, that is, they can't make things
grow back good as new. And it could be a long time
before I got a replacement eye or leg, and if I lost a
limb and had to maintain a cover, I'd have to live without the arm or leg until the cover wasn't needed anymore . . . bad news, too, but not as bad as being
captured by the Closers.

I couldn't feel sheets or anything around me, but I could feel considerable pain. So I wasn't under a twenty-ninth-century pain block, which meant I wasn't back in the hospital at Hyper Athens. Bad news . . . that left the more nightmarish possibilities . . .

I opened my eyes slowly and blinked twice. It made no difference. I was either blind or in total darkness. I tried to grope toward my face, and my right arm wouldn't move. Broken? It didn't feel like it. Pinned against my side somehow.

My left arm would move but only in a small space next to my body. I was getting the pain localized to the middle of my back, the back of my legs, and a little bit on my head. I was also trying to figure out whether I had been out at all . . . I could smell cordite, and some other explosive.

My right hand groped again and found the butt of the .45 under me, dragged it around, confirmed the barrel was warm. If I'd been unconscious, it had been for less than a minute. I knew the worst, anyway. I was buried in rubble.

I tried shouting, then, and heard nothing right away, but of course all that means is the pile was thick. Besides, from the way my ears felt, I had probably been deafened by the blast.

When you're buried in rubble, the big danger is that you'll make it collapse around your air-space, or make it shift and bend some part of yourself in a direction it shouldn't go. I shouted for help a couple more times, and then decided I'd work on getting out, in between shouting.

A lot of slow, careful groping determined that I was in a narrow space with something heavy and soft digging into my back. I was in pain from what felt like bad bruises, but I wasn't burned anywhere except a bit on my face, and I didn't seem to be leaking blood. "Help! Help! I'm in here!" I yelled again, waited for an answer, and went back to groping around me.

It didn't take much more to determine that my head was in the biggest space I had available. It was hard work feeling around behind me, but what was pushing down on me directly seemed to be a mass of cloth, hair, and wires. I tried raising my head and bumped it on the hard surface above me; a flat stick was pressing across my shoulders, not painfully, but annoying me all the same.

I yelled again, and heard nothing again. For good measure I yelled for Chrys a couple of times. The bomb blast had had a much straighter shot at her than at me, but she'd been aware it was a bomb sooner . . . and she'd been by a window. Maybe she was able to duck and cover and then get out?

At least I hadn't smelled smoke, and there was air in here, so probably the building was not burning over my head.

I yelled again, and no one answered. I decided, very, very tentatively, to try to push the "roof" upward on my little safety space. Maybe I wasn't buried by much, and even if I was, maybe I could get to a better space. And why hadn't I heard any of the search parties?

The little space I was in wasn't much bigger than a coffin, and it took a while just to get my hands under my shoulders to try this extradifficult push-up. By the time I did, I could feel sweat pouring down my back. There seemed to be air but not much.

I pushed hard, and something gave above me. Dirty, dusty, but open air hit my lungs at exactly the same instant that I realized that there was light, and I could *see*.

Forgetting the possible danger, I pushed hard and

suddenly everything broke loose, but in eerie silence. I sat up to see Chrys, still clutching her NIF, standing in the wrecked hotel room. Her mouth moved, but no sound came out, and then I reached up, touched my ears, and found blood running out.

I staggered to my feet. I had been under an armoire which had fallen, open, over me while I lay beside the maid's body; the "wires, hair, and cloth" had been hangers, coats, and clothes, the "stick" in my back the clothes rod. The great pile of weight had been the shattered plaster wall that lay on top of the armoire.

And Chrysamen was up and moving. "I can't hear," I cried. "My eardrums are ruptured."

She nodded and appeared to motion to me, but before I could read any of her signals, she stepped back and gestured.

A gate was opening in front of us, the gray void forming there. The two couriers who had passed through the airliner bathroom to ATN before—the woman, this time, tanned darker, and with her hair done like Chrysamen's—stepped out and gestured for us to get in. We did, and it became deep gray, then there was nothing at all, and after a while it all came swimming back in a way not too different from some old television sets—a glow, a sound, black-and-white, color.

We were on a small receiving dock at ATN's Hyper Athens spaceport—the overhead view is unmistakable once you've been there a few times—and a couple of doctors were converging on us. In a minute they'd sprayed something in my ears to make them stop hurting, gotten us both on stretchers, and loaded us into one of the little electric airplanes they use inside the station (when a space station is tens of miles across, and in low gravity it's easy to fly, air travel makes a lot of sense). My last thought before I passed out on the stretcher was that I wasn't going to get to hear Porter's concert after all, and that I had really been looking forward to it.

The next morning I was ravenously hungry—the "nanos," the microscopic machines they inject into your bloodstream to repair the damage, live on your blood sugar just as you do, and they eat up a lot of it doing repairs. I now had two good eardrums again, and in the places where I should have had bruises, the nanos had reabsorbed the blood and rebuilt the tissue, so I was fit and healthy, if terribly hungry.

It turned out that Chrys had been badly shaken, cracked a couple of ribs, and broken one tooth, so all that had to be repaired on her.

As we sat and gobbled down the local equivalent of pancakes with the local equivalent of jelly, Ariadne Lao filled us in on the situation.

"As far as we can determine," she said, "the attack was coordinated with a couple of people who were going to set up to take down Porter Brunreich's helicopter. They wanted you out of the way so that they could get a clear shot. We've captured one of them alive, and we're trying to find out who he was working for—not ultimately, of course, since we all know it has to be the Closers, but what organization in your timeline, how he's being controlled. We may have to resort to mind-stripping, which I'm not crazy about, but . . ." She sighed and shrugged. "This is important, and we can't trust him to tell the truth. And we can certainly tell that he is lying to us."

"Go ahead, if it's up to me," Chrys said. She can be kind of vengeful, but then she really hates getting hurt.

"I'll weigh your vote in," Ariadne Lao said, with a faint smile. "At any rate, as soon as we know, we'll be dropping you back in to finish the mission—about three minutes after your stand-ins get there. Oh, and we've surgically altered that corpse so that it won't be too obvious that she was shot, Mr. Strang. That way you won't be doing jail time while the authorities back in your own timeline figure it out."

"Great with me," I said. "I don't relish the idea of a German jail."

She looked a little baffled. "In our timeline, the Germans have an image of being rather sweet, gentle, and ineffectual," she said. "There's a comedian who does a routine about German jailers who are constantly worrying that the prisoners aren't happy."

"Not exactly the image I grew up with," I said.

A few minutes later we were once again headed back to my home timeline—and though we had spent the better part of a day healing back at Hyper Athens, we were only gone from our own timeline for about thirty seconds, just the time needed for safety. We had just traded places with our stand-ins, and the gate had just closed, when we heard screams and running. I holstered my .45.

A moment later, there were fifty hotel employees standing around, and the hotel detective was making officious noises. I showed him a huge sheaf of official paper, and while he was puzzling and harrumphing his way through that, the regular cops showed up, and right on their heels the antiterror unit out of Dresden, which had taken advantage of a *Bundeswehr* chopper that was available at that moment.

We all had a very good time exchanging stories, and fortunately although the Germans are the people who lead the world in bureaucracy (Bismarck invented it and Weber named it), that does mean that they've had a lot of practice and are pretty good at doing bureaucratic things quickly. Also, even though there was a lot to do, the computers were doing most of it, and they move pretty fast—in very little time it had been established that we were both licensed bodyguards, married, legally armed, and here to guard someone's body.

A few more checks turned up the important information that we were there to meet Porter Brunreich, and identified both my personal connection to her and the fact that she had already been attacked in Norway. All of a sudden we had crack German antiterror forces surrounding the helicopter landing area, and some serious VIP treatment for Porter.

In the middle of all the crashing, bustling arrangements, someone tapped my shoulder, and I turned around to see—"*Paula!*"

She hugged me, and it was a good thing I wasn't still sore from the bomb blast, because Paula, besides being built like a bear, seems to be about as strong as one. And a lot meaner, for that matter, when she needs to be.

"Boss, I'd ask what you're doing here, but life is full of surprises enough already. I got out here to meet Porter's chopper, and I found you'd shown up with the German Army."

I grinned back at her. It's always great to have trusted people around, and though I knew the German forces were a lot more capable than anything my agency could have put on the ground, it felt good to have Paula there as another backup.

That also reminded me that it had only been a day in that timeline since the first attack on Porter, a day since Chrysamen and I had stopped that bank robbery in New York. Time certainly flew when you were having fun.

We were set up on a parking lot, not at a regular helipad, with an eye to better security. The German troops, silent and fierce-looking, were scattered around, some visible as a deterrent, some undercover to supply backup. The whole area could be brought under interlocking fields of fire at any instant.

The major in charge of the AT troopers, a quiet guy named Kurtz, who didn't smile much and seemed a little bemused by the whole job of landing a child-prodigy pianist safely, came over to talk to me. "Herr Strang?"

"Yes, Major Kurtz?" The chip behind my ear let me speak and understand German without an accent.

"As far as I can tell, we have everything secure. I am making sure there is nothing I have overlooked. At the moment, radio contact informs me that the helicopter carrying Fraulein Brunreich is a few kilometers away. They will come in low, hopping and jigging near ground level on an indirect route, hoping to avoid the danger of a shoulder-fired missile."

"That seems smart," I said. "And your men understand that if it looks bizarre, it's probably the enemy?"

"Yes, sir. Though next to what has already happened I can't imagine what it would take to look bizarre."

I nodded. "I can understand. Nonetheless, I have good reason to think it *can* get more bizarre."

"That suggests that you know more than you have told us."

"I don't know more, but I suspect more. Don't forget, you're dealing with an organization—not just an individual but a group of them—who are interested in killing a child because she plays the piano beautifully. If that doesn't make you suspect more bizarreness may be in waiting—"

"I take your point." Kurtz sighed. "Not like the old

days, when it was just some liberation army for people you had never heard of. That was comparatively simple."

His cellular phone pinged, and he brought it to his ear. "Yes? Good. All right, we're ready. Thank you. Good-bye." He turned back to me, and said, "Well, our 'delivery' is under way. The helicopter should arrive at any moment."

I looked across the broad parking lot; they had knocked down a dozen light poles and hauled them away to make a clear landing space. There were concrete wedges of "New Jerseys"—the traffic barriers you see on highways all the time—set up in zigzag rows, with troopers crouching behind them, on two sides of the lot. The big department store across the way was empty, commandeered for the time being, and behind its dozens of windows there were crack snipers.

I didn't bother to turn and look, but I knew that in the highway ditch behind, there were another thirty ATs, all ready for action.

I also knew that if Chrys and I were to jump in here with our SHAKKs and NIFs going, we could wipe out every one of them before they had half a chance to shoot back. And I knew that if the Closers had it together enough to jump in here—and knew exactly where and what they were aiming for—they could put anything on top of us, up to and including enough nukes to cut Europe in half from the Baltic to the Med.

I didn't like knowing that. I prefer operations somewhere way the hell away from people who aren't in the war—or at least don't know they're in it. I guess if you look at it from a certain point of view, all of the possible histories the world has had are in the war. But nonetheless, I think most of the time you can tell a soldier from a civilian, and most of the time you can tell a soldier with a stake in your war from a soldier on other business, and if it were up to me, we'd be fighting the Closers in the middle of the Sahara in some timeline where life never moved out of the oceans. I don't *like* the idea of innocent bystanders getting hurt, and even though these guys were armed to the teeth, and sent to guard Porter, in another sense they truly were innocent bystanders. That is, they didn't know what the hell was going on or who they might be up against.

So I looked over the array of armaments and just didn't feel as secure as I was probably supposed to.

After a few long breaths, I heard the beat of the rotor and saw the flash of the chopper rising over the trees. The pilot was pretty good in a flashy kind of way; he bounced down, then up, coming in over the department store, and made a rapid descent to the parking lot, stopping the rotor almost as soon as he touched down. The door opened and Porter ran out toward us.

She was most of the way to us when I saw a gray shimmer forming behind the helicopter, and, without stopping to think, I shouted, "Down, Porter, down!"

I always give my ward a lot of credit for alertness and common sense, and once again she was on top of matters—she hit the dirt right away. There was a roar as something shot out of the emerging gate and hit the chopper. The fuel tank blew, enveloping the helicopter in dense orange flames and black smoke. The pilot staggered out, his clothes on fire, and was shot in the back.

From behind the New Jerseys around the edge of the lot, the ATs opened up on whatever was coming through the now-open gate. I tore my coat down the back drawing the SHAKK from between my shoulder blades, and to my right Chrysamen yanked hers out; we each took three quick sidesteps and hit the ground.

The burning remains of the helicopter flew into

pieces as another explosive round hit. Blazing wreckage and chunks of iron rained down on the lot. I could hear the steady rattle of automatic-weapons fire from the ditch, the New Jerseys, and the store windows.

But I could see it wouldn't be enough. The first Closers to charge through the gate had fallen, but there was already a ring of them surrounding their gate, setting up bulletproof barriers, getting return fire aimed back at us. I'd seen no superweapons yet, but it wasn't atypical of the Closers to push sacrificial lambs through first.

I ripped a SHAKK burst across the barriers; they fell over and shattered, and several of the bodies twitched and fell. The rest, exposed to the fire of the German commandos, were hit almost immediately. Chrysamen's burst into the gate would have slowed them further—if there had been troops in there.

Instead, what was crawling out of the gate was a silver dome floating just off the ground. I had seen those before, and I knew what this one was. Under the gleaming surface there were a dozen hypersonic homing-projectile guns, each delivering enough force to take down a house on every shot.

It was the Closer equivalent of a tank, rolling out into an ordinary department-store parking lot in our century. It must have cost them more electric power than the USA produces in a year to get that thing back here.

Chrys's rounds rang off its surface repeatedly, bouncing and then turning around to try again until they were out of energy. She might as well have been firing puffed rice. I fired, too, but more from a need to do something than from any belief that it would succeed.

The Closer "tanks" never appear to pivot; either

their surfaces are so smooth we can't see them turn, or they can fire from any point on their surfaces. There was a deep, rumbling roar, and the row of New Jerseys on one end of the parking lot flew into gravel—mixed with flesh, blood, and bone—that sprayed across the empty field behind.

Chrys hurled a PRAMIAC through the Closer gate, and a moment later the red glow was followed by the gate switching off. But she had been able to set the PRAMIAC all the way up to ten megatons because the explosion would happen on the other side of the gate—in our timeline, it didn't actually "exist" at all.

The Closer tank was already here, and anything that would take it out would take out half of Weimar with it.

5

When there's no hope you do what you can think of. I emptied the SHAKK at the thing. We knew they never appeared to be harmed, but maybe I was giving everyone inside a terrible headache, maybe I was blinding the defense system, and just possibly there was actually a vulnerable spot, and one of the rounds would find it by accident.

None of the above happened. They screamed off it as uselessly as the much slower, unguided bullets from the AT forces, and just as Chrys's rounds had, they rattled against it repeatedly with no discernible effect. The tank drifted outward, as if looking around.

Porter, staying low to the ground, crawled slowly toward us.

At least the tank no longer had its infantry cover. They're supposed to be vulnerable when that happens, but of course that's one of our tanks, from our timeline. If this thing was vulnerable, it wasn't vulnerable to anything much we had on hand.

Chrys rolled a PRAMIAC toward it, along the ground; it ran over the tennis ball–sized object.

There was a sudden red glow over the surface of the tank; just for good measure, I sprayed it some more with the SHAKK.

The red glow faded, and the tank continued to roll across the pavement as before. Shots were still pinging off it, but there was no effect.

Meanwhile, Porter was still crawling steadily on her belly toward me. I wriggled forward toward her, still firing at the tank.

Again it blasted away, this time at the other set of New Jerseys. Whatever it fired, it was hypersonic and came in a broad band rather than as individual shots. The surfaces of the New Jerseys pitted, broke up, and crumbled like a wall of sugar hit by a hot spray of water. The roar of the concrete being ground to bits was deafening.

The tops of the New Jerseys crumbled, and they began to break into large pieces. The spray of invisible hypersonic particles was hitting with such force that the remaining pieces—the size of grapefruits and softballs—flew backward like cannonballs, killing the men behind them.

An instant later, the deadly wash of hypersonic particles had sanded the rest from existence; what was left of the men was a reddish tinge in the smear that stretched into the shattered forest beyond.

The tank advanced slowly toward us.

Porter was squirming forward for all she was worth now, the black sweatshirt and jeans she usually wore getting smeared with mud and gravel, her blond hair shining in the autumn sun. (Abstractly I hoped the Closers wouldn't be able to use that to spot her; at least we were in a country with a lot of blond people.) I saw that she had managed to get the .38 I'd given her out, but she wasn't trying to get it into play—another sign of her common sense, for at that range she couldn't have hit a thing, and if the SHAKK wasn't denting that monster, and a PRAMIAC was barely warming it up, they'd never even notice .38 snakeshot.

I crawled forward toward her, not because I could do anything effective, but just to be with her. We were nearly touching when the tank suddenly zagged toward us.

Chrys fed it another PRAMIAC, and this time it glowed a much brighter red—she must have notched the power setting on the PRAMIAC up a little—and actually sat still for a moment before it again began to move toward us. Probably she'd made everyone inside feel like they'd gotten a bad sunburn. Certainly she couldn't have safely gone any higher on the PRAMIAC setting, as it was a hard gust of wind that blew out from under the tank and I felt tremendous heat on my face.

The Closer tank drew nearer; Porter was now so close that I reached out and squeezed her free hand in front of me.

"Doesn't look good at all, kid," I said.

"I'm glad you're here," she replied.

The tank was looming large as it bore down on us; I was practically out of SHAKK ammunition anyway, and it seemed futile to try firing any more.

The light shifted and changed somehow, a flickering grayish glow on the other side of us from the tank. I looked over, and then up, to see a circle of colorless gray appear in the blue autumn sky; I couldn't tell how far away as there were no reference points.

It was another gate, but was it ours or theirs?

The question was answered in a flash—literally. A

straight black line emerged from the center of the gate, and touched the Closer tank. The tank changed color, first from silver to gold, and then from gold to dull red.

Then it flew into pieces—big, hot glowing pieces that blew over our heads and crashed to the ground all around us. That settled the question as far as I was concerned—whoever it was on the other side of that gate were the good guys.

But as I was raising my head cautiously, I saw something that both startled me and explained a lot. We knew that Closer tanks were hard to knock out and that they seemed to fight as if in perfect condition right up till the moment when they were knocked out. They also never seemed to run out of fuel or ammo.

Now I saw why. Where the tank had stood, there was now a naked, gray gate.

The tanks had never been anything more than tough, mirrored armor over a gate; the power sources, ammunition, even parts of the weapons and crew themselves had been on the other side.

And now that the gate was exposed, they were still not giving up. Before I had time to react, twenty of them had raced through the gate. I gave them a quick blast with the SHAKK, and several fell dead, in that characteristic collapsing-bag way. Beside me, Porter's .38 barked, and then I heard the whiz of Chrysamen's NIF. We were back to an old-fashioned firefight around the mouth of a gate.

Except that the Closer tank had managed to wipe out most of our allies. I heard Paula's 9 mm also, and saw that the Closer troopers were now down flat. You could hardly ask for a more dangerous situation—there were superweapons around, and everyone could see everyone else.

Four of them convulsed and died from the fléchettes

of Chrys's NIF, but they were working on getting an angle on us—

A curtain of fire ripped over our heads, sounding like outsize SHAKK rounds. All of the people facing us twitched once, a bouncing motion that might have been the last gasp of the nervous system, or might only have been the physical shock from the momentum of the projectiles.

Once again, the straight black line stabbed out, this time into the gate itself, which abruptly glowed deep red, and then white—and then went out, a lot faster than any candle ever had.

We all took a long breath, and then I slowly rose to my feet. There were fewer than a dozen German commandos still alive, and none of them was an officer. Paula, Chrys, Porter, and I were all still fine.

There was an immense number of dead Closers around where the two gates had been; most of the bodies had been hit multiple times.

I had a feeling that this was not going to be easy to explain to the German authorities.

A dark shadow fell across the parking lot, and I turned to see that the gate had widened till it took up a big part of the sky immediately above us—and through it, there emerged the great, dark bulk of a dirigible.

The airship slid neatly out of the gate, which closed in a blink behind it, and descended slowly to the pavement; long, spidery legs telescoped out of it.

Though it flew and maneuvered like a dirigible, it didn't land like one; it came down quickly and precisely, like a helicopter, and it didn't bounce in the breeze.

A ramp descended, and out came a circus ringmaster, flanked by two extras from *Ben-Hur*. At least that was *my* first thought. The top hat and the tux were sort of flashy and bright-colored, and something about the centurion outfits (which really did look a lot like the Roman Meal Bread version) suggested that they weren't well cared for.

But a closer look revealed that the reason the Roman armor, helmet, and leggings looked so casually treated was because those guys were wearing them like clothes; I suddenly realized that, just possibly, this was what they always wore. Moreover, though they had scabbards with short swords, they were holding big, blocky objects that looked a lot like flattened overhead projectors—but were probably weapons, and I would guess of neither the neural-induction nor the hypersonic-projectile types that we and the Closers had been fighting with for so long.

Something about those objects told me that the SHAKK in my hand was about as up-to-date, as of that moment, as a Pilgrim musket.

The guy in the top hat and tails, on the other hand, did not look the least bit comfortable. The outfit's basic color seemed to be mauve, though it was fighting it out with enough reds and purples in the pattern to not be the clear winner. The shirt had too much lace and too many ruffles for a production of *The Three Musketeers*, and the cummerbund clashed with everything else in a way that I'd never quite seen colors do before.

He wore a waxed mustache and an enormous white tie that added to the ringmaster effect—though now that I thought about it, he might also have passed for a stage magician, or possibly for the groom at the tackiest formal wedding you ever attended.

He glanced from side to side, looked at each of us in turn, and then walked slowly in my direction. The two guys in the Roman outfits moved a little to the side and followed; that easy, practiced motion told me that

I shared an occupation with them. They were his body-guards.

I was already carefully slipping my SHAKK back into its sheath between my shoulders, under my ripped coat. I knew in my bones these guys were friendly, and, anyway, if they hadn't been, I might as well have had a kid's popgun or a fistful of soggy noodles to throw at them.

Beside me, Porter was returning her .38 to its shoulder holster, and everyone else seemed to have reached the same conclusion I had, and decided that there was no point in being ready for a fight we would be sure to lose, even if these guys didn't show every sign of being our friends.

The ringmaster was very tall and slim, and I realized now that either his blond hair or his black mustache must be a dye job. He had approached close enough to touch me, and as he did, Porter and Chrys closed in around me.

"Do I have the honor of addressing Mr. Mark Strang?" he asked, in perfect English.

"I'm Mark Strang," I said. "And you are . . . ?"

The whole thing was seeming much too real for a hallucination, and besides, I've been knocked out, beaten senseless, drugged in various ways, and hit with all kinds of neural induction, and I've never had the kind of hallucination they depict in the movies. Not to mention that if you work for ATN, you get used to seeing all sorts of things; I was in a timeline once where the King of Scotland routinely dressed like Carmen Miranda, but that's another story.

The man appeared to be disconcerted by the question of who he was, for just a moment; then he swallowed hard and said, "I'm just a minor functionary, sir. My only job here is to bring the ship to you, to Ms.

Brunreich, and to Ms. ja N'wook so that we can take you to a meeting with our leaders."

I nodded. "Nonetheless, I would prefer to know your name."

"My name is Caius Xin Schwarz," he said. "Now, may I request again, sir, that we be allowed to take you to our timeline for a conversation with people who can actually answer your questions?"

I checked the weapons, without turning my head. We sure as hell couldn't draw on them. And god knew what might be trained on us from the airship. They'd done nothing hostile; they were just a little rude, and "rude" is a culturally relative term—this might be the way they all talk to each other. In plenty of nations on Earth, people answer the phone with "Who is this?" and for that matter in California the car-rental people call everyone by first name . . . possibly he came from an even ruder timeline than our own.

So there was nothing much to be done, and it might turn out all right. I let my eyes stray sideways to Chrys, and her hand flickered in a "balancing" gesture with the thumb crossed—"better do what he says but I'll back you if you want to try something else," at least that's how I read it. Such codes have to be subtle and all but invisible, so it's never possible to be sure it isn't just a case of an itchy thumb.

"All right," I said, "we'll come along, as long as we're permitted to stick together and to retain our weapons."

He nodded. "Of course. Please come with us—er, just the three people named, please."

I decided to see how much weight I swung, and said, "Paula is very much a valued assistant, she speaks no German, and I don't want to leave her here to take the heat for all these corpses."

Again he nodded. "We may be gone for a long time, and I cannot assure her safe return."

"Nonetheless, if she chooses to go, I want her with me."

Caius Xin Schwarz nodded, and said, "All right, then. Are there any other people you wish to add to the party?"

"Not at present." I looked around at the dazed, baffled German AT troopers, pointed to one of the ones with some stripes on his shoulder, and said, in German, "You."

"Sir?" He seemed relieved to have some idea what to do; answering questions must be a lot better than standing there wondering which parts of your world had fallen away into chaos . . .

"Please inform the authorities that I will return to this spot within twenty-four hours to offer a full explanation. Don't worry about further attacks; with myself, my wife, and Fräulein Brunreich removed, there will be no cause for them, and this site will not be attacked again. Please repeat back what you will tell your superiors."

"You will return here within twenty-four hours to explain, and there is no reason to fear any further attack."

"Good." I turned to Caius Xin Schwarz, and said, "We are ready to go."

The gadget that extended down from the side of the airship, which I had thought was a simple ramp, turned out to be a moving sidewalk of sorts, though I couldn't see anything actually moving. When we stepped on it, we were carried by something that moved our feet rapidly up the ramp, and we found ourselves standing inside a large lounge or saloon within the airship.

I suppose waiting rooms are one of the things that are most alike from timeline to timeline and civilization to civilization. What you want the person waiting to do is to sit there and not do anything until he or she is wanted. And the way you achieve that is to make the environment very soothing, supply just enough distractions to keep them from revolting out of sheer boredom, and above all else make remaining seated the easiest possible thing to do. These folks were past masters at it, clearly; Caius Xin Schwarz gestured for us to sit, and we found we were all in the sort of chair that is just low enough and just squashy enough so that there is a little extra effort required to get up.

They also brought out cups of a steaming milk, coffee, and cocoa mix that was surprisingly tasty; I realized, too, that a little coconut milk must be in there, probably as a sweetener. Since all of us had just been terrified out of our minds, the combination of comfortable chairs and hot milk promptly made us all drowsy.

Porter, now that Chrys and I were there, probably felt perfectly safe. Even at eighteen, even with the terrible things that had happened in her past (she had seen her mother murdered by Closer agents), she still figured she was perfectly safe with two of her three big heroes there. (Chrys and Paula—I qualify as "good old Mark," mainly in charge of spoiling her rotten. The third hero is Robbie.) For the rest of us it just made staying awake that much harder.

But Paula is about as good a bodyguard as there is, and Chrys and I had been trained pretty well, so we didn't nod off. Instead, we looked around and watched things.

The furniture was in reds and blues; was that a clan color, national color, something the culture valued, or pure coincidence? It vaguely matched the clothing on the few people we had seen, but were they in uniform or did they just like those colors for their own clothing?

There was space in here to seat twenty, which argued that this space was not particularly for us; ergo this airship had other missions at other times. ATN, for a special mission, might have built such a ship, but it would have built it for that one special purpose, and it would have been much too expensive to operate as a regular thing. So if these people were operating it regularly, they were somewhere far in advance of ATN—or say a thousand years beyond what we had in my timeline.

We had seen nothing that resembled a flag, but besides the Roman look to the guards' outfits, there were a lot of eagles around, and since the Romans hadn't used flags and had had a major eagle fetish, I was pretty secure in identifying them as Roman. However, I hadn't noticed any "SPQR" ("senatus populusque Romanus"—meaning "this was done by the Senate and the people of Rome"), which in our timeline the Romans put on everything from roads and bridges to monuments and outhouses.

That could either mean they never got in the habit of using it, or that maybe the Senate was abolished. Or maybe their timeline was only partly descended from Rome. I could hear conversation in the distance, but not clearly enough to be sure of the language, and of course even that wouldn't tell you much about their timeline.

While I had been trying to hear, the airship had lifted off. The movement was fairly swift, but there was little sense of acceleration; one moment we were looking out at the land around us from an effective height of maybe twenty feet, the next we were rising into the sky. We turned to face the wind, and still there was no audible motor, propeller, turbine, or jet in the process; the ship just did what it did, no fuss or noise about it.

Through the windows, we saw the sky ahead of us darken. A moment later it got gray, then dark, then sounds went away, and then any sense of being there; after an eternal while, light, then sound, then definition, and finally color came back. We had crossed over into another timeline. "Some budget they have here," Chrys observed. "Rather than walk through a gate to us, they send a whole ship through and back? Either they have more energy than they need, or they don't mind burning it, or both."

I nodded. The major reason that nobody has wiped out all the other timelines is that travel is very expensive, and the more you send through, the higher the cost goes. It was just about inconceivable that anyone would send anything this big through on what seemed to be purely a diplomatic mission—but there you had it, here we were.

Which meant they were economically *far* in advance of ATN, and to judge from the way this airship performed, they were probably way out in front technologically as well.

"How do you suppose this thing is working?" I asked Chrys. "It's pretty clearly lighter than air whenever they want it to be, so it doesn't work by filling a gasbag, like our blimps, and it doesn't work by using vacuum gels like the ATN ones. How can they add or remove so much weight without making any sound?"

"We rotate it into the collapsed dimensions," Caius Xin Schwarz said, entering. "The ship is made of cells within cells; any cell can make the matter inside itself vanish, and restore it later, by causing it to rotate into one of the dimensions that didn't expand when the universe was formed. We can get right up to the edge of the stratosphere using that technique."

I had once read something about the collapsed dimensions, I vaguely recalled, in an issue of *Discover*. Chrys is from a timeline some centuries in advance of mine, and she looked as blank as I did. Oh, well, we have a saying in the Crux Ops that once you're fifty years in advance of your own time, everything is magic.

"Can you tell us where, exactly, you're taking us?" I asked.

"To Rome, of course. You'll be addressing the tribunes and the Senate."

"What about?" I knew enough Roman history from my years as an art historian to ask, "And I assume the consuls as well?"

"Of course, all the ceremonial offices. And then there will be a festival, and—" He stopped and stared at me. "What on Earth do you mean, 'what about'?"

"I have no idea why anyone in this timeline would want me to speak to them," I said. "I figured you'd be telling me what it was all about sooner or later."

He scratched his head. "You *are* Mark Strang? Native of Pittsburgh, Pennsylvania, United States of America?"

"Yep. And where I came from the North won the Civil War, World War I ended in November 1918, Elvis never entered politics, McGovern lost in 1972, and the Soviet Union broke up after a crisis in 1991." Since he was obviously familiar with our family of timelines, giving him the major breakpoints would at least let him decide whether he had a guy from the wrong timeline.

He shook his head—obviously that gesture went back a long way. "You're the right one, but I will have to talk to my superiors before I can tell you anything else. And probably they will insist that I bring you to them before explaining anything. Something is seriously wrong here." He got up and headed for the door.

"Thanks for zapping the Closers anyway," I said.

He stopped and nodded. "We were surprised to find them there, but we thought it was a last-minute counterattack. But now that you mention it, it may be a clue to the whole problem."

He shot through the door like a rocket; I guess he was a bit nervous. "Well," Paula said, "since it looks like we will have some time on our hands, I don't suppose anyone here would mind telling me absolutely everything that's going on, and then maybe following up by explaining why three people I thought I had known for years have this secret life I've never heard of that apparently involves flying saucers and armies from nowhere?"

We were both grateful to have something to do other than worry; we started at the beginning, explaining about the war between ATN and the Closers, about how I had accidentally fallen into the middle of it in my home timeline, that the three years when I was supposedly working "undercover," a few years before, had actually been the time when I had stowed away and entered a Closer timeline and conducted my own private war there. We told her about the dozens of cases, and she was even sharp enough to ask why we didn't seem to have aged much. Finally she asked, "And you've never seen these guys before? They don't look like anybody else?"

"Well, they're clearly Roman-descended," I said, "and like most of the timelines based on Greece or Rome, they've pretty well intermarried everybody, at least if our friend Caius is any indicator. Roman first name, Chinese or Korean second, and something

Germanic for the third . . . the ancient civilizations didn't worry much about intermarriage. But as to which of the many Romes they hail from, we don't know. We've only explored a bit over a million time-lines, and there's maybe a million in Closer territory we can't get to—by 'we' I mean ATN, because Chrys and I have only been to about a dozen each, not counting short visits and some training camps and things. But the best guess is that there are a few octillion timelines. Figure in any civilization that makes it all the way to modern industrial technology and so forth, there are going to be at least twenty or so turning points in their history. Figure most turning points could have gone several ways. It adds up in a hurry, once there are time travelers going back there to change things."

Paula shook her head, and said, "I will never, never say again that people don't appreciate how many alternatives there are."

I laughed; if her sense of humor was intact, we hadn't freaked her out too much. "Anyway, for some reason I'm apparently important to these people, and so are Chrys and Porter. And it looks like we were supposed to know what we did. I sure don't, and if Chrys did, she'd have spoken up. And Porter knows about ATN, but this is the first time she's been crosstime, so I don't think she'll have any idea either. No, we just have to wait and—"

Once again, the door opened abruptly, and our unhostly host came in. "We've determined that a mistake was made, and that it wasn't the fault of anyone on board this airship."

"Well, that's a load off my mind," I said.

He ignored the sarcasm, and said, "Unfortunately, as I had guessed, the mistake is serious enough so that we are going to have to have you meet with the Chief

Tribune first, and he will explain matters to you. So I'm afraid I will have to leave you still puzzled for a while; can I at least offer you refreshments or answer any other questions?"

"Hmmm," Chrysamen said, "I don't suppose you've thought of this yet, but practically any question we can think of probably leads straight to things you aren't allowed to talk about. If there's time for us to have a meal, why don't we do that? Afterward maybe we'll have thought of something."

Another dead giveaway that you've stumbled into a Rome-derived timeline is the enormous variety of chopped, pickled fish that turns up on the table. They brought in about ten kinds, and a lot of flat hard bread, and we spent a while chewing and at least making sure that whatever happened next, we wouldn't be hungry. I noticed, too, that all of us were practiced enough at the way things can get fraught so that we were all careful to visit the toilet before the ship landed.

Then, finally, we were coming in over Rome. The first thing I noticed was that several of the landmarks I'd associated with the Romans weren't there, but then if "consul" was a purely ceremonial job, there had never been an Empire—it sounded as if the Roman Republic might still be a going concern. We landed on a wide terrace on the side of a gigantic building, stepped onto the moving-sidewalk-that-moved-you-but-not-itself, and stepped off onto the middle of the terrace on a fine, warm afternoon.

Caius Xin Schwarz walked out onto the terrace with us, saluted by sticking his arm straight out, and without a word went back inside. The ramp folded in behind him, and the ship rose into the sky.

The man who came out to greet us was wearing a toga of a deep reddish purple; probably it didn't mean he was emperor, but surely it meant he held considerable power. "Mr. Strang, I'm honored and a bit amazed to meet you," he said. His English was just as flawless as Caius Xin Schwarz's had been. "I am Marcus Annaeus Scipio, and I'm the Chief Tribune here. I believe we've found the nature of our error, and it's really quite embarrassingly simple. We'd never made such an enormous crosstime leap before, and it had not occurred to us that you would be in the same place in the same small city, so far from where you live, on two occasions exactly twenty-four hours apart. We gave poor Schwarz orders to pick you up twenty-four hours earlier than he should have."

"'So far crosstime,'" I echoed. "What year are we in?"

"Oh, it was almost purely a crosstime trip. You would count it as somewhere just before your own year 2000, and we would count it as 2750 A.U.C." So they were still measuring dates from the founding of Rome . . . yes, it looked like this was a world where the Roman Republic had managed to overrun the Earth without ever having an emperor. He smiled gently. "Believe it or not we thought we were just throwing a party for you, so we sent Captain Schwarz and his gunboat to bring you along."

"Uh, he's not the most party-hearty type I've ever met." To judge from the way the Chief Tribune snorted with laughter, it looked like the translation chips were doing everybody proud. "But what was the party *about*?"

"The idea was an historical commemoration—to have one of the most important, perhaps from our viewpoint the most important, crosstime traveler of all time come and visit us on what is both a significant year since the founding of Rome, and a significant anniversary in time travel. We first developed our own crosstime equipment just fifteen hundred years ago—tomorrow is the anniversary of our first test."

Somehow or other they had managed to be two hundred years ahead of my timeline's 1990s . . . and they had done it in the 400s A.D. They were seventeen hundred years in advance of my home timeline. No wonder I didn't understand them at all.

And he had said . . . just what had he said?

"Er," I asked. "This will sound very stupid, but I don't think I've done whatever it was, that I did, that was so important to you people. I mean, I probably did it, or rather I will do it . . ." Time travel can be so confusing. "But I haven't done it yet, in my chain of experience."

"So I gathered. Well, that's easy enough to fix; we can send you back to do it, and indeed we shall. What we're celebrating is the glorious day on which you saved the Roman Republic, Mr. Strang, by assassinating Gaius Julius Caesar."

6

I don't suppose my jaw could have dropped any farther, but while I was still thinking about it, Chief Tribune Scipio looked up over his head and said, "Yes?"

He appeared to hear something from nowhere, and then said, "Yes, of course, that's exactly what I wanted you to do. Show him in at once."

A door opened at the far end of the room, and General Malecela strode in. For a guy who had probably just been snagged as bizarrely as we had, he seemed pretty self-possessed.

I even had the impression he managed to wink at us as he walked up to join our group.

"I assume," he said, "that I'm in the presence of President Brunreich and Chief Tribune Scipio, and you must be Mr. Strang's personal associate—?"

"Paula Renatsky. Who are you?" Paula was not going to let herself be thrown by the unexpected addition of another person, no matter how impressive and dignified-looking.

He grinned. "Just so. I'm General Malecela, and within Crux Operations, I'm the boss, for Mister Strang and Friend-mother ja N'wook." He turned to Scipio, and said, "Your Captain Schwarz is quite possibly the rudest officer I've ever encountered in my life."

Scipio nodded. "I would be surprised if you had found a ruder one. At any rate, were you given an adequate briefing on the matter?"

"Believe me, I would not have stepped onto your airship if I had *not* had an adequate briefing." It might have been a bit of humor if Malecela had bothered to smile, but he didn't.

"Well, then I suppose the time has come to settle on what ought to be done—and perhaps to demystify our companions, here."

"Fine by me," Porter said. Paula quietly stepped on her foot.

The biggest problem with time travel is also its greatest virtue; once you can move around in time, you often have all the time you want to get something done.

When they thought they had grabbed me for a victory celebration, they had slipped only slightly; everything would work out fine, apparently, if they just made sure they returned me to Weimar, in my own timeline, twenty-four hours after I had left.

That is, fine with everyone else. The "approaching group of timelines" that Citizen-teacher Zouck had been so excited about (and Thebenides so afraid of) seemed to be descended from this one right here. Time travel had grown so inexpensive with them, and remote sensing of timelines so accurate, that they were able to do what was only theoretically possible for the Closers and ATN—whenever a major decision came

along, they were able to try out all the possible consequences, creating a new timeline for each one, keeping
them all in touch with each other, and then, if it had
turned out badly for any of the timelines, correcting
those so that no one had to live in a failed one.

Moreover, they had been able to institute regular
and reliable communications to reshape their own
past; this meant that when they knew they would be
taking on the Closers and showing up to aid ATN, they
had relayed the information back thousands of years so
that their ancestors could put some effort into getting
ready, and take advantage of a longer technical lead
time.

This had given them such a tremendous boost over
everyone else that even General Malecela simply shook
his head and said he had spent his brief visit to their
twenty-ninth-century (or by their figuring, thirty-sixth-
century) entirely in awe of their technology; when he
tried, later, to explain to us how amazing it was, we
realized you had to be from a highly advanced civilization like ATN just to understand that this Roman timeline was doing things that ought to be impossible.

They had been willing to share, too—apparently
their first contacts had been with the timelines in
which Porter had been president of the United States
(hey, I always knew my ward had a lot of potential) just
at the time when those timelines came under Closer
attack. The Romans had sized up the situation, figured
out who the bad guys were in zip time (small wonder,
since they were already looking for the Closers), and
beaten the living daylights out of the Closers, tracking
them from timeline to timeline too fast for them to
even warn each other of what was happening until it
was too late.

According to General Malecela, the Romans

appeared to be generous with technical assistance, material goods, and everything else, and seemed to have very little urge to meddle in anyone's affairs except for a strong desire for an open trade door. This didn't surprise me—the Roman Empire, in my timeline, was noted for always starting out with as generous a policy as possible, usually by making nations into honored allies and friends.

Of course if the honored ally and friend were ever so stupid as to try to give up the benefits of Roman alliance, then they stomped them flat.

Chrys and I, not knowing what might be bugged, managed to communicate our concern about those issues to each other (her timeline diverged from mine shortly after the death of Mohammed, so we shared the same Roman Empire in our past) without coming up with anything we could do about it.

Besides, I was much too bothered about the rest of it.

They didn't want to spill any more details than they already had, but it was clear that when the Romans found ATN, they were really just coming home; this timeline had been founded by an ATN Special Agent, and it was one of the "lost" timelines, one of the cases where a timeline got started and then communication was lost so thoroughly that it wasn't possible to find it again, to pick it out from all the myriad streams of events that made up time across all the parallel histories. So whatever had happened to the Special Agent, a fellow named Walks-in-His-Shadow Caldwell, no Crux Op had been dispatched to find him.

Or rather, that was what ATN thought. Caldwell had been dispatched about twenty years before General Malecela's time, in a failed ATN project where they spent an enormous amount of energy to move a gate through a gate—in this case, moving it to Diego Garcia in the early 1200s A.D. Thus there was nobody there to be interfered with, and it was possible to erect a huge power plant to drive the gate, and to send a dozen Special Agents farther back in time than anyone had ever gone before.

Unfortunately, every one of those timelines had promptly gone off the map; the farther back you go, the more widely things can diverge, and in these cases they had diverged so far and so fast that no one had been able to track them.

Until now, when this one had shown up, won the war, and made everybody happy.

Well, everybody except certain diehards like Thebenides, who were worried about the independence of all the ATN timelines and about whether the people liberated from the Closers would ever have any free choice.

And me, of course. Because it seemed to be universally agreed that I was going to kill Julius Caesar and that this was a good thing. And now it was clear that as a Crux Op, what I should do is go back to the lost timeline in 49 B.C.—or 704 A.U.C., as the Romans counted time—and get things back on track, apparently by murdering Caesar. Indeed, they weren't sure of all the details, but it didn't look like Mark Antony or Pompey was supposed to make it through the year either. Cicero, on the other hand, was supposed to live another thirty years, till he was almost ninety, retiring to write more books, instead of being murdered by Mark Antony's agents.

"So, just to begin with," I said, "every Latin student in thousands of timelines is going to hate me." I was pacing the floor in the gigantic bedroom they had given us.

"Be serious," Chrysamen said. "It's all right to tell me what you're upset about. I'm your wife, remember?"

I sighed and flopped down backward on the bed. "Well, look, the first thing to say is that I don't really see a way out of this, and even though they haven't exactly asked, I'm certainly going to go back there and see what I can do. And you know, I've shot a historical figure or two in my time, and been there when people who should have lived to ripe old ages died, and so forth. But the fact is, Chrys, you know they always send us back in a state of complete ignorance. We know a timeline is out of whack, and we're just supposed to bring it back into line, that's all.

"This is totally different. What if, in my judgment, old Julius—"

"Gaius."

"What?"

"Gaius. His first name is Gaius. If you're trying to make fun of him by being informal, that's what you call him. Julius is the family name and Caesar is the branch of cousins he belongs to." Her eyes had a slight twinkle to them, and her mouth had a funny turn; she seemed to be enjoying needling me. I wasn't sure why she didn't see it as being as serious as I did, and wasn't sure I wanted to know, either.

"Okay, anyway, what if this guy Gaius looks to me like the good guy in the picture? It could happen, you know. The Roman Civil War is pretty complicated, there's never fewer than three sides in the game, and what happens if I look around and say to myself that the best thing is for our boy Gaius to win?"

She shook her head sadly. "Mark, you're making too big a deal out of this. What if you had jumped back into the first timeline you ever fought in and decided that Hitler was the good guy? What if you jumped back into some other one and decided Mao or Stalin was? It isn't going to happen with cases like that. And Caesar was not a good guy. He was a good administrator, but he destroyed Roman self-government for all time, he got his famous victories in Gaul mostly by breaking the laws of war of his time, and in short he's just about the model of a power-mad dictator. If you have to see that for yourself first, go right ahead. Then shoot him. And then we'll go back home, to your timeline, and live a pleasant retired life with tons of money. You can chair the Brunreich for President Committee for Allegheny County, and I'll have another six babies or so. What's the problem?"

"Well . . . jeez, Chrysamen, I wish I could explain it to you better. It just doesn't seem like a Crux Op job. We're supposed to have some kind of judgment in all of this, you know . . . we've always jumped in as the only good guys in the timeline—and what I'm supposed to be doing this time feels more like a mob hit. And I really don't like the short list of people who 'died in mysterious circumstances' in that same year, either. It sounds like I'm supposed to be a serial killer."

"So do them in parallel."

"Chrys!"

"Mark, I'm sorry," she said. "I can understand how upset you must be about the idea of just going back into a timeline to kill somebody. That's a natural enough reaction. But in fact that isn't the whole reason you're going, or even the major part of the mission. You're supposed to find out what happened to Walks-in-His-Shadow Caldwell, first of all, and secondly to do whatever you think best. It just happens to be known in advance that what you think best is going to involve shooting Gaius Julius Caesar, that's all. You could just look on it as having more information than usual going in."

I groaned. If I couldn't explain what was bothering me to Chrys, I probably couldn't explain it to anyone.

"Look," she said, "I know it's not the usual job. But it's the job that wins the war. And you seem to be bothered just because it's crossing up your ideas about free will or something. Well, all right, so it's not quite as free as some of your other jobs have been. On your first one you didn't even know that you were ever going home. And here you end up knowing in advance what you're going to decide. I can understand how that feels, but it's not the worst thing that could happen. Not by a long shot. A few days ago subjectively, we were thinking we would grow old and die with the war still going on—if one of us didn't have to see the other one blown to pieces. Now it's all different. Now there's going to be real peace and a real chance to lead a more or less comfortable, more or less normal life. And it's all going to come to us through your efforts! You're a hero for all time, Mark . . . and so I'm having a little trouble seeing why you're complaining about having to follow that particular script."

I shrugged, and said, "Well, as I said, I'm certainly not going to turn the assignment down. There's no way I could walk away from it in the circumstances. But I just don't like it. I really just don't like it."

And it didn't seem practical—partly because the room might be bugged, but also because she seemed to have no sympathy with the viewpoint—to say that I was beginning to think old Thebenides might have a point. The citizen-senator might have rubbed me the wrong way, but it did seem to me that putting ATN in the position of being a client state to a vastly superior civilization was not exactly in line with what we got into the war to do. We were the Allied Timelines for Nondeterminism—meaning all the timelines that did not want to go down the Closer road to become giant, hierarchical slave states—and it seemed to me that our Roman "friends" were bound to do a lot of determining.

It didn't seem like a change of masters was all that we should be accomplishing after all the fighting.

I got another unpleasant surprise the next day when it turned out that according to the Roman historical records, Chrys and Porter had been along on the expedition, too. Apparently we had all returned safely, or else everyone was keeping up a brave front about it.

There was no mention of Paula in the list, but if Porter was going, she wanted to go. After all, she'd been guarding the kid for years, and if Porter was going to jump into danger, Paula wanted to be there. I took advantage of that to see how much clout I had. Malecela seemed very displeased, but Scipio was actually pretty reasonable about it; he agreed that if Paula wanted to go, she could, noting only that since there was no evidence for her in the historical record, it didn't look good. "But on the other hand, our attitudes about women weren't terribly enlightened at the time," the Chief Tribune added. "We know about unusual things that Friend-mother ja N'wook and Ms. Brunreich did. We don't know about Ms. Renatsky. That may only mean she didn't do anything that a historian or chronicler of the time found interesting. Or it may mean something went very wrong, very early in the mission. We have no way of knowing. But if she is willing to assume the risk, we're certainly willing to have her assume it."

At least it ticked off Malecela, which meant I could sound him out on how he felt about our new ally.

One reason that the idea of Paula going didn't sit very well with Malecela, of course, was that this was supposed to be an ATN operation. As far as he was concerned, all we were doing was borrowing these high-tech Romans' gear to get a Crux Op back to a crux for a normal search-and-rescue operation. And Malecela didn't want to send untrained (by him) and inexperienced operatives back to a crux. He had bowed grudgingly about Porter (and I wished he hadn't!) because it was clear from the records that she had gone, but Paula, as far as he could see, ought to be sent home and told sternly not to talk about what she had seen. And having anything else happen—against his wishes— meant that ATN wasn't in charge of the operation.

That seemed like a sympathetic enough view. We were sitting out on a terrace, drinking coffee while he tried to persuade me to ask Scipio to send Paula home instead of with me, and I decided to see how he felt about the whole problem of connecting ourselves to a larger and more powerful civilization, up at the other end of time.

It didn't do me any good. He'd seen the wonders of what they could do nine centuries ahead of this, and he'd heard them declare a complete "open labs" policy, so it looked as if they really intended to share everything they knew. The mopping-up operation against the Closers was going so fast that the Romans were already opening up a lot of timelines to tourism. He himself was actually thinking about retirement and about what he might enjoy doing—horsebreeding seemed to be his choice, and with all the grasslands of all of history to pick from, he was really more interested in talking about the perfect place for a ranch.

In short, just like Chrys, he could taste the victory so thoroughly that the "free will" issue seemed like mere abstract philosophizing to him. Of course it wasn't *his* free will that was being tampered with . . .

So there seemed to be nothing more to do than get our gear together and get ready to go. Malecela had thoughtfully brought along SHAKK- and NIF-reload materials (the weapons make their own ammo, but it helps to be able to put the right mix of chemical elements into the hopper) and a fresh set of PRAMIACs; Paula got the equivalent of a SHAKK from the Romans, as did Porter. We were probably well enough armed to take on a small infantry division back home.

The step through the gate went about as it always did; over a period of time that you could perceive but not measure, the world around us went away, and then came back. We stepped out onto a bleak, freezing cold Roman road, north and east of Rome, not far from modern Bologna, in January of 49 B.C.

"Not a real prepossessing place, is it?" Chrys commented.

The road wound around a large mountain on one side of us, and crossed an arched bridge over a stream before going straight over a hill on the other side. The day was gray and a bit foggy, with an unpleasant spitting mist that seemed to blow right through the heavy, hooded cloaks we had been fitted with. As my cloak flapped open and the wind blew in and around my short fighting tunic, I had a sudden, acute appreciation of why so many women complained about miniskirts.

The land around us was a patchwork of green and brown, green on the hills where it was pasturage, brown down lower where it was tilled fields. There were some low, not yet fully grown windbreaks of trees in the distance—that hadn't been a Roman practice, so I figured it was some evidence that Special Agent Caldwell had passed this way.

In the hollows and on the north sides of trees and rocks, there were little patches of grainy, soggy snow. At least we all had new boots.

"Well," I said, "the orders were to try heading north from here. We should reach Fanum Fortunae by dusk, if they managed to put us where they were supposed to—but not if we just stand here."

We started walking. The Roman roads were rightly famous; despite the wet weather, and even this close to the coast, this one had no puddles or standing water, and it was easy enough to walk along. Of course, in the rotten weather, it was still anything but pleasant, but at least it wasn't storming, and we were probably no more than a two-hour walk from the Fanum Fortunae city gates.

We rounded one wide turn and saw the sea off to our right, the broad Adriatic; today it was gray-green and looked terribly cold. I had been along this coast several times in my own timeline. I had worked a dig here a long time ago, and we weren't far from Pesaro, where Chrysamen had dragged me a few times on pilgrimage—it was Rossini's hometown, and there's a festival of his operas there that's pretty terrific. January was just not the best time of year for this coast.

Back home in my timeline, Fano is a little fishing port and light-industrial city, just a spot on the coast road between Ancona and Pesaro—but in Roman times, Fanum Fortunae was a vitally important city, in many ways the key to Italy, because that was where the Via Amelia, the coastal highway between Ancona and Ariminum (or Rimini if you're looking at a modern map) met the great Via Flaminia, the major highway leading to Rome. If you were invading Italy from the north or the west, the Via Flaminia was your best, straightest shot toward Rome itself.

Not to mention that in time of peace a huge amount

of trade flowed through it. It was one of those places that was important because it was on the way to so many other places—sort of the Sioux Falls, or the Columbus, Ohio, of its day.

Right now we were walking into the city from the southeast, as if we were coming in from Ancona. The day before, Julius Caesar had defied the Roman Senate and consuls, just as he had in our timeline. They had ordered him to keep himself and his army within Cisalpine Gaul, the province he was supposed to be governor of (which he had enlarged by overrunning everything else up to Scotland—clearly a difference since in our timeline he had been turned back by the Britons). The southern border of Cisalpine Gaul, on this western side of Italy, was a little river only fifteen miles long, the Rubicon, and our boy Gaius had taken his troops across it—which meant they had told the general "no," and he had said, "yes." The Civil War was on.

He would have to take Fanum Fortunae within a short time, and so we needed to be in the city, undercover, waiting for him. Our best guess was that he would be there in three to five days, at the pace at which legions could march comfortably, assuming, too, that he was keeping his army close together. Thus we were walking north toward him; he was marching south toward us; and though he didn't know it, we had a date in Fanum Fortunae.

"Boss," Paula said, "I just want you to know I'm having trouble believing all this."

"That's pretty much the way everyone reacts on their first trip in time," Chrysamen said, sympathetically.

"No, not being in ancient Rome and all that," she said. "I mean that there's a guy on a bicycle coming up behind us."

7

We turned and looked. She was absolutely right.

Half a mile behind us, just coasting down the hill, was a man in the full regalia of a legate—that is, what we'd call a junior officer—riding a bicycle. We moved out of his way as he came over the hill, but he didn't bother to look at us.

The bicycle had wooden spoked wheels, but the tires were pretty obviously rubber. The "chain" was a knotted rope, which ran through large wooden pin gears, and it didn't look like they'd developed the coaster brake yet, which may have explained why the helmet was in the shape of a modern bicycle helmet and had a number of prominent dents.

Of more interest to me was the fact that he had what looked like a crude shotgun slung over his shoulder, and a brace of seventeenth-century horse pistols across his chest.

Still, apparently nothing had yet made the Romans wear pants; he was wearing a short tunic, and the bicycle was what I'd have called a girl's model, though not to this guy's face, if he was half as tough as he looked. The bicycle had pannier baskets, which seemed to be carrying dispatches, over its rear tire.

He rolled on by and vanished up the road. I noted that on the back of his tunic was the phrase "Necesse litterae transeat."

It is essential that correspondence pass, if you were being formal and trying to pass Latin class. But *The mail must go through* was close enough.

I distinctly sensed that Walks-in-His-Shadow Caldwell had been here, and I kind of liked his sense of humor.

About an hour of unpleasant, cold wet walking brought us to the city of Fanum Fortunae. Porter hadn't said much on the way; "surprisingly quiet" is the only kind of quiet that kid ever has been, at least once she got into an environment where she could play and could behave more or less normally, so I had been keeping an eye on her. Paula seemed to have crossed the timeline boundary with about as much aplomb as she crossed into Germany—maybe more, because the chips implanted in our heads allowed us all to speak Latin without an accent, and Paula spoke no German.

Chrysamen was treating it like I did, or like anyone with practice would—it was gray, dingy, wet, and cold, and she wanted to get inside. This just wasn't a big part of the job.

After a while, as Paula took her turn at tail and Chrys at point, I found myself walking beside Porter. "I don't suppose you'd be interested in telling me what's on your mind?" I asked.

"Aw, Mark, you'll pick on me for it."

"Vicious accusation, unless what's on your mind is

some worthless guy who wants to date you, or some lunatic notion you have like getting another hole punched in your nose." We'd had a few go-rounds about nasal jewelry, which, in absolutely typical fashion for me, I'd lost. Probably because ultimately it was her nose; one way that I'll never make parent material, I suppose, is that I tend to see too much value in such arguments.

"No, it's not a guy, and it's not piercing," she said. There was a long pause while we walked along, the fine grit of the road crunching under the heavy leather of our boots. Finally, after a very long while, she asked, "Are you going to say, 'So, what is it, then?'"

"I was trying to be quietly supportive."

"I think you're easier to deal with when you're repressing me. Okay, here's what it is, Mark, and you can go right ahead and tell me how silly you think I am. Uh—is this a timeline where they could have us bugged?"

"It's not very likely that there would be any listening devices around here," I said, "and even less likely that anyone is going to have a station to pick up something planted on our clothes. I don't think you have to worry about any outfit that does time travel. And to judge from the looks of the bicycle that went by, I'd say you don't have to worry at all about the locals."

"Okay, then." She took a deep breath. "When you hear this, please don't tell me to grow up, or anything like that."

"Wouldn't dream of it. Really. What's the matter, Porter?"

"Well, it's that . . . a couple of people slipped, and I don't think they were supposed to do it, but they addressed me as President Brunreich. And I know that I'm supposed to be very important in history and all that, so I just kind of put it all together. I'm going to be, uh, president of the United States, I guess?"

"It sounds that way," I said, noncommittally.

"Well, what if I don't want to be?" It came out kind of choked and strangled in sound, and when I looked closer I saw that she was crying. "I mean, I *like* music. I *like* playing the piano and organ, and I really want to get more composing done. All right, so maybe I'm famous, but nobody's ever even asked my opinion about anything—though if they did, I could certainly tell them that things aren't being run very well—but that doesn't mean I want to run them myself . . . ." She was actually blubbering now, and wiping her face with the back of her hand, though a slight spitting rain was picking up so much that her face was hardly getting any dryer for the process.

"Aww, Porter," I said, because I couldn't think of anything better to say, and threw an arm around her.

She hung on to me for a second, and seemed to be sobbing. "And another thing," she added. "If that's all the way it is . . . if the Closers always knew that the timelines where I was president were ones they wanted to prevent . . . then that's why they tried to kill me, isn't it? And they ended up killing *my m-m-mother!*"

That made my mind flash back to when I had been working for ATN for less than three days—when Harry Skena and I had managed an impromptu rescue from a hostage situation. Ostensibly the Blade of the Most Merciful had been a Mideastern terrorist group noted for being erratic to the point of psychotic. Really, they had been a Closer front whose whole purpose was to eliminate the two biggest threats to them in our time-line: me and Porter.

Porter had been alive when we arrived only because

her mother had switched IDs with her; at the age of ten she'd seen her mother shot to death in front of her.

For that matter, it had only been a few years before that I'd seen about half of my family die at the hands of the same outfit.

There's a bond Porter and I share that's a little hard to explain to other people . . . and now, of course, poor old Harry Skena had been dead for years, and so were a lot of old friends and comrades, just to get us to this point.

"Porter," I said, "the way you are feeling is the most natural thing in the world. Really. You're suddenly finding out that the whole world had big plans that turned around you, and you never got to have any say in them. You were just sort of dropped into the middle. It's no wonder that you feel upset. And of course you're wondering how much of your actions are really your own, and it doesn't seem fair at all—plenty of people get through life without anything like this happening. Even geniuses and important people. You never asked for anything like this to happen, and there are better things you could be doing with your time. Am I right?"

She snuffled. "Good guesses all around." She smeared her face with her hand, still trying to get the tears and snot under control. She'd really been bearing up pretty well in a completely confusing situation; though I had never kept my work for ATN secret from her, or from my father or sister, it still must have been bewildering.

"Well, it's pretty much how I've been feeling lately."

She looked sideways at me. "Really?"

"Yeah, really. It is not normal for them to tell us what we do back in the past timelines. In fact usually they don't know. Usually the job is, go back and fix things so that they come out right. How is up to you. This time the job is more like a mob hit; go shoot old Gaius in the back so that a civilization can come into being. Not even a suggestion that I ought to help decide whether Caesar needs shooting. And the worst part is not just being given the order—it's knowing that I'm going to carry it out, whether I decide I want to or not. They've got it down in their history books that I shot Julius Caesar. No getting away from that one—I'm going to do it. Just like you're going to end up as President Brunreich, and apparently to hell with whatever time you need to practice."

She sighed. "I just figured they must always know how it was going to come out."

"No—they only know in a general way that it did come out okay, sometimes. The details have always been up to us. But this is one hell of a detail to have them take control of. And I just think you probably feel exactly the same way about having to be president."

"Yeah." She sighed and snuffled once again; I was getting to hate that hopeless little sound. "Mark, do you suppose I'll be the first woman president?"

"I don't know. I suppose it's possible. Why do you ask?"

"Well, 'cause—well, I'm only eighteen right now. Do you realize how long that means we'll have to wait for a woman president? And what a mess things are likely to be in by the time I get the job?"

I laughed and gave her a quick hug; it was hard to believe this little wisp of a young woman was ever going to command anything more imposing than a piano keyboard, but then how could one know? Abe Lincoln must've looked like the class geek, or would have if he'd been able to get to school, and I always kind of suspected that they used to take Teddy

Roosevelt's glasses and make him bob for them in the boys' room toilets.

"You'll be fine at the job," I said, "if that's any consolation. Hell, considering who ran the last few times, I'd be perfectly happy to vote for you next time."

She shrugged. "Yeah, but that's not the issue. Thanks for listening, though, Mark. I do feel better."

That left me alone with my own thoughts until we had a change of positions, and the thoughts were not the kind to be alone with. The overwhelming thing that kept coming back to me was that where at least Porter only knew that she would have a job and be important in the job, I knew something I was going to do. I was going to take a person of extraordinary energy and ability, one of the great complex figures of history, and turn him into a heap of meat.

We had just changed over, so that I was on point (despite her protestations, we kept Porter in the middle for the whole journey), when the gate of Fanum Fortunae came into sight.

It was a pretty typical Roman walled town—apparently the new military hardware had not yet strongly modified architecture, or maybe Fanum Fortunae just hadn't been forced to adapt yet. The wall was high enough so that you would need a ladder to climb it, and wide enough for soldiers to be walking around on top of it. There were three big stone arches set in the wall, a large one over the road for carts and carriages, flanked by two small ones for pedestrian traffic.

On this cold and generally rotten day, the city was sending up a substantial plume of brown smoke from its many chimneys—and that, I realized, was the most un-Roman thing about it, and another sign of Caldwell's influence—the chimney was a late-medieval innovation in our timeline. Before that they had used various kinds of open hearths and smoke holes.

But here was Roman Fanum Fortunae with belching chimneys. Moreover, as we drew nearer, I saw that the guards and watchmen on the city wall were wearing rubberized-fabric ponchos. Not elegant, but a sight more comfortable than what we had on.

This guy Caldwell clearly valued comfort and had clearly exerted quite some influence. I was beginning to look forward to finding a place for the night.

That turned out to be remarkably simple. As we entered the city, we saw the typical layout of a Roman town—stepping-stones over the major thoroughfares because streets doubled as sewers, and streets laid out in straight lines, with everything of military importance kept near the walls. We were coming in through the main gate, so the military parade ground was the first thing we walked past.

But as we topped a slight rise at the end of the parade ground, I saw a beautiful sight: a billboard.

The face on the billboard was rather startlingly piggish in aspect, with a kind of cunning expression that didn't breed trust. All the same, he was smiling, and below, in Latin, was the announcement that we need only continue for eight hundred paces to reach the "Crassus Inn Fanum Fortunae"—"low rates and available throughout the Roman world."

I found myself wondering at once . . . a fast review of history was in order—

"Hey," Chrysamen said, "remember the data we memorized? Does this mean Crassus is still alive? In our timeline he was killed with his troops in Parthia, six years ago. If he's still around, that really changes the balance of power."

"Sure does," I said, "but I see more of the handiwork

of Caldwell than I do Crassus here. The chain of hotels exists, anyway—and not a minute too soon because there weren't any in the ancient world of our timeline. But just because Crassus's name is on it doesn't mean he'll be at the front desk. Colonel Sanders is dead, but that doesn't stop KFC."

"Well, then I guess we walk up there and find out," Chrysamen said. "Which I do believe was the original plan."

The organization of the Crassus Inn was so much like a modern hotel that I suspect you could have checked in without knowing Latin—they must have had plenty of foreign travelers. In short order we were being shown into a large room, which they assured us was the cleanest and most modern in the place.

I handed over the sesterces from the pouch on my belt, and they were gone at once. Only then did Porter say, "I see a problem here."

The problem was that the room was furnished with one bed—large and circular—and one tub—ditto.

Modesty was going to be a bit tricky to serve, at least if I stuck around. "Well," I said, "looks like Porter and Paula bathe first, while we go reconnoiter for what's to eat. Then we take a turn. Then we all sleep dressed tonight."

Paula nodded. "Uh, boss, I didn't stay awake in Latin class, but I just thought of something funny." She had a slight crooked grin.

"Yes?" I asked.

"I think the desk clerk, if that's what the guy was, figured that all three of us are your harem. He's going to be mighty surprised when two of us depart."

"Well, it'll broaden his horizons. All right, we'll see you in about an hour."

As we were walking out into the street, Chrys

commented, "You know, there are people back in your home timeline who would be freaked by what you just did."

"What did I do?"

"Well, um, you know that Paula—well, of course you know that she and Robbie are—"

"Of course," I said.

"And you left her alone with a teenage girl, to take a bath together."

"In case it hasn't occurred to you," I said, "I'm attracted to women myself, and *I* certainly wouldn't attack Porter. And Paula's devoted to her. You've been listening to too much talk radio, and it's given you a dirty mind." I was really annoyed.

"Mark?"

"Yeah?"

"I love you. Don't change."

I swear, it is not possible for a married guy to understand his wife even when they come from the same history. So I don't know why I expected the present situation to make any more sense.

Anyway, we found that though Fanum Fortunae was pretty much battened down against the bad weather, there were plenty of shops open, even if you did have to knock for admittance. One of the shopkeepers finally explained to us that on days like this, any ship out in the Adriatic was running for harbor early (when they could, Roman ships put in to port every night), and so you never knew how many seamen might turn up in the afternoon; the shops that were open would get all the business.

A little exploration revealed that Caldwell had introduced a lot of other things. There were printed posters, for one thing, which meant he'd brought the press, movable type, and paper here (along with the secret of postering glue, as well, to judge from the dates on some of the posters, which had clearly been on those walls for years). There were a few very expensive horse cabs in the streets, with double-bowed axles and horse collars, the kind of thing that in our timeline wasn't developed until centuries or millennia after Rome fell. There were mailboxes everywhere, so apparently among the other benefits of modernism, Caldwell had given them the post office. It made me wonder just how benign his intentions really were.

The other thing we found was that employment seemed to be running pretty high. The background from my own time had suggested that this was an age of the urban mob, fueled by unemployment, when lots of people without jobs wandered around with nothing to do other than join riots and political campaigns. (Of course a riot and a political campaign were pretty much the same thing at the time.) This had no such aspect to it; everyone we saw was busy, and the harbor was a wild confusion of longshoremen and sailors getting things on and off the ships, merchants looking at the wares, captains announcing bargains. Fanum Fortunae looked like a city that had a lot to do.

"Caldwell is one hell of a Special Agent," I muttered to Chrys. "Can you believe the work he's done?"

"It's remarkable," Chrys agreed. "And if all the timelines really do open up for tourism, we're coming back here. Have you noticed the silverwork on display?"

We found a place that sold sausages in rolls, something not a lot different from the modern hot dog, and stopped to eat there; by then we were fairly damp and cold and figured that it was about time to head back to the room, get a hot bath ourselves, and see how the other two were doing.

Just as we started to stroll back to the Crassus Inn,

there was a great uproar that seemed to come from everywhere at once. We looked around and saw that the guards were running back and forth on the walls like madmen; a moment later we heard the crashing sound of the big city gates being dropped, and we began to hurry toward the inn. "What do you suppose—"

"Caesar might not be sticking to schedule," I said. "That would be just like him, from everything we know about his history. And if he's got enough bicycles for his legions, he moves a *lot* faster than we estimated."

We had to flatten ourselves against a building the next minute, and were splashed with the nasty mix of slush and sewage that ran between the stepping-stones, as fifty soldiers on bicycles shot by, moving fast and not looking much where they were going. "They're in a hurry, and they looked scared," I said. "This is bad, whatever it is."

I took Chrysamen's hand and we ran through the streets together, trying to find a way to the inn that wasn't hopelessly blocked with people. We had no luck—everywhere, people were rushing into the street to grab children or bring in a mule or horse. Shutters were slamming closed all around and everywhere there was the sound of hammering as shopkeepers and property owners boarded up their belongings.

From a quiet city on a slow winter day, a few minutes ago, Fanum Fortunae had whipped into a panic; these people were on the brink of fleeing.

All around us we could hear the word being shouted again and again—it sounded like "Kye Sarr," in Latin, and it was the way they pronounced Caesar. Apparently his legendary ability to move an army fast—probably plus the technical boost of the bicycle—meant that he had gotten south much faster than we had thought he would.

Caesar was not a nice guy; aside from the testimony of generations of Latin students, let me just mention his habit of accepting the surrender of cities and then abrogating the terms he had promised. Lying under a flag of truce is treacherous and needlessly imperils the lives of soldiers, but it does have the advantage of utterly crushing a helpless enemy. And his carefully constructed reputation for utterly crushing his enemies was helping him now—the city was ready to surrender.

Or parts of it were. With a crash and jingle, a group of men armed with pistols strode into the square we were struggling across. The crowd parted around them, and the leader of the group began to read, very loudly and not at all well, a proclamation that the "Citizens for Caesar" were going to assume command of the town for everyone's safety and that as long as they were permitted to surrender it "in good order" no harm would come to anyone.

He was just beginning to announce the proscriptions—which citizens he was putting a price on the head of—when a shot boomed out from the crowd and he fell dead. An instant later another shot hit one of his followers in the back, and then the mob closed around them. I didn't look; I've seen before what mobs do to people they don't like, and even though I felt no sympathy at all for the men (whose groans and screams I could hear), it's a hideous way to die.

The shift in the crowd freed up Chrys and me; we turned and ran, though she wasted one step to take a snap kick at an older man with a cane. The man flew over backward, his face spraying blood from his broken teeth and nose.

"What—?" I asked Chrys as we raced down another street, fighting fleeing civilians the whole way.

"Old bastard groped me in the crowd. Taking

advantage of the situation, I guess you'd call it. I hope he learned some manners."

We kept running. It was just a short way now.

High above us something that sounded like a freight train rumbled; an instant later, there was a low, thudding boom. Caesar's cannon were within reach of the city.

We put on an extra burst of speed, but it gained us less than fifty yards before we were hopelessly pinned. The Latins of Fanum Fortunae had never heard cannon fired before—they were far enough from the frontier so that they had not seen battle up close in a couple of generations. Moreover, cannon themselves were only about twenty years old in this timeline.

But they had been reading Caesar's *Commentaries on the Gaulish War* and his *Commentary on the Conquest of Britain*. They had read his vivid—maybe a better term would have been "lip-smacking, gloating, joyful"—descriptions of what artillery fire did to cities. He had spread more than enough terror of the cannon ahead of him; these people fell apart at the thought. When you've dreaded something long enough, imagined it hard enough, you don't stand up and fight when you encounter it.

I found out later that most of the garrison of the city wasn't even able to get to the walls through the mob of panicking civilians. The cannonballs booming into the city were solid stone shot, not incendiary shells, but they might as well have been filled with napalm, because there were thousands of cooking fires and fires on hearths everywhere, and where one of the massive stones fell, it overturned braziers, threw stoves into thatch, made people run away in a panic from the fires they had tended. Before Chrys and I could even struggle off the wall that our backs had been pinned to by the howling mob, there was a distinct scent of smoke.

And as the cry of "Fire!" spread among them, people began to pour away in every direction. There was no hope of getting bucket brigades formed to fight the fire; most people standing next to burning buildings couldn't even get away thanks to all the pushing, shoving, and snarled traffic.

From the walls came the sounds of fusillades of musket fire. The gadget Caldwell had introduced had been about as good as you could do with Roman iron—basically a length of drilled-out iron pipe (because any seam would be sure to split) with a rammed-paper cartridge, a separate percussion cap, and a lead bullet that was based on the same principle as the Minié ball—designed to expand against the walls of the barrel on its way out, so that it would form a better seal and pick up some velocity. Necessarily that had to be limited in its effectiveness, because Roman iron wouldn't take the pressures that a really effective seal would have made.

Still, you could get just as dead standing in front of one as you could get from a twenty-ninth-century SHAKK.

The percussion cap, cartridge, and Minié-ball design had leapfrogged firearms far past what would have been their "natural" pace of development if the Romans had merely been given gunpowder and some introduction to the principle. They loaded a lot faster than any gun in my own timeline had until close to the American Civil War, and though not accurate at any great distance, they required little training to learn to operate and were more than deadly enough for their purpose.

The first volleys were sweeping the guards from the walls; moments later we heard a huge, booming crash, which we only realized later had been a particular innovation of Caesar's for taking walled cities—a battering ram driven by gunpowder.

The smell of smoke and the screaming were everywhere. The crowd hesitated and then began to pour away from the gate where the crash had happened, knowing full well that the first hour or so as soldiers invaded the city would be much the worst; if they could avoid coming to the attention of Caesar's troops for one or two hours, they stood a chance of surviving with their property and without severe injury.

Unfortunately, the crowd was flowing exactly opposite the direction we wanted to go. There seemed to be no way to get through them.

"NIF?" Chrys asked. "We could stun a few hundred."

"And they'd be burned, trampled, or raped by Caesar's troops," I shouted back into her ear. The wailing, shrieking crowd, the rumble of cart wheels, and the crashes of musketry were so loud it was hard to hear each other without shouting directly into the ear. "Plus the ones we didn't get would be screaming that we were wizards or in league with spirits or something, and they'd stone us."

She nodded, clearly not liking it. The smoke was growing thicker, and I realized with a grim, sinking feeling that it was thickest in the direction of the Crassus Inn. Caesar must have circled the city before attacking from the unexpected direction—another favorite tactic of his.

With a terrible thunder, the wall opposite us came down. I don't know if it was the mob pressing up against a weak structure, an internal fire, or perhaps a cannon shot that landed inside, but the whole thing fell outward like a house of cards, and the three-story-high masonry wall slammed into the crowd below, crushing many, wounding others with sharp pieces of rock. The building stood for one instant in cross section, as if it had been cut away—I saw people in the uppermost story, mouths wide with horror, and a mother with her baby on the second floor turn to run for a staircase that was already falling out of reach— and then with a twisting, grinding sound, it all came down in a heap, forming a steep pile that then slid and broke out into the crowd around.

Immediately, smoke curled up from the pile; the gods alone knew how many braziers and stoves had spilled into the mess.

There was a great wail from the crowd; hundreds rushed onto the pile, seeking to rescue those inside (or to rob them); hundreds more fled as if the bad luck might well be contagious. The ones in the back pushed forward, the ones in front pushed back, and brawling erupted everywhere. Meanwhile the smoke grew thicker, more musketry and cannon fire crashed in the distance, there was a rumbling of horses' hooves, and then, with a great, thudding *whump*, the center of the pile of rubble went up in flames.

The toga, tunic, and chiton were never designed for situations like this. Dozens of men, women, and children went up in flames and staggered into the crowd, desperately trying to peel their burning garments off themselves. A woman in front of us tore her blazing garments from her body, only to be pulled down by two strong men who pinned her to the ground and forced her legs apart—

Before they both fell over dead, as empty bags of bloody skin. Chrys, beside me, held her SHAKK level and ready. In the volume of noise, I had not even heard her fire.

I drew my own SHAKK from between my shoulder blades and looked around. The naked woman had fled; we would never know what became of her. The crowd had not noticed our weapons; they were still milling and groaning.

Then there was an astonishing sound. All the voices seemed to stop at once.

There came the tramping of horses' hooves on cobblestones, and people pulled away from the middle. As if by magic, room began to appear.

There were about thirty of them, a troop of Caesar's auxiliaries, and they rode into the middle of that panicked mob as if they were out to give their horses a little light exercise on a spring day. When they reached the center of the crowd, the legate heading the group looked around and bellowed, "Citizens of Fanum Fortunae. It is hereby ordered that you are to cease resistance at once. Your city is on fire. Go immediately to your stations for fire fighting. No one who is fighting fires will be harmed. As soon as resistance in the city ends, Caesar's troops will also help you put out the fires. Now, if you wish to save your city, *hurry!*"

It was like magic, and magic of the strangest sort. There had been a rioting mob there, in a panic, ready to trample the helpless and filled with people whose only motive, besides stark terror, was to take advantage of the ones around them—and at the word of the legate, with the command of Caesar behind it, they were suddenly tough, disciplined Romans, getting the job done. In moments the square had more than half-cleared as people ran to pump water or to join the bucket brigades. As others milled around, not having definite fire-fighting stations, the legate would point, and bellow, "All of you, there, over to that pile of rubble, and pick it apart carefully to see if anyone is alive inside" or "You people there—start pulling rubbish out of that well, see if we can get some water."

Before he looked our way, Chrys and I holstered our

SHAKKs and slipped off into the winding alleys between the buildings. Roman cities were laid out in a geometric grid for the major streets, but what happened inside the blocks was pretty much improvised on a catch-as-catch-can basis, so there were a lot of narrow passageways and winding alleys to move through.

It took us another ten minutes to reach the Crassus Inn, because there were so many patrols and work parties on the street. One hour before, Fanum Fortunae had been slumbering through a cold winter day; half an hour before it had been enveloped in flames, rage, and terror; now it was rebuilding itself in an orderly way. Caesar sure knew how to make an entrance.

When we finally popped out of an alley facing the Crassus Inn, I had steeled myself, but still, what I saw made me gasp. The building was falling apart in flames; a firebreak had been cleared around it, but they were letting it burn itself out. From the yardarm where the sign with the picture of Crassus had been, the body of the desk clerk hung, his face black, clothes smoldering; someone had fired a shot into him after he was dead, to judge from the mess of his belly.

There was absolutely no sign of Porter or Paula, and that was the best news there could have been at that point. "God, of all the places to be when Caesar attacked," I said, softly. "Next to Pompey, Crassus has to be the man he hates most on Earth. The mob probably did this just trying to appease Caesar."

"As a matter of fact, that *is* what happened," a voice said behind us. We turned to find ourselves facing a young legate, with several tough legionaries behind him. He had a horse pistol leveled on us.

"You look very much like the people Caesar told me to look for," he said. "So I shall take you to him to find out if you're the right ones. If you are worried about friends inside, I would not be. I believe only that wretched slave died in this, and several of the guests were taken as personal prisoners by Caesar. Chances are your friends are alive and well, though they are no longer free. And this is after all a circumstance you are very likely to share with them soon."

It took me a moment to remember what that all meant, as we marched along, the legate's pistol at our backs, toward our meeting with the man I was supposed to kill. In the ancient world, prisoners taken in war—especially including civilians—were sold as slaves. All four of us were going to be auctioned off, and as far as the Romans were concerned (even ones who might prove friendly to us) once that had happened, we were slaves until we bought our freedom or our masters freed us.

The boots I was wearing were new, and I tried to savor their crunch on the pavement; they would go to some poorer supporter of Caesar, along with the good clothes I was wearing. Slaves did not dress this well.

8

Caesar had set up his headquarters in Fanum Fortunae's Praetorium. The Praetorium originally meant where the praetor, a high-ranking government official, stayed, but the term had come to mean first the place where he stayed when he was in town (so that every town had a praetorium) and later simply the center of government. This town was large enough to have an impressive one, about the size of a modern basketball gym, with many benches and tables for the public business inside, and a second floor on which there was a courtroom.

That was the room Gaius Julius Caesar had appointed his own. When we arrived, there was a long parade of prisoners ahead of us, but it appeared we were something special, because they marched us straight to the head of the line.

The man sitting next to Caesar was not wearing a toga, like a Roman, or a chiton, like a Greek, or even pants like a barbarian. He wore a simple one-piece coverall that looked like practical work clothing anywhere—in my timeline or in any advanced industrial one.

It was not any ATN uniform I recognized, and then, as we drew closer, I saw the symbol on his breast—a black-on-white image of two hands, crossed at the wrists, one forming a fist and the other held up like a cop stopping traffic.

This was a Closer agent.

His hair was very dark, his skin a coffee color not unlike Chrys's. His nose was small but hooked, making him look a little like a parakeet, but his expression was sharp and intelligent. He looked very much like a man who knew what he was doing.

And he was on the other side.

The SHAKK between my shoulders could not have been farther away if it had been on Mars; the NIF in my boot was equally far. So far I had not been searched, but they would find both with any kind of a pat-down—ATN's superweapons may be very high-tech, but they are also large, solid lumps on the human body where it normally doesn't have them.

There was also my old, reliable Model 1911A1, the military-make Colt .45 that sat in my shoulder holster. My best guess was that I could draw that before anyone realized, and I might get off one shot.

Now here was an interesting dilemma. I could accomplish the mission—as far as I knew it—with that one shot, assuming fate didn't decide to intervene. Caesar was right there, and I could just put a round through him and trust to the fact that we were somehow alive back in the future.

But for my money the most dangerous man in the room had to be that Closer agent. He alone had the potential to turn the whole timeline permanently against us; he was the source, I had no doubt, of much of Caesar's advanced weaponry. (I was just realizing that one reason Caldwell had done so well was probably that an arms race had gotten started, and that always accelerates technology.)

I had a few seconds before they searched me; all I had to do was decide whether to get the designated target and hope to have time for the vital second shot, or get the one I thought most dangerous and hope to have time to get Caesar as well.

I've never had any trouble gunning down a Closer bastard; I owe them more deaths than I'm likely to repay, as far as I'm concerned, and knowing what their idea of fun is (they teach their children to kill favorite slaves in order to harden their hearts, and thirteen-year-old Closer boys often kill or mutilate the slave girls they have just lost their virginity to), it didn't seem like such a bad idea to get both of us killed abruptly and immediately. On the other hand, I was still having a major set of butterflies in the stomach about assassinating Caesar. Maybe I'd seen Shakespeare's play once too often or something.

So I walked forward, calmly drew the Colt and leveled it on the Closer in one smooth movement, and squeezed the trigger.

There was a roar from the muzzle, but the Closer had been alert, and while it must have scared hell out of him, he had sidestepped just as I fired; the round sprayed gravel chips from the wall behind him, but that was all. I squeezed the trigger again and nothing happened; I looked down to see the open top of the spent casing sticking up out of the .45.

Smokestack jam. I had barely brought my left hand to the pistol, still working to clear the jam, when the butt of a spear knocked the gun from my hand, and a solid fist swung in under my jaw and put me on the floor. Then there were hands all over me, and I could feel the rest of the armament being stripped off.

Over to one side there was another flurry of struggle, by which I knew Chrys was being disarmed in about the same way.

The world was still spinning from the force of the blow to my jaw, and anyway there were just too many bodies holding just too many parts of me down. I made myself relax and stop struggling—sometimes that will help somebody let their guard down—and waited.

After a lot of rough poking around, including being turned over for a cavity search, they all agreed that I was harmless, or at least unarmed, and braced me up facing Caesar. I was naked now, which didn't exactly help my self-confidence.

Beside me, Chrys was braced up in exactly the same way, hands locked behind the back in a double hammerlock, feet wide apart, three men holding on to her in a very businesslike way. I had the sudden, sad thought that my wife was very beautiful and that if I had been granted a last request just before execution, one more look at her might very well have been it.

They pressed me forward so that I was now facing Caesar, who sat on the raised dais, where the judge would have sat in a Roman court, with an expression of alert amusement. The Closer agent beside him seemed to be tense and ready to spring, though whether at the prospect of working over two ATN agents or with anger at my attempt to kill him, I couldn't say.

"And so then," Caesar said, very conversationally, as if we were just guests in his living room, "I suppose that you are yet another person sent to dispose of me. I believe I am in the presence of Marcus Ajax Fortius, if the registry of that inn is to be believed. You really might have had better taste than to stay at Crassus's place, you know; if you had gone to one of my Barrel Tile Roof franchises, I might still be looking for you."

"My mistake," I admitted. "I'm new here."

"You will be happy to hear, I'm sure, that both of your female companions—in addition to this lovely one here—are quite well and safe; in fact if I permitted you to look all the way behind you, you could see them both. I'm afraid their proclivities are a bit like yours; Hasmonea here made some not quite tasteful remark, and the larger and stronger of the women struck with remarkable force. I don't suppose you've actually found the land of the Amazons? You certainly seem to be surrounded by women who are proficient in a fight."

"They're just well trained," I said. Anything that kept us talking was likely to be better than anything that would happen when the talking stopped.

"Now," Caesar said, leaning forward, "I could understand that it was entirely possible that Hasmonea's insulting behavior and lack of decent breeding"—the Closer beside him stirred a little at that, but not enough to take his eyes off me or Chrys—"might have provoked your female guard to doing what she did. On the other hand, I note with some interest that you looked at both of us and chose him as target with almost no hesitation. At the time that happened you probably believed you were also a dead man.

"It so happens I am not noted for my modesty. I find myself wondering what about this advisor is of such value and interest that you prefer to kill him rather than to kill Caesar. I know, of course, that there is a deadly war between your kind and his, and that to some extent you have made the Triumvirate and the Senate into mere pieces on the board for your purposes. Thus I can suppose that your reaction was without thought.

"But this I do not believe. And while Hasmonea has been of immense value to me, I find myself thinking that should anything happen to him, those who sent him will most likely send another. I think this in particular because the most likely reason you are here—or so Hasmonea told me—is to find out what happened to that barbarian fellow Caldwell.

"Thus if you had killed Hasmonea, I have no doubt his people would have sent someone after him, perhaps someone whose fighting skills and knowledge were as superior to Hasmonea's as yours are to this Caldwell's.

"So it could not have been for a mere momentary advantage that you decided to pass up your opportunity to kill me, and instead decided to kill this agent of the 'Masters,' as they style themselves. You had some other reason behind that decision." Caesar now leaned forward, letting his elbows rest on his knees in a not-at-all-patrician way, and peered intently at my face. "Now, I suggest you explain yourself to me. Think for a long time about how matters are apt to go with you, and decide to tell me the truth."

I looked back into his eyes. At the time, Gaius Julius Caesar was just past fifty years old, a vigorous and strong man in the prime of life. He had spent ten years fighting in Gaul and Britain, and though he had certainly had it easier in this timeline than in my own, it was still remarkable that so much warfare had taken so little toll.

His cheekbones were heavy and relatively low, his brow unusually wide, giving most of his face a flat look, but his nose was thin and sharp, his lips a mere slash in his face, and the intelligence that stared out of his wide-set eyes was terrifying. He was mostly bald and did nothing much to hide it; his face had exactly the kind of "lean and hungry look" that Shakespeare's

Julius Caesar claims to find frightening. This was a man who had made a life out of devouring everything in his path, and he liked that about himself.

He would be difficult to lie to, not for moral reasons but because he was so sharp, and because he had no sentimental expectations that anyone would ever tell him the truth.

I let his stare rest on me for a long moment, then watched as his eyes roamed speculatively over Chrys's naked body. I knew he was doing it to provoke me, to see if he could get my thinking to muddle, and I held myself in check, much as I wanted to grab him by his wisps of remaining hair and batter his face on the table in front of him. I let him have his long pause to challenge me in that way, so that he could see that we were equal in that sense—we didn't scare each other.

It occurred to me then that if I did go ahead with killing him, later, that it would be a good idea to get him from behind, when he wasn't watching out. And that it might be a very long time before he wasn't watching out.

Finally I spoke, and I kept my voice soft and reasonable but firm. "Let me tell you of these ones who call themselves 'Masters,' but who we call 'Closers.' Did Caesar ever speak to my comrade Walks-in-His-Shadow Caldwell about this?"

"I have not spoken to him in several years; as you well know, he has taken the part of Crassus in these matters. I first met Hasmonea while I was in the field, in Gaul, and he has proved an invaluable advisor on weapons and tactics, though I'm afraid he has a bit of a weak stomach for the real necessities of warfare."

So Caesar apparently made the Closer uncomfortable . . . I wondered if this was a matter of his treatment of prisoners and civilians (which seemed unlikely) or probably just a matter of anyone from a more advanced civilization being used to killing at a distance rather than by shoving a sharpened slab of iron into a human body. I took a long extra moment to consider, and then Caesar said, "So tell me what you know of them."

"You know well that they are descendants of Carthage," I began, "and one might well ask what one of the oldest families of Rome is doing in consorting with a Carthaginian."

There was a low stir in the room; a lot of Caesar's soldiers had heard that, and it sounded like it was news to them. But Caesar himself nodded, and said, "We have suspected this though he has not told us; his native tongue is a bit like Punic. Tell me, then, why it is that you oppose these people."

"For the same reason Rome opposed Carthage," I said, milking it for all it was worth. "Because they are the sworn foes of everyone's freedom."

"Great Caesar—" Hasmonea began.

"You will remain silent until Caesar has need for you to speak," Caesar said, without taking his eyes off me. "Now tell me everything, Marcus Ajax Fortius. Tell me why they are called 'Closers' and what they are after."

For the next half hour I did myself proud at speech-making. It wasn't the easiest thing in the world, but at least I had a lot of material. I talked about the Closer view that divides all the timelines, everywhere, into Closers and prey. I talked about the deliberate hardening of their hearts, the systematic extermination of sympathy among them. I talked about the pleasures they took in cruelty and in being obeyed.

I admitted to my personal biases and told them a little of Closer crimes I had encountered, that my first wife, my mother, and my brother had died at their hands, that my sister Carrie had lost both legs and an arm at the same time. I went out of my way to detail their barbarities in a dozen worlds where I had known them, and laid it on fairly thick that they were still worshiping Moloch.

That seemed to be getting the kind of attention I wanted; Moloch was a concept that horrified the Romans nearly as much as it would us. He was the cruelest of any gods, an enormous metal idol, hollowed inside to form a furnace, into which Carthaginians threw children to be burned alive in his belly. Once, in a very distant timeline, I had burst into a temple of Moloch and had the pleasure of slaughtering the priesthood there. It would never trouble my conscience one iota.

The reaction around the room was fairly satisfying, but Caesar continued to stare. Finally, he said, "You make your case well. Cato himself could hardly have made a better one."

At that name, Hasmonea stirred uncomfortably—in the Closer timelines, Cato had been the last great opponent of the Carthaginians. His stirring did not go unnoticed—I could hear people muttering and pointing—and I realized that the Closer agent had probably not made himself popular with the common footsloggers in this timeline. Closers think it's degrading to treat inferiors well; I've seen Closers stick knives in their bosses' backs, literally, because the boss treated them too leniently and thus lost their respect.

"Now," Caesar said, "tell me of your own cause."

I drew my breath and began with the phrase they always hammer into us. "It is our desire only that each history should find its own way into the future. We would have no quarrel with the Closers had they left every other timeline alone. It is only in their seeking to make everyone else conform to their ways, in their attempt to reduce all of history to a set of identical timelines, that we oppose them." I went on to sketch out, briefly, as much of ATN's history as I thought was germane. It took a while, and my first sign that things were going well was that servants arrived with clothing for Chrys and me, plus some warmed wine that Caesar extended with the comment that he had forced me to spend a great deal of time talking without adequate shelter from the cold.

I would come to realize that that was like him. Caesar could be brutal, perhaps even could enjoy being brutal, but he never did it without cause, and, most especially, he also knew that kindness extended to an opponent could be a powerful weapon as well.

After the pause for refreshment, Caesar asked some more questions. I knew the Romans admired all things Greek, so I stressed ATN's connection to the Athenian civilization and to Perikles; I knew they admired courage and soldierly virtues, so I made sure they heard much of ATN's long-running war, and of our heroes. I kept that notion that Closers were followers of Moloch firmly in front of them, and since it had been only about a hundred years since Rome decided to solve the Carthaginian problem once and for all by leveling the city, this worked pretty well.

I had anticipated that it would. There are hatreds in the modern world, of course, but few like the one between Rome and Carthage. The wars between them were wars to the death from the outset, and if the Romans had made something of a hero out of Hannibal and his brother Hasdrubal, they had done so only once both men were safely dead. Hannibal's army had come "within the third milestone"—that is, so far along the road to Rome that they passed mile marker three before being turned back. They had succeeded in turning substantial numbers of Rome's allies in Italy against her, and this was a thing that stirred Roman paranoia as nothing else did; the Romans believed in being generous to their opponents, in making the enemy from this war the ally for the next one, but necessarily this bred the nervous feeling that their "friends" were not entirely friendly. Anything that involved turning the sympathies of Rome's allies tended to get Romans at least as freaked out as anything that involves race does the average American.

All in all, I thought I gave a damned fine performance.

The question, however, was what Caesar would think of it. He sat there, listening carefully, studying me and my face, occasionally raising an eyebrow to make me nervous or seeing if a glance at Chrys could rile me. (Not at all, now that she was dressed. I thought any hetero guy who didn't stare at her was blind or crazy.) He was sizing me up at least as much as he was concerned with the case I was making, and we both knew that. There would be a decision of one kind or another, but he wasn't going to make it till he knew what he thought.

Then he would probably make it without any regret or remorse in either direction.

When I finished, he sat back and thought for a long time. "Hasmonea," he said, "do you deny the essential correctness of Marcus Fortius's charges? Or do you merely propose to offer me more advantages than Fortius is able to offer?"

The Carthaginian licked his lips and seemed to take a long time to think. That was probably a mistake—it made you wonder what he was going to say, rather than what he actually thought. Finally, he said, "It is true, Caesar, that I worship Moloch, and you yourself have long known this. And it is true that we of the Masters are destined by our gods to rule all times and places. But we can be generous to those who accept the will of our gods, and in any case the end is not yet—it would be many centuries before direct rule was imposed here."

"And thus," Caesar said, his eyes narrowing, "you tell me that Caesar will not be enslaved, but only his grandchildren, and thus Caesar ought to welcome you?"

Hasmonea looked a little pale.

"Moreover," Caesar said, "I deny absolutely that I had any knowledge of your vile worship. This is a lie made to separate Caesar from his army, and it is a very clumsy lie."

Hasmonea seemed to stagger; I realized later that it was only that he had seen that expression on Caesar before, a certain narrowing of the eyes and tightening of the mouth that meant that something unpleasant needed to be done, that Gaius Julius Caesar was just the man to do it, and that he was going to make people pay for forcing him to do it.

Then the general sat back, stared into space, and said, "It seems to me we have an insoluble problem here. We are told that Hasmonea is from a civilization which is in all ways repugnant to us and threatens to enslave ourselves and our posterity. We are also told that this ATN has supplied a military advisor and engineer to Crassus, our onetime friend and bitter foe." He appeared to hesitate over the options, and then finally said, "Let us settle this matter by putting it in the hands of the gods. We will prepare the arena here in Fanum Fortunae, and tomorrow, using only their own skills and with no weapons, these strangers from other times will fight each other to the death. Venus, who guards my family, and Mars, whose servant I have ever been, and mighty Jupiter himself, will send victory to he who is deserving."

The way Hasmonea turned green told me two things—first of all, that he probably wasn't trained much at hand-to-hand, and secondly, that he had figured out the same thing I had. I was supposed to win the fight tomorrow.

I also realized just how he had sealed his doom, and that he had not had any choice in the matter. By telling the truth he effectively sentenced himself to death—that was clear. Caesar's army were Romans, and patriotic Romans, and the notion of yoking themselves or their grandchildren to Carthage was impossible to accept. Add to that Hasmonea's worship of Moloch, and you had an open-and-shut case against him; the army would gladly see him executed.

Moreover, he had accused Caesar of knowing about the Moloch worship. That particular stain had to be scrubbed off right now; Caesar couldn't afford the kind of evil reputation that would give him in Roman politics.

But if Hasmonea had lied, it would have gone worse. It would not have *forced* Caesar to act, as doing this in public had, but it would have shown Caesar at once that he could not trust Hasmonea, and that would have been a different sort of death sentence.

Could Caesar somehow be aware how the timeline wars were going? Was he trying to get in with the side that seemed to be winning? Did he genuinely prefer us?

It was impossible to say, and, anyway, tomorrow I apparently had to kill a man with my bare hands. I was glad it was at least a Closer.

"Let both men be watched, but restore them to their companions for the evening, and let the legates see that they are comfortable and well fed," Caesar said. "That is Caesar's decision. Let the combat happen at the second hour after sunrise. Let these men be escorted away and let them be kept away from each other and from their weapons."

The "let"s were a minor defect in the translating software, I figured; Latin tended to use the subjunctive to give an order, particularly when who carried it out or how it got carried out was being left up to the discretion of subordinates, and there's no real subjunctive in English, so instead it kept saying, "Let." But the message was clear enough; we would be treated well tonight and then tomorrow one of us would kill the other.

Not the most heartwarming thought I've ever heard, but at least it was clear. That night, the bed was comfortable, the food was good, and we got caught up on what had happened to Porter and Paula. Apparently the inn had been hit by one of the very first cannon rounds, and Caesar's cavalry had been there by the time the two of them had managed to get out the front door. The desk clerk was already hanging from the yardarm at that point; they had both been scared silly, and both were deeply annoyed by the cavity search, but "It wasn't that big a deal, boss, these soldiers are disciplined as all get out. They told us what they were going to do—poke a finger up and see if we had anything hidden—they put oil on the finger first, and they were at least as embarrassed as we were. I think 'cavity searches' are probably one of Hasmonea's innovations—there's not any really significant weapon in the local technology you could hide there."

Paula seemed so anxious to reassure me that I

turned immediately to Porter, and said, "So are you all right? Were you scared or hurt?"

Porter shrugged and kept looking at the floor.

"Porter," I said. "It's me. You can tell me."

"Well, it made me feel gross. I wanted to throw up, having an old man feeling around like that. He tried to be polite and all that, but it was still gross."

"Yeah," I said, "it must have been." I sat down next to her without quite touching her.

"But I feel like a big baby," she said. "All you guys just shrug it off—"

Chrys sat on the other side and took Porter in her arms. "Sweetheart," she said, "we're all professional killers. We get strip-searched and messed around with a lot, all the time. Sometimes by people a lot ruder than that. We're used to it. We all felt terrible the first time it happened. And it's still not a good thing to do to a person. The fact that it doesn't bother us is something wrong with us, really."

Porter started to cry, quietly, and Chrysamen held her for a long time. I sat and stared like a fool; you can spend an eternity of time and a fortune in cash on keeping bad things away from your family, and they find a way to you anyway. I realized, too, that bad as things had been for Porter, she had probably felt safe after she started living with me and my family and employees—something about the presence of so many people who love you (and who are armed to the teeth and good with what they carry) must breed the feeling that the bad things are all in the past.

A lot worse could happen, of course, and easily might, but this was the first time she was really aware that it could.

As usual, I felt like an idiot in the situation, and wondered what I would do without Chrysamen.

After a while Porter stopped crying, dried her eyes, and tried to apologize for upsetting everyone. We all told her not to worry about it, and by then we figured we were all tired enough to sleep.

Caesar's courtesy even extended far enough to supply us with three beds, smaller ones for Porter and Paula and a big one for Chrys and me. The room was warm and comfortable—one of those Roman inventions that should never have gone out of use was central heating—and pitch-dark with the blinds pulled. Paula snores now and then, and Porter occasionally mumbles in her sleep; after a few minutes there was enough snoring and mumbling so that I figured they were both out.

Chrysamen is hard to tell about; she's so silent and wastes so little energy in her movement, like the superb natural athlete she is, that when there's nothing that needs doing she simply doesn't move. Thus in the dark you can't really tell if she's asleep or lying awake.

I certainly knew that I was lying awake. I couldn't quite figure it out. I had shot Closers, pushed them from high places, set buildings on fire and shot them as they ran out, exposed them to the naked fury of nuclear reactions. In all this I felt about the same way I did about killing copperheads or rats—i.e., it was a job, and it badly needed doing.

But somehow this thing with Hasmonea was different. Maybe because I would have an audience—it was quite clear from hints dropped by the servants that most of the staff were looking forward to this in exactly the way they looked forward to gladiatorial combats. The Romans were a people of war, whatever they thought of themselves, and they were always interested in seeing how strangers fought. Having people applaud and cheer while I was killing a Closer seemed too much like having a cheering section while I cleared a poisonous snake from a trail.

Or then again, maybe I was just afraid; I'm a great believer in using whatever advantage you have, and I've never in all the fights I've been in worried about "sportsmanship." When only one of you gets to walk away afterward, it's pretty stupid to worry about whether it's with honor. Violence is dirty and ugly, and you can't beautify it by treating it like a sporting event.

Not that there would be a referee here, but it was going to be an absolutely fair fight, and I had always preferred having it rigged in my favor, and doing the rigging myself.

Or then again maybe it was that I knew a little too much. I knew that Hasmonea was his name, and I knew what he looked like, and that he was easily rattled and sometimes said things that weren't wise. I knew he was frightened by something about me and didn't carry himself in the well-balanced way of an athlete or a fighting man. And he didn't have either my reach or my muscle development.

Chances were good, in short, that I was going to win, and much as I despised what he was, it's one thing to hate a set of ideas and a culture, like the Closers, and quite another thing to take away the life of a single human individual, especially when you have a pretty good idea of what he must be feeling and experiencing while you do it.

So there were a lot of good reasons not to be able to sleep. The only good reason for falling asleep, actually, was so that I could win tomorrow. *If* I won. Which got me back on the same train of thought, and around the track we went again . . .

Chrys's hand gently stroked down the side of my

body, running over the hard muscles of my chest, finding my stomach. Her soft lips brushed my ear. "Mark?"

"I'm awake."

"Tell me about it. You're wound up like a spring. What's the matter?"

"Everything, I suppose."

"Yeah, I guessed as much." She snuggled against me; her breasts were still high and firm after our years of marriage, and her skin was still soft and smooth. Her hands worked at my chest muscles. "Jeez, how can a guy clench his chest?"

"It's easier than it sounds."

"Shh. Don't talk. Let me fix a few things. Roll over."

So I did and she started working on my back. It was great, but I noticed that the lower back was getting all the attention, and then my buttocks. After a while her hands moved around to the front.

"Do you want to do this?" I asked.

"I want to because you need it, husband. And if I didn't usually want to do it with you, I'd never have married you."

"Okay."

"And if you give me any crap about it slowing you down or spoiling your eye tomorrow, I'll tie your dick in a knot."

I couldn't help it; I giggled a little at that, and then she licked my neck, which always seems to hit a magic switch. When I rolled over and pressed her thighs apart, she was already warm and ready for me. We had to keep the noise down so as not to wake the others, but occasionally that's an amusing challenge in its own right.

Afterward, as we lay together, I kissed her very tenderly; she pressed my head back and returned the kiss—and that's the last thing I remembered till morning.

When I woke up, there were pancakes and honey for breakfast, together with a little goat cheese. It was a decent enough way to start the day, but I ate just enough to keep hunger pangs at bay. It's undignified to throw up on your opponent, even if you go on to kill him.

The guards arrived promptly, one set to take the women to the arena—they were being "honored" by being allowed to sit in Caesar's box—and another set to take me to a different door.

It was cold and clear today; everyone was bundled tight, but the sun was shining brightly, and it made the great plumes of everyone's breath shine white and silver in the narrow, dim street they led me up. The last couple of blocks, several young women turned up to throw roses at me. I wasn't at all sure what that symbolized, and I was even less sure I wanted to know.

9

What they put us in looked more like holding pens for animals than anything else; it was a stone cell with a barred door and window looking out on a hallway on one side, and a barred door into the arena on the other. I made the mistake of getting too close to that door just once, and suddenly the crowd was going crazy, whooping and cheering.

They had stripped me to fight; I was wearing a leather jock, a pair of boots, padded fingerless leather gloves, and that was all. They gave me a blanket to keep me warm as well.

When I backed away from the window, a voice said, "They did the same thing for me, but more of them whistled."

Whistling was a sign of disapproval, the chip in my ear informed me. I looked around and saw that Hasmonea was in the cell across the hallway. "I was trying to sleep," he said.

He looked about as scared and miserable as a human

being can; I decided then and there that since there wasn't any getting around killing him, I would make it quick. I knew if he had the chance, being a Closer, he would naturally kill me without compunction, and quite possibly torture me first, and I knew how dangerous his kind was—but I saw no reason to inflict any more pain than I had to.

Hasmonea hung on to the bars and looked at me a little hungrily. "The woman you were with is your wife? The girl is your daughter?"

"My ward, actually."

He sighed. "That's the tough part of all this. I know what the odds are, which is not going to help my chances any. But I wish I had some way of saying goodbye to my family. Not that they would want me to— that's a disgrace and so forth. But I've noticed, after a lot of missions, that other cultures manage to say goodbye, and mourn for their dead, and it doesn't seem to hurt their fighting ability."

"How many timelines have you been to?" I asked, to keep the conversation going. I didn't want to be alone with my thoughts, and I doubted he wanted to be alone with his.

"Just over thirty. Thirty, uh, three, I think. You lose count after a while."

"Yeah, I've only been to a dozen."

"You're a Crux Op, aren't you?"

"Unhunh."

He half groaned. "I knew I shouldn't ask, and I did anyway. This doesn't look good for me at all. I'm not even a soldier—I'm just a Slave Searcher."

Slave Searchers were the equivalent of our Time Scouts. When a new timeline was identified, there was only so much you could accomplish with hidden cameras, listening devices, and so forth. Sooner or later somebody had to walk through a gate and go see what it was really like over there.

After that the equivalency ended. Sometimes our Time Scouts were sent into known timelines, to start new branch points that could eventually grow into timelines that might join ATN. Other times a Time Scout just jumped through the gate into a timeline that needed investigating—usually not knowing whether the Closers were active there (and had perhaps started the timeline), whether some independent time-traveling civilization had started it, or whether (perhaps—there were arguments about whether or not this ever happened) it had just occurred naturally.

In every case the mission was the same. Make contact. Decide whether the civilization was advanced enough and psychologically stable enough to open full relations crosstime. If no, then help them move toward maturity as fast as they safely could (and hope the Closers don't show up before you do). If yes, then open up relations and see if they'd like to join ATN. Even if they didn't want to join on, at least they would know where to call for help if Closers invaded, and they could be on their guard.

The Closer approach was much simpler. Find the most militarily formidable civilization in the timeline. Assist it in conquering the Earth. Find the most ruthless potential dictator and assist him in taking power. When the whole Earth was under the rule of one man or at most a few families, kill the top people and move in to run the show yourselves, turning the whole Earth into one big plantation.

It had never occurred to me before that there might be any other resemblances between the jobs, but life can surprise you; obviously their Slave Searchers had to know something about the cultures with which they interacted, and perhaps even study them and learn to see things from their point of view. Know thy enemy, and all that, especially if you can know him thoroughly before he knows you're his enemy.

Morbid curiosity caused me to ask the next question. "So have you liked this timeline?"

He shrugged. "At least slaves are cheap, and there's a wide variety of them. The wine isn't bad, and the baths are pleasant. But it's really much too far north, and there are really too many people in the middle class. Most of them would benefit from being owned, even if only by other people like themselves."

"Benefit?" I asked.

"Of course. How many people are really fit to run their own lives? And let's be honest here . . . how many servants are any good if they can change masters? They only learn to please when they have no choice. That's why we always say that an ugly girl you own is better than a whore you rent, and both are better than a wife. They have some reason to be."

There might be things worse than being alone with your thoughts, after all. But I asked, "And yet you say you miss your family?"

He shrugged. "It's an emotional weakness. Like most of my weaknesses. They couldn't do anything with me, and I was too high-ranking to sell or kill, so they put me into the Slave Searchers because I was medically unfit for the Army. Every so often I write home to them, and I've occasionally gone and visited my sister and her children. They find me very embarrassing—Moloch's jaws, *I* find me very embarrassing—but duty is duty, and they let me hang around. Which comforts me a great deal, weak though it is."

"Have you liked being a, uh, Slave Searcher?"

"Oh, actually, a lot. I like observing other cultures. You can learn a lot from them."

For an instant there, I thought I might have to kill a Closer I liked, but then he went on, "For example, the Romans make such effective use of crucifixion in keeping slaves in line. It takes the slave a long time to die, and it's right out in public, so it gets the message through to every single slave without wasting much of the stock. And, of course, it's fascinating to see how easy or difficult it is to domesticate the various cultures. The Romans are tough and independent and so forth, but they will make better slaves exactly because they are used to seeing the world in terms of masters and slaves. Where some very gentle, even servile populations are hard as Moloch's teeth to enslave because they don't understand what it means when we tell them that they are property and they exist only for us." He sighed. "At any rate, it hasn't been a bad life, really, and I have few regrets. I wish I had spent more time at home with my mother—I liked that a lot—and I wish I had pleased my father more. It will please him to know I died as a Slave Searcher, heavily decorated, and thus kept up the family honor, but that will never wipe out his memories of how weak I really am."

By Closer standards, I realized, this was a sentimental and rather sweet poet-type. Any more sensitive (or any less politically connected), and they'd have fed him to Moloch. But the real reason he was still alive was probably that fundamentally he agreed with them; his impulses toward sensitivity, his interest in other cultures, his preference for real affection—he and his culture both agreed that this was an illness, something that regrettably had not been cured yet.

"But you're fond of them?"

"All babies are," he said. "Some of us just have more trouble growing up. I've even gotten fond of my wife, even though she's a low-status type and has just as big an affection-craving problem as I do."

Whatever he had actually said, "affection-craving problem" was probably as close to the meaning as the translator could get, taking it from his language into Latin and then from Latin into English. But there was something in his tone that made it sound like it was a disease, and a shameful one.

"And you wish you could kiss her good-bye, hold hands, maybe even hold each other a little or have spent a night sleeping next to each other?"

He gave me the strangest look I've ever seen from anyone, and his voice choked. "Is this a tactic?"

"If it is, it's backward," I said, and suddenly realized just how tired I felt. "Look, it might surprise you, but what you're feeling is what I think it's healthy for human beings to feel. That's all. I probably feel a little less like killing you because of it."

He sat there on the cold floor, wrapped in his blanket, and very quietly said, "You know, if anyone had talked to me that way when I was ten, so that I had grown up with maybe a slight idea that it was all right to be the way I am . . . I'd have ended up fed to Moloch by the time I was twelve."

I couldn't help it—I laughed, and so did he. "Make it quick," he said, "if you win. I'll do the same for you. Caesar likes to see people play with each other, but there's not any reason to do that. As long as Crassus still has the one from your timeline, Caesar will have to keep at least one of us alive. As soon as one of us is dead . . . well, there you go. Perfect security for the other one."

"You've got it," I said.

Unfortunately, there were two acts ahead of us. One was a couple of Gauls, big crude types who were handed short axes, had their knees tied together, and who simply whaled away at each other until one of them fell over. They came out and cut them apart, carried off the bodies—I wasn't sure either of them was alive—and then a big cart came out, a lot like the Zamboni at a hockey game, and slaves threw sand all over the arena.

Caesar hadn't shown up yet. I guess when you head an army of tens of thousands who all think you're god, you can be as late as you like, and just enjoy your breakfast.

The next little crowd-warmer was four naked girls, not much out of puberty, armed with spears, against a very large and not happy bear. It took a long time, and I just kind of sat in the corner away from the front grating, not watching it, hoping Porter and the others had sense enough not to watch. As it ended, Hasmonea said, "It's over, and, if you want to know, it looks like two of the girls will live."

"Were you rooting for the bear?"

"Moloch's jaws, no. These Romans are much, much too crude. I tried to enliven their gladiatorial games a little by suggesting that perhaps they could move away from professional killers and explore what happened with amateurs and with animals. After all, in the time-lines where there's a Court of Nero, there are some wonderful shows. Unfortunately I underestimated their crudity."

"One thing I can't stand, it's *crude* barbarity," I said.

Hasmonea chuckled. "I think we have again reached the edge of the cultural divide."

"Pretty clearly. Has the big cheese shown up yet?"

"I think so. I think that was all the crowd noise in the middle of the act. Nothing much was happening at the time in the arena. If you want to look again, they've carried off the bear, the dead girl, and the one who I think is going to bleed to death. The other two walked off some time ago."

"I'll wait till they get the sand down, thanks."

I had the grim and slightly sad realization that if Hasmonea and I had ended up in the same prison together for years instead of hours, we might well have worked out a way to stand each other, and even begun to like each other. Even though I knew, for example, that as a high-ranking Closer he had probably tossed his first child into Moloch . . . it's funny what loneliness and stress will make you overlook.

There was more wild cheering from the arena, and a couple of priests came out to bless all the fresh sand that had been thrown down. Then a bunch of standard-bearers carrying the eagles of Caesar's various legions came out, and paraded them around while the crowd cheered loudly. There was one voice that sounded like it was coming through a megaphone, and I figured it was probably someone rattling off everything each legion had done.

That took a while, because the crowd had to cheer loudly each time an announcement was finished, and also because since there were four main banks of seats in the arena, each eagle was also collecting a cheer as it was presented to each bank. So that added up to five cheers per eagle, and that took some time.

"Are there any more curtain-raisers before us?" I asked.

"Couldn't say; they didn't give me a program," Hasmonea said. "If you win, make it *quick*, remember."

"It's a deal. I'd like you to know I won't enjoy killing you," I said.

"And I'd like you to know I'd rather kill somebody else than you," Hasmonea said.

Hell, by Closer standards that probably made us *compañeros*, blood brothers, and best buddies forever.

There was another delay or two while they got everything blessed, but now there were plenty of criers standing out there making all sorts of announcements about the two of us, building us up into a couple of exciting supermen versed in every art of death-dealing there was.

At least we were getting star billing.

I didn't speak to Hasmonea again, nor he to me; there was nothing really left to say, and we shared nothing except the arena, when you came down to it. Still, there have been times since—late at night, say, when I wake from dark dreams that I can't recall— when I see his face in my memory, and hear his voice, and strangely enough the thing I really regret is not having asked him what his wife's name was or if they had any kids.

It doesn't happen often.

Anyway, by now it was close to noon, and the sand outside was bright enough to stab at my eyes a little. The various criers were spewing steam with each announcement, and it sparkled in the sun.

The moment came. The grates rumbled up. The guard behind me said, "Leave the blanket." I felt a lot more like killing him than Hasmonea.

We entered the arena, and the guard who was waiting inside said, "Turn left and walk all the way around the arena. When you get back to me I'll tell you what to do."

So I did, and the crowd applauded wildly. Hasmonea had turned the other way and gone around the other side; I could hear him getting whistled at and people yelling various terms that the gadget in my ear kept translating as "Carthaginian. Carthaginian. Punic. Poenian. Carthaginian. Worshiper of Moloch."

I suspected the terms were a lot more pejorative than that.

We passed each other just in front of Caesar's reviewing stand. I saw that Caesar was lounging comfortably, obviously enjoying a warm bowl of wine. Paula, Chrys, and Porter were dressed in better clothes than they had brought, and they all looked unbearably tense. I wondered—if I lost, what might Caesar do to them? Put them into the arena? I'd pit Chrys and Paula against anybody . . . give them to Hasmonea as a reward? I hoped his gentle impulses might win out . . . so that Chrysamen would get a chance to kill him.

It was fruitless to worry about it. The thing to do was to not lose.

Walking around the arena had at least given me some idea of how the boots fit—pretty well, actually, so I wasn't expecting any trouble from that quarter. The fresh sand didn't seem to be too slick, and, with the sun reflecting off the sand, it was quite a bit warmer than I would have expected it to be out there.

I had also been flexing my hands like mad, trying to get them loose and relaxed enough to be effective. And I had noted that the leather jock wasn't too terribly uncomfortable, though in a long fight it would probably chafe my thighs. Probably they had a lot of experience with fitting these things.

That gave me another thought, so I tripped and fell; people laughed, and while they were laughing I got a nice big wad of damp sand in my left hand. Years ago, when I was stuck in an airport waiting and had nothing to read but a cheap adventure book, I ran across the phrase, "The first rule of unarmed combat is to not stay unarmed." It works for me, anyway.

I passed the last part of the crowd and was almost

back to my guard—second? trainer? handler? I didn't really know what his function was in all this.

He led me out to the middle; Hasmonea's guard led him out to face me. We stood facing each other, about ten feet apart. A little guy with a megaphone came out and announced that we would be fighting to the death, unless it was voted to spare one of us, and that this was to be no-holds-barred, any-which-way-you-can fighting. Then he told us to face Caesar, and to extend our right arms and repeat after him, loudly.

It was the phrase you've heard in a thousand movies—"*Salute, imperator, we who are about to die, salute you.*" The Latin "Salute" means something a bit like "Hail" and a bit like "Viva." "Imperator" later meant "emperor," in our timeline, but at this time it meant "guy with real good mojo." The Romans had the idea that an army whose leader had *imperium*—which you might as well translate as "the Force was with him"—was invincible, so it was a heavy-duty compliment. Calling him by name would have been a bit more normal and a lot more modest. But as I was to learn, old Gaius could never really get enough of praise of himself. Even from people who he'd decided ought to fight to the death with each other for his amusement.

Then we turned to face each other, the crowd started whooping, and they signaled for us to start.

For a guy with a tenth of my training at fighting—and maybe one one-hundredth of my experience—Hasmonea put up a hell of a fight; he didn't really hurt me, but he forced me to worry about it.

We closed with each other right away—after all we had said we'd be quick—and I shot what looked like a left jab at his face. He blocked, but of course the fistful of sand I had picked up went into his eyes, blinding him. I sidestepped and snap-kicked as hard as I could; my boot flung his elbow upward and connected hard with his rib cage. He made an "oof" noise, but it hadn't felt like I'd cracked any ribs. I closed in.

I don't know if he was lucky or had already gotten one eye cleared of sand, but he managed to swing an arm around my head, forcing it down, and got in a respectable knee to my nose, not hard enough to break it because he didn't really know what he was doing, but certainly hard enough to hurt. He followed through, too slowly, with a solid punch to the side of my jaw. (If he had known what he was doing he should have hit me, two or three times, in the temple or the throat, or driven a thumb into my eye.)

It hurt like hell for a short instant, but as my jaw went numb, I scooped his supporting leg with my free hand and shoulder-rolled out, planting my shoulder in his ribs as I went.

I spun before I hit and lunged forward for a grip at his throat, but he was too fast and had already gotten turned—my hands clawed at sand, and then his were on my face, groping for my eyes. He was beginning to learn, and that was bad news.

I pulled my head back and trapped one of his hands, turning it against the little finger, taking up the slack skin around the wrist, and finally levering it against my opposite arm. He screamed then, as his elbow joint went, and I flung sand into his open mouth, making him choke and gasp. I rolled to my feet and circled toward his left arm, which now hung at a funny angle, the palm facing uselessly out from his body.

He was half-blind and choking, but when I tried a driving kick into his ribs on that side, his leg rose to block and turn mine, and in as neat a little motion as you've ever seen in dojo, his leg extended hard. He was shorter than I was, and a fraction too far away—otherwise, he'd have nailed my scrotum to my backbone with his boot toe. But since he missed, and didn't hit my thigh with enough force to make a difference, I continued the motion, planted the kicking foot, and whipped a roundhouse at his head. It connected, badly, but enough to throw him off-balance—which is serious when your arm is out of joint at the elbow.

He staggered in a little spiral and barely righted himself. I took two giant steps and felt my blood go cold as ice; now I would kill him.

I had finally slipped behind him. Most of the good places for killing a human being quickly, if you've only got your hands to work with, are behind him.

I kicked hard again, and caught one of his kidneys. From the way he grunted I had hurt Hasmonea badly at least, and if I was lucky, I might actually have ruptured the kidney and started the hemorrhage that would finish him in a minute or so.

He tried to turn to face me. His face was now a mask of hideous pain, with one eye swollen shut from the sand, and his mouth hanging open to breathe. I skipped sideways and used the leather on my left palm to smash his septum, sending a spray of blood from his nose. The odds of driving the bone into the brain that way are practically nil (though it does happen), but the pain is blinding and incapacitating, and that was all I needed.

He fell forward to his knees, and then sat back as if trying to rise. I turned and kicked his other kidney, harder than I had the first. With a moan of pure agony and despair, he went forward onto his hands and knees, his left side buckling at once as his broken arm would not bear the weight.

From here on it was by the book. I slapped a half

nelson around his neck, using his good right arm as a brace (and thereby taking his working arm out of the contest). From the way his hand was beginning to twitch, I think he may have been passing out by that point.

I surely hope so. I had promised him that I would be quick, and I was being as quick as I could. But still, he was bound to suffer horribly before it was all over. If both people know it's a fight, and both are fighting, it is not within the power of bare human hands to be painless.

With his head locked, I wrapped my other arm around so that it would brace against my own arm and against his carotid. I twisted my two arms like a rope knotting, shutting off the blood flow to his brain, and then used my own arms as a fulcrum to somersault over his body, stretching him out and further crushing his neck. My legs whipped around to brace his thighs apart, my hips lifted his buttocks, and the move was complete; nothing shielded the arteries of his neck from the crushing force of my arms. I counted thirty seconds, slowly, to myself, while keeping his limp body torqued as hard as it would go; when I released my grip, I wanted to be sure he was dead.

At twenty seconds into my count, on the front of my leather jock, I felt something warm and wet; a moment later the stench told me that he had voided his bowels. I kept the lock on and kept counting. Hasmonea was a clever man and it could be a last-instant fake.

Could have been, might have been, but whether it was or not, I kept the lock on long enough. When I finally released his limp body, he was thoroughly dead. I flung him off me like an old towel and stood up; Hasmonea's body lay crumpled and still, and a legion doctor ran out to check him. It didn't take much of a look, apparently, because he announced at once that the man was dead.

The place went up in wild cheering, then into rhythmic clapping like you hear at the Olympics. Caesar stood up, nodded at me, and then turned to the crowd, raising his arms. The crowd went so crazy you'd have thought Caesar had been doing the work.

It was a strange moment. The sun beat down through the icy air, reflecting off the sand onto me, and I realized I was getting a little bit of a sunburn. The glare was blinding, the roar of the crowd deafening.

Behind Caesar, I could see Porter looking pale and sick with what she had seen. Paula was impassive, Chrys clearly just relieved, but all of them had managed to sit as far away on the bench from Caesar as was practical.

I looked down at my arms and saw that the sweat was not only drying but freezing on me, and that it was mixed with blood, though whether mine or Hasmonea's I had no idea. I began to shiver all over, and I wanted desperately to heave up breakfast.

It was then that I found myself wishing I had asked that poor sad crumpled heap of broken bones leaking blood into the sand what his wife's name was, what he loved about her, how many children they had, and so forth. It would have been far better than what I had heard him talk about, and it would have comforted him to talk about it.

I looked back up into Caesar's eyes. That slash of a mouth was drawn in a tight smile, the kind that some people put on when they think they must appear pleased and don't feel it, but Caesar's pleasure seemed real enough; his eyes had that strange, farseeing look to them again, like a thousand-yard stare but with every intention of coming back in just one more moment. He thought a little farther ahead than most people, lived in a slightly wider mental space and time, and it showed through now and then.

He turned to the guard next to him, and an order was given. I couldn't hear it over the noise at the distance, but the crowd began to quiet at once.

Behind me there was a squeaking sound. I turned to see a twin-drive pedicab—I don't know how else you could describe it—pulling up behind me.

It was built like the bicycles we had seen the other day, or rather like two of them stuck on the front of a chariot. The men peddling it seemed to be slaves, probably Gauls or Britons to judge by their blazing red hair. A legate rode on the back.

He stepped off, and they stuck out their feet to stop. Then he walked up to me, threw a heavy robe around my shoulders, and put a wreath of some kind onto my head. "Get into the chariot," he said. "We will circle the arena once. You will wave to the crowd. You will lead them in cheers of 'Caesar! Caesar!'"

The horse pistol he held under his cloak seemed very persuasive.

I always had a hard time understanding how anyone could be a cheerleader—my brother, my sister, and I were always participants and bouncing around and looking pert didn't enter into our idea of how to spend our time—but let me tell you, there's no skill easier to acquire when, first of all, you've got a man with a gun making you learn, and, secondly, you've got a crowd that has been terrorized into cheering as if their lives depended upon it. Which, in a certain very real sense, they did.

We ended up circling the arena three times, and when we were done, my throat was good and hoarse from shouting "Caesar! Caesar!" to them. They cheered back wildly, and then finally, after it was all done, I got to go back to the room where we had slept the night before, and they had a hot bath waiting for me. They also had a slave girl that I would have guessed was about thirteen, who I gently sent on her way, pleading that I had vowed to my gods to have sex only with Chrysamen. In a little while they brought all three of my companions back to join me, but I sure wasn't in the mood. Mostly I just wanted to sit in the hot water and let the feelings of the day soak away.

I hated killing Closers who had names, and it occurred to me that probably all of them did—I just usually didn't know them. There were a lot of things I didn't like about this mission, but if it really meant an end to this war, I was all for it.

"One thing you can say for the Romans," Chrysamen said, "they don't do things quickly unless they have to. The games were the big event of the day. Caesar has gone back to his quarters to think about things and isn't expected to come out till tomorrow morning. We have sort of a lunch date with him, I guess, in which he'll finally explain what he is going to do with all of us. Meanwhile, we're here, we're warm and well fed, and you don't have to kill anybody tomorrow morning, at least not that we know about."

"What's been going on out in the city?"

"Well, Caesar's supporters posted a long list of proscriptions, but Caesar ordered that taken down and commuted the sentence of anyone who will formally surrender and swear an oath of allegiance. So there haven't been many executions so far—everyone who could had already fled, and everyone who couldn't swore the oath. So I'd say the city is thoroughly in his hands."

"What's he going to do now?" I asked.

She shrugged. "We were thrown in with slave women for a while, and all of them had picked up gossip. Everyone agrees he's going to take Rome. The only real question is whether he'll cut over to one of the coasts and then head south, or take the direct route south. But the last word from bicycle post is that the direct road, down the Via Flaminia, is open. And with bicycles, if he goes that way, he's only a two-day forced march from Rome. All that's between him and the capital is whatever Pompey has scared up—assuming Pompey hasn't just cut and run like he did in our timeline."

"Where's Crassus? I thought everyone figured *he* was Caesar's main opponent. And from what Hasmonea told me, if our boy Caldwell is still alive anywhere, it's with Crassus."

Paula made a face. "Well, then don't bet on the cavalry turning up soon. Word is that Crassus made his winter encampment in Egypt. I'm afraid we're stuck with Caesar for quite a while."

10

At least he was slow about getting around to things the next morning as well, so there was a lot of time to just hang out. It might have been tough on the nerves, but on the other hand we didn't have too much to fear just then, so we played some silly word games, talked about nothing, and generally enjoyed being bored in comfort. Or at least Paula, Chrys, and I did. People in violent occupations learn to enjoy boredom.

Porter was sulking. Teenagers, even when they know there's violence around, don't appreciate boredom enough.

We had played "Categories" about one time too many, and we were actually starting to wonder if we should ask the guards for a midday meal when the summons came, and when we got there we discovered we were all supposed to stretch out at the table for Roman-style dining.

There was the expectable vast load of pickled fish and the heavy flat bread; the soup was good, the wine was plentiful, and Caesar seemed mainly interested in talking about the political structure of ATN, and about the people who headed it, and why exactly they might object to one person or support another.

This was making me slightly more uncomfortable than before, but I think I did a decent job of hiding it. It would have been one thing if he had given me the creeps, but although I had certainly seen that he could be cruel and arbitrary, nothing about him was really bothering or repelling me. Which was what the problem was—thus far Caesar had done nothing that would even remotely make me think of shooting him.

Of course he was a first-class jerk, but if I went around shooting all of those, I'd never have to leave my own timeline, and I'd still never get finished. And then again orders were orders . . . but they hadn't told me where or when to shoot him. In fact Chief Tribune Scipio had told me that there was a certain amount of historical confusion about the whole thing and thus they figured it would be better not to tell me, because I could easily end up staking out a place where it didn't happen.

When he had told me that, my judgment had been that he was lying. But he had told me in front of General Malecela, and when I tried to talk to Malecela about it later, Malecela had strongly discouraged the question.

Now I wondered why, and more than that, I wished I had extorted everything they knew from Scipio and Malecela—because I was sure that was much more than they had told me.

And just when had I started distrusting Malecela? It had been a relief to have him show up in the timeline to which we had been carried off, but by a few days later when our party left to come here, I had already begun to wonder what was up. Whatever it was, Malecela was in on it, and something smelled really bad when an agent with a record as long and as good as mine—I had known him back when he was a captain—couldn't be trusted with whatever the secret was.

I tried to remind myself to cool down, *after all, it may be something that mustn't fall into enemy hands, and if you don't know it, they can't get it out of you.* For that matter there could easily be a good reason I hadn't thought of, or maybe there was a reason why they couldn't tell me why they couldn't tell me . . . my thoughts were beginning to go in circles.

Naturally I was trying to have that argument with myself while I also listened to Caesar and attempted not to drop all of the food onto my chest, eating lying down. It's not as easy as it looks, at least not if you don't want to end up shaking dinner out of your toga for the next three days.

The real trouble was that I knew Malecela well enough to figure that in any normal circumstances he'd at least have told me that there was something he couldn't tell me. That would have been enough.

But just to try to hide it from me entirely . . . that didn't sit well. It made me think that what he was up to was something I wouldn't have liked, and he knew it.

I did my best to distract myself by paying attention to the conversation. After a while I noticed that Caesar was paying a lot of attention to Porter, which might have worried me for a second—technically we were all spoils of war and she, like all of us, was his slave—except it was mostly her music that interested him. She, in turn, had never seen a lyre; he had one brought in, along with a Roman version of a flute, and she spent the rest of the time softly noodling around over in the corner, getting the feel for the instruments. I guess when your setting is totally unfamiliar, the most comforting thing possible is a familiar task, one you find easy—and for Porter nothing was easier than learning a new instrument.

At last the wine came in, and the conversation turned serious. Caesar was a blunt man by nature, but capable of subtlety when he needed it; this time bluntness suited him. "So this timeline in which I live is to be a very important one," he said. "The Republic will flourish, the tribunes will gain power, and the Senate and consuls lose power, and eventually Rome will rule the entire Earth, even the two whole continents across the sea, that Caldwell led us to sail to, where the colony of Terra Elastica was planted. And in a few thousand years we will be the most advanced timeline of all.

"This interests me. It has always seemed to me that my destiny and Rome's are intertwined to our mutual benefit. You say that in your timeline, I became dictator after taking Rome—"

"And emperor for all practical purposes, until you were assassinated in 709 A.U.C.," I said. "March 15. I would suggest that on that day, you don't go to the Senate house, and listen to the soothsayers." What the hell, it was five years in the future; by that time either I'd have done it, or things would be drastically changed.

Caesar nodded. "Though of course all things have been changed by your intervention, and the Closers'."

"Things that have been changed have a way of turning out the same," I said. I was thinking of the fact that twice I had seen John Glenn be the first American to orbit the Earth.

"I see. Well, then, 709 A.U.C. And the conspirators—"

"Mostly are your allies nowadays," I said. "They turned against you when you became dictator."

He nodded. "I see more and more advantage in working behind the scenes. And young Marcus Antonius is a fine tribune; through him I can exert more than enough control. I think I will avoid the step of becoming dictator. Yes, once we are off to a good start here, I think much can be done." The general sat up a bit more and poured himself some wine. "And there is something wonderful about it, you know. That silly old Pompey has a tendency to think he is Alexander reincarnated, merely because he has some flair for tactics and logistics, but then what Roman general doesn't dream of just extending conquest till we have the whole Earth sworn to alliance? And then, of course, we realize that if we were to accomplish that, men like Pompey and I would be nothing again . . . and much like Alexander, we would be left weeping because there would be no more worlds to conquer.

"But what you describe is wonderful. Not just more worlds to conquer, but an unlimited number of worlds with an unlimited number of challenges. Room for the biggest heart, spirit, and intellect. A man with the right *genius* could go farther than most men could imagine." It took me a moment to realize that he had said "genius," because the word came out with a hard *g*, like GENN ee oose, and the translator in my ear just let it through because there's no such word in English. Your *genius*, if you're a Roman, is the god you're assigned at birth, who looks after you and your interests as long as you're careful to say the right prayers and do the right rituals. Which means if you've got a real hotshot *genius*, and you take care of him, you're going places.

Caesar seemed to just sit and watch quietly while I thought. I don't think he realized that I had had to take a moment to figure out what he had said. When my expression cleared, and I stopped looking confused, he smiled and explained further that, "It was just the thought—the question really . . . well, if it should happen that the world is unified during my lifetime, or that there is no longer an urgent need for me here . . . do you suppose your ATN might want a general or an administrator of some kind?"

I was startled, and Chrys looked like she'd choke. "We do sometimes recruit from other timelines," I said. "The founding leader of my nation—which only exists in some timelines—became an ATN agent in one timeline where there was nothing much for him to do. So it is not impossible. But we do know that contact was lost for a very long time, so the odds of your being able to cross over are small."

Caesar shrugged. "It was a thought, only. I've got at least twenty vigorous years left, if I can contrive not to be shot or stabbed, and chances are that the possibilities of this world will not be exhausted at all by that time. But I hate limits of any kind, you know. The Senate was very foolish to draw a line and tell me not to cross it—I can't imagine anything that would make me want to defy them more." He sighed and stretched. "I'm looking forward, one of these days, to having a villa on the Bay of Naples, and sitting there warm and comfortable, with no bigger question in mind than what book to read that day. All in the sun. The Gaulish winters are horrible, and the British winters make them seem bearable by comparison.

"Meanwhile, however, there's a delicate question that I've refrained from asking for some time. When this Caldwell person set himself up as a business partner with Crassus, it seemed of very minor interest to me. He had come in with his strange 'rubber,' showing off how many uses it had like any vulgar tradesman, and only a complete boor like Crassus would have been taken with him. We all thought it was the end of Caldwell when he set sail in his ten ships with all those free craftsmen and skilled slaves—we figured Crassus had truly thrown the money down a rathole—and yet just three years later, back he came with a load of rubber and requests for more colonists. Even then, we just thought, 'Well, no matter, a plebeian is growing wealthy. They have grown wealthy before.' Even when he introduced his firearms and his bicycles, and suddenly all of us had to relearn the art of war, we thought only, 'Now that Rome has these things, we are truly invincible.' But now I see how much he has changed us, and how much Hasmonea has changed us as well."

"Did you know him well?" I asked.

"Too well. He disgusted me; his worship of Moloch was the least of it. He was a coward when he could get away with it, soft in the worst ways to be soft, and hard-hearted where any real man ought to have some compassion."

"Then why did you have him—"

Caesar made an irritated chopping gesture with his hand. I'm not easily intimidated but I stopped, right then, with my mouth open. "Because," the general said, "I knew that eventually I would have to contend with Crassus for leadership of Rome, and that might well mean fighting. And Crassus has your Walks-in-His-Shadow Caldwell advising him, or did until recently, anyway—my spies tell me he has disappeared, and Crassus seems to be frantic with worry. At any rate, having seen what one man could bring with him, I *had* to have an advisor of my own. It took me no time at all to realize this was a real Carthaginian, a truly unrepentant child-sacrificer, and all the rest, but I had absolutely no other choice, as a practical matter. As soon as I had another option, I took it; I had no doubt at all that you would win, and thus Caesar disposed of an unpopular person in favor of one who could do him more good."

I had another moment to think, and what I thought was that his reasoning was cold, logical, and exactly the kind of thing Thebenides might have said.

On the other hand I wasn't supposed to shoot Thebenides.

"What are you hoping, exactly, to arrange with us?" I asked Caesar. "And you should be aware that Chrysamen is fully my partner; if you're going to deal with ATN, you should learn that we practice equality of the sexes."

"Mostly," Chrys said.

Caesar appeared slightly amused, though whether at Chrys's comment or at the notion of "equality of the sexes" I couldn't tell. "Very well, then. Let me make a suggestion as to our course of action. Clearly ATN wishes this timeline to succeed, and will want to deal with whoever is in charge of it. It so happens that both Crassus and I also want this timeline to succeed—I doubt his competence but not his patriotism. So in a real sense it is a matter of indifference to you which of us eventually emerges on top. Thus my suggestion is only that you and your wife act as advisors to me in exactly the same way that this Caldwell acts as advisor to Crassus." I started to speak, but he held up a finger. "I understand fully that you cannot be expected to assist in injuring the agent you came here to rescue. Thus I offer this—if you take my offer, I shall do my utmost to see that Caldwell goes unharmed, even at peril to my personal safety, and even at some peril to my potential victory. If I know he is present on the battlefield, my orders will be that he is to be captured unharmed, and permitted to escape if there is the slightest potential he may be harmed.

"Thus ATN will secure the relations it wants with this timeline, I will secure an even footing against Crassus—and believe me, no one knows Crassus better than I, and with an even footing I cannot lose. ATN will have Caesar as its ally, and surely you know—from what you know of my many timelines—that this is no bad thing?"

As a matter of fact, I knew Caesar's record was so mixed that nobody in his right mind would try to sum the man up. He accepted surrenders on easy terms, then turned around and plundered the cities and enslaved their inhabitants. But he also systematically forgave and forgot once he took power. He used his admitted military brilliance to smash the armies of his own nation on his way to power—but then he treated the veterans of both sides of the conflict with tremendous generosity and fairness. He was known to be ruthless, but he could be very kind; known to care passionately what people thought of him, but able to completely ignore public opinion when it disapproved of something he wanted to do.

In short, he was utterly his own man. If he was inconsistent, it was because he chose to be; he didn't live his life with an eye to the history books, the way that a lot of recent presidents had. That was about all you could say. And compared to a lot of my own timeline's pussyfooting, PR, spindoctoring, and other forms of lying, it was sort of refreshing to run into a guy whose two interests were 1) ruling the world, and 2) ruling it better than anyone else possibly could.

"And what if I don't take the offer?" I said. "Let me

say first of all I find it attractive, but I also want to know every option you are offering us."

"If you don't take the offer," Caesar said, taking a sip of his wine and staring off into space, "then what I would say is that after all, whatever ATN's rules might be, you are among Romans now, and among Romans you will live by Caesar's rules. And under those rules, my dear Marcus, all four of you are slaves. That would mean you will do what I say or you will suffer punishment—and I remind you that in our law, I may kill my slaves at any time I wish. But you did say you found the offer attractive? Surely I don't need to speak of such terribly unpleasant things?"

The strangest part, I realized, was that he was sincere; he really wanted to have our loyalty and service because it was what we thought best, and he really didn't want to have to talk about what he would do if we didn't offer it to him. It was part of that strange inconsistency that ran through his character like hot lava pouring through a forest; on either side it was familiar, and in the center of it all, it looked like the dark side of the moon.

I had never been quite so afraid on a mission before—but I also felt oddly comfortable. "We'll take the deal, then," I said.

Gaius Julius Caesar's face broke into a real, honest-to-all-the-gods grin of pleasure; I'm sure he had not forgotten his threat, and neither had we, but the business was settled, and that was all he cared about.

We went back to our quarters soon after; he told us that he would make arrangements for us to travel with him, and as the merest afterthought, presented Porter with the lyre and flute, suggesting that she continue to practice.

At least I wouldn't have to amuse a teenager along with all the other things we needed to do.

The next morning, we found out what the difference was between a day Caesar spent in camp and a day Caesar spent on campaign. Servants came and woke us two hours before the cold winter dawn, gave us five minutes to wash with the pitchers of warm water they had brought, fed us bowls of warm gruel with beef chips, and stuffed us, our clothing, and our baggage out the door and into a spitting predawn rain, all within seemingly no time at all.

By the time we were out there, Caesar had been up for two hours, and the legions, allies, and auxiliaries were all there in full array, on their bicycles. While we waited for it to be light enough to start, the centurions and legates roamed back and forth, shouting at men and getting the units together.

"How do you tell what rank everybody is, and why aren't there any uniforms?" Porter asked, shivering beside me.

"They have a pretty flexible notion of rank," I said. "A legion is sixty centuries, and a century is one hundred men. A century is commanded by a centurion—see, it's easier to remember than you thought, right?"

"Wise-ass," Paula muttered, but I noticed that she, too, was leaning in to hear. I suppose nobody wants to go to a battle without a scorecard.

"The centurions have a mixture of power and authority that sort of ranges from what in a modern army would be a sergeant, all the way up to what might be a captain. A legate is any guy who can speak for the commander. He sort of assigns them any way that makes sense to him—kind of like a free-floating officer corps. So a very respected and experienced legate might command a legion, but a very young and inexperienced one might be assigned to run alongside an experienced centurion until he got some idea of what was going on."

"Then there aren't any real tight rules about that?" Porter asked.

"There are Caesar's rules. You can't get any tighter than that," Chrysamen said.

Paula nodded. "I understand that. Okay, boss, that's legions. Who are the other guys?"

"Well, the auxiliaries are cavalry, or sometimes other specialty troops like archers, slingers, and that kind of thing. It looks like Caesar's guys are equipped with stirrups, which weren't invented for a few more centuries in our home timeline. So they're probably a lot more effective than Caesar is used to."

"Because they have stirrups?"

I nodded. "Think about a knight jousting. If he has no stirrups, what happens when his lance hits something?"

"He lands flat on his ass. Got you, boss. And I suppose that applies to almost anything else he could use; the stirrups would give him firmer footing for using a pistol or a bow, too."

Another troop of auxiliaries rumbled by, and I turned and then stared.

"What is it, Mark?" Porter asked.

Chrysamen sighed, then spoke before I could. "It's a field gun. I don't think they were supposed to have anything more than big siege guns at this point in their accelerated development. The idea was supposed to be to get the world politically unified, technologically progressive, and sympathetic to ATN, as far back in history as they could go. The weapons that were introduced here were bound to accelerate the killing, too, but we were trying to hold that in check. Unfortunately I bet Hasmonea wasn't . . . so he gave Caesar the neat idea for how to kill a whole bunch of people at once. Those field guns are going to send the death rate sky-high."

"What's the difference?" Porter asked. "Doesn't any cannon kill a lot of people?"

"Siege guns like the ones that were supposed to be introduced here are mainly aimed at walls and towers," I said. "They take so much effort to move and re-aim that you can't use them very much against troops in the field. So what they're good for is taking a city, where you have a wall or a fortified part to batter apart. And naturally people don't just stand there and die while the battering happens, so the casualty rate isn't necessarily very high.

"But a field gun is intended to be wheeled onto a battlefield and pointed and fired wherever it's needed. That's why those things have wheeled carriages and limbers—the things the mules are pulling them by. So a field gun is fired against troops in the open field—and it kills a lot of them."

"I wonder if that hole in the shield and the musket rest is Caldwell's trick, or Caesar's?" Chrysamen said, as another legion went by. "And will the armor stand up to the shot, anyway?"

"If they're far enough away," I said. "But I have a feeling we'll know way too much about it before this is over."

"It was my invention, by the way," Caesar said, behind us. He was smiling again, that tight-lipped look that I was coming to realize meant he felt very alive and full of energy. "It took me quite a while to figure out how men could fire muskets from behind a shield wall—and I had to modify a lot of things to make this practical."

He was perched on a bicycle of his own, and now he slapped the seat, and said, "My other great invention is the idea of springs under the seat. My men can ride a lot farther than anyone else's."

I didn't have the heart to tell him, and besides, why shouldn't he be proud? He had indeed thought of it himself.

"I assume you all can ride these, since the device came from an ATN timeline," he went on, oblivious to us. "I'm having four of them brought to you; naturally, most of your things will be in the baggage wagons." Then he jumped on his cycle and pedaled away; I noted how straight and stiff he sat as he rode, and figured the springs were getting some extra workout. I also was surprised at just how dignified he seemed to be.

A dozen young legates formed a squadron dashing along behind him on their cycles, and then, in the dim predawn gray light, he faded into the huge crowd of armed men, all in process of assembly.

Half an hour later, we were sitting on our bicycles—all "girls' models" since everyone in this timeline wore a skirt—with a whole party of miscellaneous slaves of Caesar's. They were a lively bunch, and educational in their way; they all seemed to be competing for the position of Caesar's favorite bed partner, and I didn't notice that the men were any less competitive than the women. There was a vast array of skills among them—cooks, musicians, poets, painters, a couple of very attractive young redheads of each gender whose skills were probably not displayed in public much—bodyguards, dancers, actors, everything you could think of that went into making life comfortable. There were half a dozen strong young men whose major duty was putting up the several large tents that served as field quarters for Caesar's party.

And whose minor duty, as far as I could tell, was to look great in a jockstrap and a coat of oil.

I'm not a prude, per se; Caesar was a powerful man in a culture that kept slaves, and I wasn't terribly shocked that he liked to be comfortable, or that he tended to mess around in his own household. What was bothering me was that Porter was getting ears full of all this. Girls a lot younger than she were vying with each other over who "dearest Gaius" had dragged into bed how often. If it had been just Chrysamen and Paula, the three of us might have found it all amusing, but I was dying of embarrassment on Porter's behalf.

I guess it showed, because Porter suddenly whispered to me, in English, "Oh, grow up, Mark, these are Romans; of course they have sex all the time."

"You're confusing the late Empire with the late Republic," I stammered. "Caesar is a bit unusual for his day, and a lot of people thought this was all made up by his political enemies."

People were beginning to stare at us because we were speaking a language they couldn't understand, so we clammed up at that point. But I figured as long as Porter wanted to pretend she could be sophisticated and cool about it, it wasn't my place to get bent out of shape on her behalf.

I even began to find some of the razzing the cooks were getting amusing.

At last the command came to mount up, and the whole vast column of bicycles that had been painstakingly assembled on the Via Flaminia got into motion. Because the knotted rope as chain, and the wooden pin gears, did not permit a derailleur or a hub shift, the cranks had to be a little outsize, so against the just-turning-light skyline in front of us, the legions seemed to bob up and down in great waves, their round cycle helmets and the shoulder pieces of their gear giving them a strangely uniform look in silhouette, like a vast horde of beetles doing the Wave. The weather was improving a tiny bit—the rain wasn't freezing, and there was less of it—and we got off smoothly.

An hour later I was beginning to admire the hell out of Roman training. My bottom was promising to be sore soon, if it wasn't already, and my thighs were killing me. Chrys, beside me, seemed a bit more comfortable, but I think her cycle fit her better. Porter looked like she'd die rather than complain, and like the choice was coming up pretty quickly.

Paula was chugging along strongly, apparently enjoying the ride; she was more athlete than any of us, actually, and back home she was the sort of person who enters marathons at the last minute because she's not doing anything that weekend.

It was a pretty long ride. Forum Sempronii, the next big town, was about fifteen miles away by road, almost all of it uphill—a day's march for the legions in the old days, but now just a three-hour ride, with a break of about five minutes every hour.

The second break was prolonged quite a bit for most of us; we saw a group of cyclists leading strings of horses start out in advance of us.

"What's that?" Porter asked.

About all I know about horses is that you put oats in one end and the feet move, and that the maintenance is a lot more complicated than it is for a motorcycle, which is saying something. They made us learn to ride and to care for horses (and camels, llamas, mules, donkeys, water buffalo, and several things you don't find in our timeline) at the ATN training camp, and I spent just as little time on it as I could get away with.

But Chrys and Paula both loved riding, even though

they'd never gotten Porter very interested in it, and so it was Chrys who answered, "Human beings are actually some of the most efficient distance-running animals there are. The reason people ride horses is because the horse does all the work, not because the horse does it better. And the bicycle drastically improves human performance. I was noticing before that they keep switching off horses on the baggage wagons—they pretty much have to—and that most of the time most of the horses are completely unloaded. So my guess is that we're getting ready for battle, and the horses—oh, and look, there's a string of mules—have to be sent on ahead, or given a head start if you want to call it that, and then the cavalrymen will ride up on bicycles to join them."

"There's something strange in the balance of power," I said, "when people are working that hard for horses."

"Human chauvinist," Paula said.

"Species traitor," I retorted. "Yeah, that makes sense. And it's sort of in keeping with the Caesar we know; systematic and thorough. This way he arrives with a whole army ready to fight."

"Is there going to be a battle, do you think?" Porter asked.

"Forum Sempronii is a lot smaller than Fanum Fortunae," I said. "It's really just a garrison town and a way stop for traffic. If they have any sense, they won't fight at all; the garrison might even have been pulled back toward Rome. I'm surprised they haven't just sent a message out to surrender; surely they've known Caesar was coming."

An hour later, as we rolled into Forum Sempronii, the mystery became clearer. The city government had taken one look at the situation, and being all pro-

Senate, had fled toward Rome, taking the whole garrison and the militia as well, leaving no one in charge to surrender or even to keep law and order. Caesar's scouts had found a certain amount of petty looting and rioting going on, which they had suppressed (the bodies of several looters were still dangling in the town's forum), and a large crowd of people in the forum looking for something to do, which they had taken charge of. The citizens of Forum Sempronii, who had been frightened out of their wits, were given the basic course in Caesar's approach: be cool and nobody gets hurt. Within hours he had appointed a new city government, distributed the property of those who had deserted to Rome, and made most of the people still there into passionate Caesar fans. It was a hell of a performance; watching him, I thought that if there were an election, I might have voted for him myself.

11

There wasn't room enough in Forum Sempronii to put everyone up for the night, but luckily we were either privileged advisors or pet slaves, depending on how you looked at it, so we got a small room in a confiscated villa. The scuttlebutt was that the next day would be much the longest ride, and considering the way my thighs and ass felt, I was dreading it. We all traded around back rubs, put warm ointment where we thought it would count, and worked out ways to put some additional padding on the seats, though, as Paula pointed out, that meant being a little more wobbly and what we saved in butt bruises would be paid back in harder work on our thighs.

Porter was tireder than the rest of us—she'd never much liked athletics of any kind and was in crummy shape—but she had the resilience of youth and bounced back a lot faster. As the rest of us were getting ready for bed, she sat and picked at the lyre.

"Hoping to revive the instrument in our timeline?" I asked.

"Just maybe, Mark, just maybe. It's got some interesting possibilities. With this alternate tuning, check out this bit from Praetorius." She played a little baroque passage, picking it carefully. "Just happened to be a piano piece I knew well. You see what I mean? Interesting sound, but the instrument is technically demanding." She set it aside. "Now try this one—it's the flute part for a Handel sonata, the part I never get to play when I play harpsichord with that nice old French guy. I think with the softer, rounder tone, it sounds pretty neat on this thing."

I had to admit that it was beautiful, but Porter is a world-class musician, and I pretty much have to admit that everything she plays is beautiful.

"You're still going to wish you'd taken some extra sleep in the morning," Chrysamen grumbled—which wasn't like her, but I think she was tiredest of all of us.

"Sure," Porter said, putting her instruments away and heading for bed. She was so pleasant and cooperative, especially compared to the way she had been a couple of years ago, that I wondered if she were feeling well.

Sure enough, the next day's ride was truly a ride from hell, or maybe *to* hell.

The problem was this. The Apennine Range runs down the spine of Italy like the plates on a dinosaur, and there are large parts of it, even today, that are a hassle to go over on the ground. Back in World War II, when the Allies and the Germans were slugging it out on the peninsula, both sides left a fifty-mile gap in their lines between east and west, just to accommodate the Apennines, and neither side could find a way through the other's fifty-mile gap. And that was with jeeps, bulldozers, and trucks available.

So you had to go through one of the few passes. Since Caesar had been at Ariminum, after he crossed the Rubicon he could either go directly down the Via Flaminia to Rome, or he could backtrack a long way north into Cisalpine Gaul on the Via Aemilia, all the way to Bononia (which was where Bologna is on the modern map), and then come back down through Clusium on the Via Cassia. And off of the *viae*—the paved military roads—travel was just plain impossible in the Apennines in the winter.

Thus Caesar had picked the shorter way; the moment he had struck down to Fanum Fortunae was clear. Dispatch riders on cycles would be reaching Rome soon, if they hadn't already, with the news (which would come as no surprise—it would not have been like Caesar to leave his own territory exposed and take the long way around, just for a surprise that was sure to collapse soon afterward).

Now, the problem with all that is that it's tough to march or attack uphill; the old thing about getting the high ground. So it was vital that Caesar reach and cross the divide—the high pass between the eastern and western watersheds of Italy—before Pompey did.

Unfortunately, at least for our little group, that divide was right around the city of Spoletium—just under a hundred miles away by the Via Flaminia. And since we were riding with the legions, somehow or other we were going to have to manage to ride these silly contraptions a hundred miles the next day. So early bed after a big meal seemed very much in order.

The ride wasn't quite as bad as I had feared. Even though the Via Flaminia had been built for marching troops rather than bicycles, it was well banked and had plenty of switchbacks; parts of it are used for highways even today, because it takes the easiest route through that part of the mountains. Moreover, though we were up just as early, we'd all slept well, and though it was just as cold, it was a bright, sunny day. And with the exercise, we didn't feel cold for long.

Still, by midafternoon we were only halfway there, and I for one would have said it had already been a long day. We did the last ten miles with soldiers leading each contingent using candle-lamps mounted on their bicycles.

Spoletium was another military-base city, which had been built there to guard the road and provide services to the soldiers who did the guarding, and then had grown because the road was the logical way for freight to travel, and the people who moved the freight needed somewhere to stop for a meal or for the night. We ate because they ordered us to, and then fell into our beds.

I also let myself feel a certain amount of awe at the legions. The pass was actually a few miles east of Spoletium, and two of the legions riding out front had actually managed to get there during daylight, dig entrenchments by lamplight, and then settle in to guard Caesar against a surprise attack coming up from Rome.

But the next morning we could all sleep in; with forces up at the pass, and with entrenchments dug there, Caesar was as secure as he could be. According to scuttlebutt, the spies in Rome said Pompey's army there would not be moving against us for at least another day, and we now occupied a strong position. Thus a couple of days could be spent gathering and resting our forces.

So we spent most of that day groaning and stretching out from time to time. Caesar was busy and didn't pay much attention to us, which was fine by me; late that evening he invited us to dine with him, and Porter played some Praetorius, as well as some Bach, Handel, and Haydn. He seemed to like it a lot, and made a point of congratulating us all around.

While we were sitting over wine, he was quizzing us both very heavily over all the histories of all the timelines we knew. Another thing I got to admire and respect about Caesar—he had one of those minds that picks up theory and detail, fitting them together seamlessly, and absorbing it very rapidly. I knew of six different important battles, in six different timelines, that had been fought at Dien Bien Phu, and eight at Gettysburg (I had been to one at each place), and he not only wanted to know what the ground was like and how each battle had gone, but he seemed to have no trouble, after hearing it once, keeping all the different cases straight in his head and comparing them. Indeed, he rapidly developed convincing opinions about the style and methods of different generals, and could at the least persuade me that he had a good take on why the Patton–Rommel tank duel at Gettysburg, in one timeline, was so much more difficult for Patton than the equivalent battle had been for Meade in 1863 of my timeline. I began to think that if he was sincere in his interest in working for ATN, perhaps we ought to consider carrying him off.

Then again he was also a crafty, sneaky, devious, master politician, and we seemed to have more than enough of those already.

A messenger came in just as we were saying good night; Caesar took the dispatch, looked at it for one long second, and said, "Well, then, it begins. Plan for a long ride tomorrow, but it will be downhill. Pompey is moving, and I know where he thinks he's going. We're going to hand him a surprise."

The next morning, well before it was light, we got up and walked up the hill with Caesar's slaves, who were giggling about Caesar having abruptly helped himself, after we left, to one of his female food servers, a Gaulish girl who didn't look like she'd hit puberty yet and spoke Latin very badly. They were laughing; she seemed to be in tears, which they all found made it much funnier; whatever her name had been, all of them were now referring to her as "Face Down," which was apparently as much as Caesar had talked to her. I was beginning to see why freeborn Romans despised slaves, and why many people especially seemed to dislike Caesar's slaves.

Considering our position, maybe I should say Caesar's *other* slaves, but Caesar was being fairly careful not to rub it in that officially he owned us; he wanted real partnership, and he was prepared to act like it.

Dawn found us just saddling our bicycles on top of the divide; behind us, to the west, water flowed to the Chienti; in front of us, it flowed into the Tiber—which is to say, down to Rome.

Nobody knew exactly how far we were riding that day, but it stood to reason that if Caesar was going to be fighting a hostile army, he wasn't going to have us ride all day long. On the other hand, he had said a "long ride."

The mystery got solved fairly quickly, but by the time it did I wasn't much worried. It was downhill most of the way from the pass, and so for a large part of the trip everyone was coasting, which the bicycles did pretty well. Every half hour we had to pull over and let the bearings cool—no ball bearings meant that moving, as we were, at twenty miles per hour would eventually overheat the axles, most especially with only bacon grease as a lubricant. Every so often one of the bicycles would begin to smoke at the hub, and once the younger slave riding one was so negligent that by the time he pulled over the hub and two spokes were actually on fire, and with no water handy in that dry part of the mountains, the whole bike ended up going up in flames. They sent him back several miles, to walk with the prisoners.

That was about the peak excitement for the day. It was bright and sunny, and a bit warmer, and we made excellent time. When the time came for the noon meal, we were told to eat a couple handfuls of hardtack and about a half cup of chipped dried beef, and then get back on the road; it wouldn't be long till we were there.

When the valley opened out in front of us, it was really very beautiful, even in January. The dark green grass showed through the thin snow in many places, the little farmsteads were decorated with thin drifts of snow, and the bare trees stood out with every twig in sharp detail against the bright blue of the early-afternoon sun.

Far down below us, as the road ran straight down the gentle slope, the Tiber wound its way through the valley; the land rose a bit afterward, and just where low hills lay on the horizon we could see a town.

"That's Falerii," said one of the slaves riding with us. "I hear that's where we'll be stopping."

I had come to have a great respect for scuttlebutt, at least in this timeline; when communication is not terribly fast, nobody is very careful about security, and things leak pretty fast. Besides, I could see about half the army stretched out in front of us on the road, with occasional glimpses of parties of riders on the road beyond the Tiber, also headed for Falerii.

It made sense, too—it was the first big town after the

pass, so it would have to be Pompey's staging area if he were going to attack uphill. Moreover, because it sat on the other side of the Tiber, which was covered in large places around the bank with thin ice, and infested everywhere with blocks of floating ice, Caesar could approach only over the bridge, which Pompey could easily hold.

Or he could have if he had gotten there first. Now I saw Caesar's plan, and like so much of his best strategy, it was a very simple idea executed well. Pompey's army was going to have to ride uphill to get here; clearly he had planned to do it in a single forced march and dig in, so that at least there would be a stalemate—Caesar couldn't get to Rome at an acceptable cost, and would have to squat at the Tiber, with nowhere to go except backward (or try to break out and face terrible losses).

But now the plan had been turned against Pompey. Caesar's men were good at entrenchments, and the city fortifications themselves would help. Pompey's army would arrive, having worn itself out with a long uphill ride, late today, and would either have to fight while exhausted and cold with night falling, or (more likely) build a field fortification far into the night, and then get up for a dawn attack (or face one). All Pompey's options were bad.

If you're looking at a map, Falerii was a little west of where Civita Castellana is now, and on a low rise; in addition to everything else, Pompey would be forced to attack uphill, whether he fought on the offense or defense, and whether he gave battle that night or the next morning. Reports were that his army was a full four legions smaller than ours, and had many fewer cavalry—plus, I had learned, the horse pistols I had seen so many of had been an introduction of Hasmonea's—the Gaulish cavalry with Caesar had them. Pompey's Roman cavalry (which was less skilled than Gaulish cavalry anyway) would have only lances.

In short, this had all the makings of a massacre.

I rolled down the long hill and over the Tiber bridge, lost in my own thoughts. There seemed to be trouble if Chrys and I spoke in English, particularly if other slaves finked on us, so we weren't discussing it, but I learned later that she had figured it about the same way I had.

The Tiber bridge was one of those things the Romans built to last forever, or maybe longer; their system of paying for public works was that the contractor got half on completion, and half after forty years, *if* the structure was still standing. It was a bit rough on contractors, but everywhere in Europe you can see what it did for buildings.

That night I slept uneasily; Pompey's army had not come all the way up to Falerii, but that only meant that he had found out his situation. I didn't like what tomorrow was promising.

Well before dawn, I heard footsteps running and orders being shouted. Leaving Porter back in the room, and Paula to guard her, Chrys and I ran to the battlements to see if we could find out what was going on.

There was almost no one up there except townspeople sightseeing, but as dawn rose we saw the two armies opposing each other. Caesar's forces had their backs to us; Pompey's faced the city.

"Did you manage to smuggle anything when they strip-searched us?" I asked Chrys.

"Distance glasses, holy-shit switch, transponder tracker, that's all," she said. "I don't see any of the gendarmerie around if you want to try the distance glasses."

"Hmm. I saved the distance glasses and the thumbnail atlas. Please don't pick on me, but I didn't manage to hang on to the holy-shit switch."

"Mark . . ." She sighed. "Are they ever going to teach you that it's okay to push that thing now and then?"

I shrugged; it's a bigger issue with her than with me. The "holy-shit switch" is actually the call for help communicator; it contacts an Earth satellite that's been placed in the same timeline with you and triggers a crosstime signal to let them know you're in trouble. I had only pushed it a couple of times in my career, a lot less than most senior Crux Ops. Maybe it was because my first mission had been an improvised affair, without even a SHAKK for most of it. I had just sort of lost the tendency to call for help, even when it would have made sense.

So there was probably a little truth in what she was implying; I hadn't kept my holy-shit switch because I hadn't thought it was that important. And considering how much trouble we were already in, that was a pretty hard thing to justify.

Years of marriage had taught me that whenever you realize your partner is right, you should agree, and then change the subject. So I said, "Well, you're right, of course, but at least you kept yours, so no harm done so far. Anyway, I don't see anyone who looks enough like a cop to ask nosy questions about the distance glasses." In fact the wall was rapidly getting deserted except for the few soldiers standing at the towers and firing positions; civilians were too nervous to stick around.

We put on our distance glasses, and since they only require one finger to control, we held hands.

"Weird to be on the sidelines for a battle," I said. "Especially without a weapon."

The two lines advanced slowly toward each other; I had a few minutes to see what the differences were.

The classic Roman way of fighting is sort of a zone defense; you keep your *gladius*, a short sword that's about the size and weight of a machete, in your right hand, and your *scutum*, a small shield, in your left. You are in charge of staying in your position relative to the other legionaries, and whacking anything in a rectangle that extends about three feet in front of you and a bit under three feet to each side of your right foot. If you're in an interior rank, your zone is bordered on all sides by other legionaries' zones.

It worked because the Romans had nearly perfect discipline. They would die in their tracks before allowing a hole to open in the ranks; if someone fell dead or wounded, his buddies would step over him, close up the hole, and keep going. Furthermore, after a few years of training, they were effectively martial-arts masters with those *gladii*; they had the same kind of perfect concentration and ability to strike hard and accurately without having to think first.

The classical way of attacking was that each man carried two *pila*, or javelins, and as they closed with the enemy, on command the soldiers flung two volleys of javelins, then closed in for sword-to-sword fighting.

But I could see there had been modifications. Pompey's men still carried *pila*, but mixed in with each century there were ten musketeers, armed only with the musket, forming a back rank. Caesar's men had no *pila*, and every man carried a musket; from behind we could see there was something different on the shield, too, but we couldn't see what exactly.

"Pompey is treating muskets as auxiliaries," I said. "Caesar's made them the primary weapon. Bet on Caesar, if you weren't already."

The lines drew closer, and as they did I let my eyes wander farther out on the plain. The first thing that caught my eye was a strange shape—like a forest of pipes—

"Don't look now," I said, "but I think Pompey has invented the Stalin organ. We just might be in deep shit."

We clicked in on it, taking things up to highest magnification, and it was clear as a bell. The round objects lying next to the sets of tubes were pretty clearly rockets; Pompey had found out about rockets one way or another.

"I'm surprised he doesn't just build big cannon," Chrys said.

"Roman iron won't take the pressure very well," I said. "For a long-range weapon, if you can't hold much breech pressure, rockets are better. Even if they're just fueled with black powder like old-fashioned skyrockets."

The first volley of shots rang out from Pompey's lines; at the extreme range for the muskets, they did no damage, for with breech pressures so low, velocity fell off rapidly, and a hundred yards away they weren't hitting hard enough to pierce the shields of Caesar's men.

Immediately on firing the volley, Pompey's legionaries had broken into a trot, obviously intending to close the distance and create a shield wall behind which the musketeers could reload.

But as Pompey's men formed their shield wall, something strange happened. Caesar's front rank knelt; with distance glasses now I saw that a little shelf had been attached to the bottom of each *scutum*. They put their knees down on those shelves, so that the *scuta* stood up like a garden rake with a man standing on the tines, and withdrew their left arms. The muskets slid neatly through the small holes; a moment later, they fired.

The second rank advanced past them, and repeated that procedure; then the third. Meanwhile the first rank reloaded, then picked up their shields and advanced again.

"They're firing about six volleys to Pompey's one," Chrysamen said. "It looks like this is it."

Pompey's forces took the first couple of volleys on the shield wall, with only a couple of men falling, either by stray rounds that had enough energy to penetrate the shields, or more likely shots that had found their way through niches between. But as Caesar's force worked its way inexorably forward, shots began to break through, and the wall wavered. The next time Pompey's front centurions turned their shields for their own musketeers to fire a volley, two of the musketeers and several of the legionaries fell; before they could reorganize, another volley tore into them.

Centurions bellowed commands, and Pompey's legion broke its shield wall and trotted forward. A half dozen men in each century fell over dead as another of Caesar's musket volleys struck, but they kept coming, like the real Romans they were, maintaining their positions.

The centurions barked almost in unison, and a flight of *pila* sailed toward Caesar's forces; unable to raise their shields quickly, many men were killed and wounded. The second flight of *pila* found them better prepared, but still many hit home. Moreover, the two flights of javelins had disrupted Caesar's volleys, which were now coming more raggedly along the line.

If Pompey's men had somehow been carrying two more *pila* each, for a total of four, they might have carried right through. But with that much weight, they couldn't have moved.

And when the javelins stopped falling, most of

Caesar's legionaries were still alive and well. As I watched from the wall, distance glasses set for a fairly wide view, the second rank of Caesar's troops moved forward and knelt beside the first, forming a tighter line. All of them slung their shields to their backs, but stayed kneeling.

The third and fourth ranks closed up into a single line, and now there were just two lines. The troops in the rear line also slung their *scuta,* and stood up.

"*Street Firing!*" I said.

"What?" Chrys asked.

"Street Firing! I recognize it from my trips to Revolutionary America. It's the system for getting the highest rate of fire out of a unit of muzzle loaders—"

The first rank fired; a great cloud of black-powder smoke belched forth, and the field was obscured as it blew back. I clicked to infrared, and saw the soldiers stand, as the second rank stepped through to kneel behind them. Even as they stood, their hands stayed busy—"Of course! Caldwell gave them percussion caps! It takes a lot less time to load than a flintlock—they just ram down a paper cartridge whole, set a cap on the nipple, cock the hammer, and shoot. No tearing the cartridge open, no firing pan or priming powder to deal with. Right now those troops could—"

The new first rank, now kneeling, fired, but this time when they stood they stepped back. "Now that Pompey's men are trying to close up," I said, "they're backing up to prevent them from closing, and make them take more volleys before it gets down to cold steel. I wonder if Caesar invented all of this? It would be like him—"

There was another huge boom as a volley ripped into Pompey's troops. Through the smoke, using infrared, I could see what was happening—Pompey's men were struggling through the thick, choking clouds, trying to keep their positions, their lines being raked by the volleys coming at them. Meanwhile, Caesar's centuries were leapfrogging backward, firing at what had to be six rounds per minute—twice as fast as the best British troops had done in 1800. It was turning into a slaughter.

The Romans had a verb, "*superare,*" for what Caesar's legions were doing to Pompey's—usually it's translated as "overcame" or "defeated," but it means more than that. It means "they threw their swords and shields down and ran like bunnies." Which is exactly what happened at that moment.

I saw Caesar's men stand up, form ranks, draw their *gladii* and bring their *scuta* back to guard position, and advance on the double. Now it would be naked butchery.

Something moved in my peripheral vision, and I scanned the back of the battlefield. No question they were loading the "Stalin organs," which I had expected, but—

There was a big, dark mass there, and it was splitting in half like an amoeba. I stared . . . I considered . . .

"Shit," Chrys said. "This is all a setup for Hannibal's double bow."

"I think you're right."

It was just about the most famous battle plan of ancient history. You advance in a long curved line with the center contacting the enemy first. The center fights hard, then turns and runs away. Since there are no radios on the ancient battlefield, no general can tell his men to "hang back." The enemy pursue into the center, as your big curving line turns inside out.

Then your center meets up with your reserves, your flanks close in, and the enemy is caught in a crossfire and surrounded.

The giveaway to all that is when troops in the

reserve body at the rear start to flow toward the flanks, instead of up to the middle where the fighting is.

And Chrys had just spotted that.

I scanned the field. Sure enough, Pompey's flanks were moving in fast. Moreover, the legions on the flanks were, all of them, equipped with muskets, and the cavalry had long heavy lances like a medieval knight's. "They're going to crash in any second now," I said, and even as I spoke, the legions went to double time, and the auxiliaries broke into a trot.

Gaulish cavalry from both of Caesar's flanks charged to meet the threat.

"Looks like we're going to see whether the pistol or the lance is superior," I said.

And then we heard a familiar sound—a deep, bass buzz that is made by only one thing in the universe—

—a SHAKK firing on full auto.

It took me a moment to find where the sound was coming from, and then I saw—Caesar himself stood on a small wooden tower, holding the SHAKK, spraying one of Pompey's flanks.

He didn't really have to aim and he didn't bother. The S in SHAKK stands for "Seeking"—each individual round was finding a target. There are two thousand rounds in the magazine of an ATN-issued SHAKK, and Caesar had two of those; he sprayed down Pompey's left flank with one of them, picked up the other, and sprayed Pompey's right flank with the other. Then he calmly pulled out the SHAKK-equivalents that Porter and Paula had been given—they had smaller magazines because they had smarter ammo, rounds that communicated with each other in flight and picked targets based on maximum coverage and evaluated threat. He emptied five hundred rounds from each of those, again spraying each side equally.

I was finding myself thinking of a lot of Latin today. Our word "decimate" comes from the Latin for "ten"— if you killed ten men out of a century, the century was usually too disrupted to fight effectively.

That was approximately what Caesar, single-handedly, had just done. Everywhere out there, men or horses were converted into bags of red jam and collapsed. It was terrifying and inexplicable, and the scent of so much blood maddened the horses. Furthermore, the more-advanced SHAKKs from the Roman future apparently had some way of spotting officers, for every centurion and legate on the field seemed to fall victim to them.

By the time the Gauls got to the front ranks, neither Pompey's legions nor his cavalry had any effective command at all. They collapsed in a screaming mess, some trying to fight, many to run away, some just to hide and stay alive. The Gauls didn't make any fine distinctions—they used their horse pistols on everything that wasn't Caesar's.

Even the ones who were trying to surrender.

Sickened, I looked away, and scanned to the back. Pompey's center didn't know that when the trap had sprung, its jaws had broken. Thus they moved forward confidently, not knowing the battle was lost. At the range I couldn't see exactly, but I knew more or less what happened from the clouds of smoke and the glimpses I was able to catch.

Caesar's forces advanced until the last of Pompey's old, false center fled into the reserves ahead. By now Pompey must have known something was wrong, but not quite what it was, by the fact that so few of his front line had returned. They were supposed to *fake* losing, not get clobbered.

Then the legions of Caesar stopped as one man,

formed up for Street Firing, and waited for the surge out of Pompey's reserves. They didn't have to wait long.

As Pompey's legions attacked, this time all carrying muskets and *pila*, Caesar's troops opened up at long range. Pompey's men formed the shield wall, turned the shields to fire from behind it, and continued.

"Not as dumb as we thought he was," Chrysamen commented.

"Well, historically he had a good rep," I said. "But look how tricky Caesar is here—his troops are backing up in Street Firing, and between lugging a firearm *and* javelins, Pompey's troops are weighed down. Caesar's men can fire and retreat faster than Pompey can advance, and Caesar's giving them several rounds for every one of theirs. They may not know it yet, but they're going to lose."

A moment later we saw exactly how they would lose. Caesar's mule-drawn field artillery had finally gotten into place on the flanks of his legions, now that Pompey's flanks were eliminated. It became quite evident that Hasmonea had given him grape and canister shot—the trick of loading a cannon with musket balls, to make it work like a giant shotgun, or of putting the musket balls in a paper canister that would then burn away in flight, leaving them in a tighter pattern.

And the reason it became evident was that Pompey's troops went over like bowling pins. They were packed in close, and the field artillery simply tore huge holes in their lines, slaughtering dozens and hundreds at a shot. Within two minutes, as the guns continued to boom on both flanks, Pompey's center collapsed really, and for good.

It was an utter, smashing victory for Caesar, and though I couldn't say yet what difference it would make, I knew that all of history had just been altered;

Caesar would not have to pursue Pompey to Spain to beat him, at least—

There was a white-hot flash on my distance glasses. I had set them for infrared; now what had they picked up? I was all but dazzled—

"Shit!" Chrys said. *"Down!"*

I trusted her reflexes too much to ask; I was on my belly before I had really figured out what she had said. I drew a long deep breath, and heard a high-pitched scream—

There were a dozen powerful explosions nearby. I turned, and looked to see flames leaping up from several places in the city. I heard a distant rumble and realized—"Those Stalin organs!" I set my glasses back to normal vision so as not to be blinded, and peered over the wall.

A dozen bright flashes in less than a minute meant that perhaps two hundred rockets were on their way, and behind me I heard the first few land in the city. A preindustrial city has no pumped running water, and its alleys are full of hovels that burn like matchwood. The city was going to die in flames; nothing and no one could stop it now. Curtains of flame were leaping into the air, and sobbing and screaming resounded in all directions.

I looked back the way we had come to the wall, to the villa six blocks away with Paula and Porter in it. It was already on fire.

Grimly, Chrys and I vaulted down the ladders and raced up the street, hoping to reach the burning villa before the hysterical mob, just beginning to form, could block our way.

12

Within two blocks I started to doubt that we would make it. I found out later that Pompey's rockets were his own invention—he wasn't a stupid man, in fact he was one of the best generals the world has ever seen, but his reputation has always suffered a bit because he was up against Julius Caesar.

In this timeline his luck was even worse than it was in mine. When the Senate realized how fast Caesar could move, they still didn't act like people with an emergency on—they acted like rich people who needed to save their financial assets in a hurry. This was perhaps not so surprising, since the Roman Senate was not elected—it was made up of retired high-level civil servants, almost all from the hereditary nobility, plus a few who had bought their way in. Thus they decided they needed a few days to get their more important possessions onto ships and out of Caesar's reach, and this mattered much more than the lives of Pompey's men, so to get those few days, they told Pompey that either he could give up his army (and let them send it to its death under some political hack) or he could go fight Caesar right now.

Pompey wasn't nearly the shrewd politician that Caesar, or even Crassus, was. He had actually disbanded his army when he was supposed to, once, when he was younger, and been horribly shocked and disappointed when the Senate promptly kicked his veterans in the teeth and undid all the arrangements he had made for them. Still, he knew he was being had—but there was a simple problem. The Senate was the real soul of the Roman state, and everyone knew it. If you didn't have the Senate, you weren't really the leader, and whatever you did was never quite legitimate.

On the other hand, if the Senate made you consul, or dictator—even if they did it with your army's bayonets at their throats—you were in. You were legit. Anyone else was a usurper.

Pompey didn't have an army the size of either Caesar's or Crassus's. He didn't have Crassus's vast empire in the East or tremendous wealth, and he didn't have Caesar's new possessions in Britain and Gaul, let alone the more advanced tech both of them had. All he had was a good record, the admiration of many citizens, the respect of his soldiers—and a claim to legitimacy, via the Senate, that the other two did not.

When the Triumvirate had been organized among the three men, to divide up power, Pompey had thought he was the senior partner—he was higher ranking and had a more distinguished record than Caesar, and he certainly had more prestige than Crassus. But in a three-way contest between glory, brains, and money, don't bet on glory.

So it was not a surprise to discover that he had been tinkering with some of the toys that Hasmonea and

Walks-in-His-Shadow Caldwell had brought, and made some improvements of his own. I later learned that what Pompey had come up with amounted to a crude kind of napalm—Hasmonea had introduced distilling, and Pompey had played around with distilling petroleum—in little "bomblets" with percussion-cap tips, all tied together at their tails with a gunpowder-filled knot. When the rocket burned out, it lit the gunpowder knot and set the cardboard nose cone on fire; long before the bomblets hit, they were all tumbling freely, and came down widely scattered.

There were ten bomblets to a rocket, and each bomblet was about five pounds of napalm, to be blown apart with half a pound of black powder. That meant that, when Pompey fired his two hundred rockets into the city of Falerii, he set somewhere just under two thousand fires.

Preindustrial cities burn very easily. That's why in all the cities in all the timelines that haven't advanced far enough to have piped water and regular fire companies, there is always an unwritten but important rule—no matter what else is happening, if fire breaks out, everyone fights it, because any fire could lose the whole city for you.

Unless, of course, the city is already lost—and if that's the case, then the rule is, run and save yourself.

Three big fires, or five, would have been a struggle for Falerii to fight in normal times. It wasn't a large city. And ten separate fires would probably have been too much to hold against.

Many hundreds meant there was no hope, and everyone knew it.

I never did find out whether Pompey's rockets were fired as a sort of last "spite hit" to stop Caesar from pursuing his army and let the remnants escape, or if perhaps the rocketeers had their orders and carried them out because that was when the launch was supposed to happen and no one told them not to.

But whatever the reason, when Chrys and I tried to fight our way up that street, there was little hope. Dozens of buildings were on fire, and the air was thick with the stench of burning thatch, rich and heavy like a compost heap on fire. Underneath it, already, there was the more acrid smell of wood burning and plaster roasting, the wet ammonia smell of blazing stables, the occasional scent of charred meat where some luckless soul was trapped.

You've probably never heard a whole city scream at once. My suggestion is that you avoid ever hearing it if you can help it. Horses, men, cows, women, chickens, cats, sheep, dogs, children, everything that had a voice was roaring its terror into the street.

As the crowd packed thick around us, Chrys and I found it harder and harder to push and shove our way through. We were trying to figure out what we could do; you can use martial arts to get through a mob only if none of them are armed and there's somewhere for all of them to go. We were bare-handed, and no one could hear us or would have much cared that we wanted to go the opposite way. There was no likely way to get through, and the side streets were already turning into seas of fire as the little lean-tos the poor built there went up in blazes. As I was pinned for a moment against a wall by an alley, I saw a woman in rags rooting through a collapsed, blazing lean-to; a moment later she pulled out a bundle, and I realized it was her baby.

The child must have been dead, for the woman screamed, and as her head cloth fell back I saw she was a lot younger than Porter. Then I saw that her clothing was burning, smoke pouring off the hem of her skirt, about to go up in flame.

It's senseless but true—in the middle of a burning city, surrounded by a mob, you can be as ruthless as anyone, but when you see one single isolated crisis, you can suddenly find yourself forgetting even an urgent errand or self-preservation, because even though we all have plenty of the beast in us, we also all have plenty of civilized training. Neither one wins all the time.

I darted into the alley, tackled her, tore off the biggest burning piece, stamped out the rest, and yanked her to her feet. Her legs were horribly red, and I expected that the blisters of second-degree burns would start at any moment, but I shoved her hard to get her running before she collapsed, toward the city gate. I never saw her again. I have no idea what became of her.

I looked around. Chrys had not followed me. The alley was filling with smoke and getting unbearably hot as stone walls reflected the burning junk and hovels; I did not try to run back to the street I had been on, but instead ran around the corner to see if the side street there was as yet unburned.

It was. That meant I had a clear passage, and I managed to run a long way toward the villa before, very suddenly, a huge load of roof tiles from one of the buildings plunged into the alley in front of me. I leaped back, choking from the hot dust and smoke that came with it, and looked up to see evil orange flame licking the sky from the three-story building that had burned to a shell; I dove sideways to the left, down another alley, and then was flung flat by the gust of blazing wind as the wall came down behind me with a grinding, ripping crash.

Jumping to my feet, I hurled myself down the alley—the jet of flame that had passed over my back while I lay prone had ignited dozens of flammable surfaces, and I had to get out of there in the seconds before the alley became a furnace.

I made it with not much time to spare; there was a sort of "whump" sound behind me as the fresh fires grabbed a lot of the oxygen and pushed out a harsh wave of heat.

I was back in the main street. The building across the way was blazing, the one beside it had fires inside—and the next one was the villa where we had left Porter and Paula asleep that morning. I ran toward it; its roof was being licked by flames from under the eaves, but perhaps—

I rushed toward the building, and was just approaching the main doorbell when something knocked me flat. A moment later I was being held down on the ground, and, inexplicably, somebody was slapping at me and pounding me with hands—I placed my hands to roll suddenly and get at them—

"Boss-don't-it's-me-and-you're-on-fire!"

It was Paula, and what she had been doing was beating out the blaze on the back of my tunic, which must have gotten set on fire while I was getting out of the alley. She let me up and I rolled over. The air was unbelievably hot and dry, the smoke terribly thick, and I was gasping, not least because even when she's doing it to help, if Paula slaps you, you have been *slapped*.

Porter was standing beside her, looking very worried. "Chrysamen—" I gasped out.

"She's not with you?"

"We got separated." I sat up, wheezed, and gagged. Here, in the open street, it was blazing hot in January, and dark with smoke despite the sunlight, but we were far enough away from any individual burning building to take stock for a moment. "I last saw her about two hundred yards back—" When I pointed, I looked. "Shit."

There was one vast sheet of flame across the street; one whole side of the Praetorium had come down into the street, and the rugs, furniture, tapestries, and all were burning there.

"Well, it's for sure she didn't come that way, and she won't," Paula said. "Do you think she followed you?"

"I'm pretty sure she didn't," I said. "And if she did, the way got cut off in front of her. I'm going to try not to panic about this. She can certainly handle herself, but, on the other hand, *anything* can happen out there. Anybody could have bad luck. We didn't have time to set up a rendezvous point—we were trying to get back to you guys."

Paula nodded. "Well, it's for sure she won't stay in the city. And neither should we. What happened in the battle? Caesar must have gotten clobbered."

I shook my head. "Caesar won. This was sort of Pompey's last gasp. I don't know how much baggage train they lost, but his legions still have all their fighting gear and their bicycles, and with Pompey's army in a shambles, this force can be in Rome tomorrow. It's down to Crassus versus Caesar. And from what I've seen, I'd bet on Caesar."

"Me too," Porter said. "Why are you so down on him? Is it because you're looking for an excuse to . . . you know?"

"Could be. Could also be that I notice how many other people suffer and die for his great achievements. To paraphrase a great poem, 'Caesar conquered Gaul / Did he take no one with him? / Not even a cook?'

Meaning he does great things—for Caesar. And what I just saw out there was an ingeniously orchestrated murder of a whole army—of his fellow Romans, mind you. There are probably twenty thousand dead, or more, out there, for Caesar's ambition. I don't exactly call that patriotic, no matter what he does for the country afterward." I peered at her intently. "Are you being pulled in by his charm? Do you want them calling *you* 'Face Down' sometime soon?"

Porter sighed. "No, not really. I mean, no, I'm not falling for him or anything. All I meant was . . . well, he's fascinating. And of course he likes my music, and there's something about flattery from a famous genius . . ."

"I understand," I said, thinking of how it felt when I got to meet and become friends with Wernher von Braun, Dr. Samuel Johnson, Daniel Webster, Leonardo da Vinci, and George Washington, among many others. For that matter I certainly hadn't taken them up on it, but I'd kind of enjoyed the attention from Oscar Wilde and Michelangelo. So I knew some of what Porter was feeling.

The trouble was that Caesar was still a spectacularly dangerous man, in every sense of the word.

"Anyway," I said, "chances are good that Chrysamen will find us." Inspiration hit, and I said, "And she probably still has her transponder-tracker. She can find me with that, for sure. So she will."

"Transponder-tracker?" Paula asked. "Are you wearing a transponder?"

"Yep, inside one of the bones in my pelvic girdle. Approximately the same place Chrys wears hers. Unfortunately I'm not quite the wizard smuggler that Chrys is—she managed to hang on to her tracker. But if I'm within about two miles, she can find me."

"And if you're not?"

"Then she'll keep looking until I turn up at the right distance. She's as good at this as I am, you know. Let's get going." The very last thing I wanted to do was to worry about Chrysamen any more than I already was—and I was already feeling sick with worry. True, the Romans from the future of this timeline had acted like they expected her back when they showed up to take me to the victory parade . . . but, on the other hand, they'd gotten some things wrong. And there was something or other they didn't want to tell me about the whole assassination of Caesar bit, as well.

So the range of things I had to worry about was so large that if I had had the time, I could have sat down and spent the next several hours doing nothing else but worry about them. And that would get nothing accomplished toward alleviating the problem.

So I needed to shake off the fears and worries, remind myself that Chrysamen was not just a big girl but one of the toughest people in a million timelines, and focus on the problem at hand.

"Probably if we move fast, we can escape from Caesar," I said, "but it's an interesting question whether we want to. He has most of our gear and all kinds of valuable resources, and I have no doubt he'd help us look for Chrys. And his offer of a temporary alliance seemed perfectly legit to me. We could just link backup with him and take advantage of what he has to offer—not to mention build quite a bit of trust in him."

"And if we escape?" Porter said.

"Well, then we have no money, no tools worth speaking of, zip for weapons other than bare hands—"

"And this," Paula said, producing a .38 snubnose from somewhere or other, "and I've got a nice little switchblade, but it would take me a second to fish it out, boss."

"You've got a lot of talent," I said, "and I hope ATN processes your job application a long time before they process Caesar's."

"Might take you up on that." The pistol vanished, and this time I was watching. It didn't help.

"Well, then, we'd be lightly armed. Otherwise out in the cold. Hard to say how we'd solve the problem," I said.

Porter nodded. "You've worked that way before."

"Yeah, by myself or with Chrys. Paula, I think, has had some relevant practice. But I'm afraid we don't know whether you have any talent for all this, Porter. How'd you feel about the guys you shot after Robbie got hit?"

"I threw up a lot, and I was pretty upset."

"And you know you have the same habit any musician does, worrying about hurting your hands. Could you forget about your hands for the duration, and just figure ATN would fix them afterward? They have the medical tech to do anything up to and including growing you new ones."

"Looking out for my hands is kind of a habit by now." She sighed. "I'm a little scared of Caesar, but I guess the advantages are all that way. And besides, I'm sorry, but I have a pretty good memory for what sleeping rough was like—and it's not a good memory."

I nodded. I wasn't comfortable myself with those months she had spent on the street at age thirteen. "All right, mixed bag on that side, leaning toward going with Caesar. Paula?"

"Caesar makes me nervous, too, but if we leave him, the first thing we will have to come up with is some way to keep track of him," Paula said. "And we have no idea which side is the most desirable; no reason to think Crassus is any better, except maybe that he's old and fat and couldn't rape kids if he wanted to. So we might as well stay put; right now nobody is mad at us, and Caesar would be a bad person to have mad at us."

"Then it's unanimous," I said. "Let's cut through this alley to the next major street, head out the gate, and see what we can find; for all we know, Chrys is standing around waiting for us to be smart enough to leave a burning city."

The big square we were in was a lot safer than most other places—Falerii was neither large enough nor built high enough to have a firestorm like a modern city might—and the real problem was figuring out the safest way to get from it to a gate. We finally settled on walking through an alley that was already burned out to the next large street over; that turned out to be unblocked, so we walked up it toward the city gate.

There were a few bodies in the street; most of them were probably disguised crime, people bashing a rich guy to get the jewels or gold he was carrying. In the age before plastic, credit cards, or banks, disasters were the best possible time for robbery.

We emerged from the gate. There was no trace of Chrys, so we walked toward the side of the city on which the battle had been fought. We might as well have been all alone on the planet.

Now that we were out of the burning town, it was very suddenly clear just how cold the day really was, and that evening was coming on. The sun was just barely above the dark blue of the western hills, the sky had turned a deep blue smudged with a little black, and the cold air was finding its way through the holes in my clothes. I shivered; this would be a bad night to spend in the open, with as little gear as we had. We might end up going back into the city just to find a fire to sleep next to.

I glanced back behind us. Falerii's walls still stood; no shot or ram had touched them. But from behind them, there were columns of whirling sparks, streams of ink black smoke, and occasional still-rising flames. The city's gates were thrown open, and through them there was only the flickering light of fire; the arched gates in the white walls of the city looked like the eyeholes of a skull, and the fire was like the delusion of a madman, capering and dancing visibly in that empty city, through those empty eyes.

I shivered, and we continued on around, aiming to join the Via Flaminia as it ran toward Rome, for surely Caesar would be on it or near it.

"You!" a voice shouted.

I turned. A legate was riding up on a bicycle. "Are you speaking to us?" I asked.

He stood very straight and erect. "I am ordered by Caesar himself to bring you to Caesar; he has need to confer with you. I am ordered not to harm you, but to use force if necessary."

"It won't be necessary," I said, "but I'd like to know how you would have used it without harming us, if it had been."

There was a faint twitch in the legate's stiff upper lip, which he contained, and then he said, "Best, then, that we don't try. I am not sure what I would do either, sir. But I was instructed to find four of you; where is the fourth?"

"Gods, I wish we knew," I said.

13

"So she has simply vanished," Caesar said, that evening. We had only a few minutes to meet with him, for the victory celebration was extensive, and he was expected to put in an appearance at many different parts of it. He had dropped by the tent where they quartered us; little more than a pup tent, it was originally intended for two people at most, but the army's supply of shelter had been severely stressed by the need to get the town in out of the weather.

"That's about it," I agreed. "If she were nearby, she'd have contacted me by now."

Caesar nodded. "I've given orders that any body looking at all like hers is not to be buried; we'll let you check for her among the dead. But from what you say, it seems terribly unlikely that she was killed."

There was something deeply reassuring in the way he said that; it made me feel, at once, that he believed it, too. I don't know if that was just his amazing political sense, or if it was just Caesar facing facts as he always did. Either way I was comforted.

And that kindness he had just shown made the next thing I had to do all the more difficult. "You realize," I said, "that since it is ineffective to upbraid you, I won't, but I'm quite annoyed by your appropriation of our weapons to your cause this morning."

Caesar nodded. "I can understand that you might be. I ask only that you understand that I am a general; men's lives depend on what I do. It is my job to keep my men alive, and to make sure that the dying is done by the enemy. I could not and would not do things any differently. I can also imagine that you will be in some trouble over having allowed those weapons to fall into my hands. You have my sympathy, but I think an apology unwarranted."

"I understand," I said. And strangely enough, I no longer seemed to be angry. I even thanked him. He asked if Porter had been able to save her flute or lyre, and when it turned out she hadn't, he told her he'd have new ones sent around in the morning. Then he smiled, said that this stop was more interesting than most of the others, and was out the door. I heard later that he visited everywhere that night, from enlisted men drinking around a bonfire to officers throwing orgies with slaves, and at every one he was friendly, polite, a little distant, and warmly appreciative of what the legion, century, cohort, or tribe of Gauls or Britons had done that day.

I suppose you can never really explain how someone has that kind of effect. You can only note that they do, and marvel at it.

Meanwhile, Chrysamen was still missing, possibly staying loose but nearby, possibly off on some promising tangent of her own, and possibly in real trouble.

The bed was pretty lonely that night; you can remind yourself a lot of times how professional someone is, and how many bad spots she's been in, but at three in the morning the thought that she could be dead in a ditch tends to keep coming back anyway.

Even though it was terribly cold, I was glad to see the sun come up the next morning—and I rolled out of the too-big bed at the first sign of light through the fabric of the tent. At last I could stop pretending that I could sleep, get up, get moving, and see what I could do about the problem.

The attendant, a little British kid who spoke some Latin, went to grab me some breakfast from a legion mess, as I hastily dressed. He came back with a heavy, brownish glop that was made by boiling wheat and rye flour, a small pitcher of scalding-hot milk, two hard-boiled eggs, and a fistful of prunes. I wolfed most of it down in just a few minutes, and gave the rest to the kid, who was just hitting that age when you can't possibly get too many calories.

"Are they feeding you?" I asked, wondering how the remnants had vanished so quickly.

"Oh, yes, they are, I'm just hungry all the time, master," the boy said. "Is the lady going to come back? Is she all right?"

"I'm working on that," I said.

"She's very kind," he said.

This didn't surprise me; Chrys wants to keep every stray kitten that finds its way to our doorstep back home in Pittsburgh.

"She is," I agreed. "I'm doing what I can for her. When the others rise, tell them I'll be back for the midday meal, unless something comes up."

"Yes, sir."

Soldiers get up early for a lot of reasons, and in

wintertime anyone who works outdoors gets up early because there's only so much time that the lights are on and you don't want to waste it. So the camp was already bustling and busy, with legion messes going full blast, legates drafting orders for the day, centurions checking on the readiness of their centuries, farmers driving in livestock that they hoped to sell to Caesar. Even as worried as I was, it's pretty hard not to crack a grin when a guy in a big straw hat, which looks sort of like a sombrero with a pointy top, cuts across your path herding a dozen squalling geese.

I hadn't gone far when the little British attendant came running up behind me, gasping, "Word from Caesar, sir. He says he's heard something about the lady, and he will see you in his tent as soon as you can get there."

I tipped him five times what you're supposed to and got to Caesar's tent at a dead run.

Caesar wasn't a guy who lived cheap, or who roughed it on purpose. That tent was a lot more comfortable than most of my student apartments, or than Marie's and my first apartment. They had spread ground cloths and put heavy carpets over them; there was a second, inner tent to hold the warmth, and slaves brought in heated rocks from the fire outside to keep the place warm—indeed they ran in and out constantly, always careful to pull flaps closed behind them so that hot air didn't escape.

The rocks were great big thirty-pounders, so hot that you could see that most of the slaves had a lot of little burns from wherever the cloth in which the rocks were wrapped had slipped; they ran frantically, and I knew they were probably scared to death of what might happen if they screwed the job up.

It might be a hell of a place to be a slave, but it was

pretty comfortable to be Caesar. He was naked when I got there, just stepping into his tub, which was steaming hot and perfumed with dried rose petals. (I could just imagine Generals Patton, Washington, Gordon, Giap, Crazy Horse, Sherman, or Marlborough—all of whom I had known fairly well in one timeline or another—having "rose petals," "perfumed soap," and, for that matter, a "large bathtub" in the baggage train. It was a bad century to be a grunt, and a pretty good one to be a general—but then most centuries are that way.)

Over in the corner, I saw a couple of slave women tending to the little girl that seemed to be Caesar's current favorite victim; she was crying, but all they were doing was first aid. I thought seriously, then, about a way the world would be better if I pulled the trigger on Gaius Julius Caesar, and that might have been a great moment to do it, but if there was news of Chrys . . .

"Thank you for your promptness," Caesar said, lowering himself into the tub. I noted abstractly that, at least in the light of the little oil lamps, he looked pretty good for his age; his body was still hard and lean, with little extra flesh, and though he was almost entirely bald now and his skin was lined and wrinkled from all the time he spent outside, still the muscles underneath would have looked good on a man twenty years younger than he was. It was the kind of body that fascinates a modernist sculptor, not classically beautiful or perfectly proportioned, but worn and shaped by its work and habits until the body becomes a perfect expression of the character, until if you can capture what he really looks like, you've captured the man's soul.

I thought about what it would be like to pull out Paula's .38, jam it behind that lean jaw just by the ear so that the round would cut the carotid on its way in, and pull the trigger. The little girl in the corner started to sob, and one of the slave women slapped her silent.

It would feel pretty good to shoot Caesar, on the whole. Just as soon as I found out about Chrys.

"We received a message earlier today," Caesar said, "from Pompey. I have never been very fond of Cnaeus Pompeius 'Magnus.'" The way he said "magnus," which means "the great" and was a name awarded to Pompey by the Senate, was loaded with such vicious bitterness that you'd have thought Caesar was spitting out rat turds. "And I think you and I may share this opinion." A slave brought up a small silver salver, on which was a written note and something else. He held it out to me, and Caesar said, "Read."

I lifted the message and read:

To Gaius Julius Caesar from Cnaeus Pompeius Magnus, greetings.

I have something here, the evidence of which I enclose, which will be of great interest to one who travels with you. I shall await you in Rome, and there I will treat with you for whatever terms you care to offer me for the safe return of this thing.

That is, if Great Caesar is still his own master, and not the lackey of the one he travels with. I offer the thing I have to either of you, indifferently; I wish terms, and honorable terms, and will hold this thing only so long as is needed. While I hold it, however, you will neither enter Rome, nor fire upon the city, nor surround it or blockade it, upon pain of losing this much-valued thing forever.

I await your reply.

The "Great Caesar" was a calculated insult; Caesar had not been granted such a title as Pompey had. The message seemed alarmingly clear, and when I looked back at the salver, it confirmed my worst fears—there was a hank of Chrysamen's dark, curly hair. I looked closely, but, speaking as her husband, friend, and lover of many years, I was quite certain it was hers.

Then I looked again, peered closely, and hissed with fury.

"Yes," Caesar agreed, "it looks very much as if it has been pulled out by the roots."

"I don't know how he could have—"

"Quite. But I am told that when his damned rockets flew yesterday, he was quite near the point of launch, and when my men closed in to overthrow the launchers, Pompey escaped on his bicycle, back through my lines, into the confusion between my army and the city. We would guess he hid among the refugees after dark—

"But he's one of the most widely known faces in Roman territory!" I protested.

"Just so and part of that boldness of his," Caesar said. "I've never faulted his manhood or his guts. He is, after all, Rome's second-best general. At any rate, one of my agents thought he saw Pompey in the city, shortly after the rockets fell and the fires began, but unfortunately failed to take steps because it seemed too impossible to him. It's the sort of disaster that happens whenever a slave attempts to think.

"At any rate, I have learned a few things from this. One is that, as I should have anticipated, Pompey's intelligence is first-rate, and he already knew the significance of you and your party, including knowing enough to be able to recognize all of you. Probably he struck within minutes of your being separated."

"He'd have to be hell on wheels at hand-to-hand," I said. "In a fight to the death between Chrys and me, you'd have to bet it fifty-five me forty-five Chrys, but that's just based on difference in body size. She's a bit faster and a little more skilled than I am."

Caesar scratched his head. "It doesn't entirely make sense, I admit; I had thought of that myself. But his evidence does look like evidence—and we hardly want him to produce anything more convincing, after all."

I shuddered. "Right. So we at least have to assume he's captured her and is taking her to Rome with him. I'd call that more than enough bad news. Now what can be done about it?"

Caesar smiled grimly. "Exactly the question to be discussed. It seems to me that you are used to operating by yourself, that you have a notable ability to improvise, and so forth. That's my first reason for sending you after her."

"You have others?"

"I doubt you'll be any use to me until she is rescued."

I had to admit, silently, that he had a point.

"Therefore," he went on, "I am deputizing you to go rescue Chrysamen, and you are authorized to do whatever you think fit for the purpose. If by some accident a few of Caesar's enemies should die—" Caesar said, grinning, "—do remember that I am currently the most popular author of histories, and, moreover, that most of Rome's better-known prosecutors, notably that prissy prude Cicero, are on the other side and will have no authority. So little harm will come to you from such circumstances."

"I understand," I said.

"Now, there's the matter of armament," he said. "If

you would like to reload one of the weapons I used yesterday, and take it with you, then—"

I had been thinking ahead of him, and I said, "I'm sorry, but there's no way to reload them in this timeline. We don't normally use them on full auto, so the number of shots in the magazine is far in excess of what we can be expected to need—but now that it's drained, it's drained. It would have to go home for a refill."

I was lying to him. If he knew that, he would probably kill me right now. If not, then he wouldn't be able to use the SHAKKs again, and his plan of world conquest would take a big step backward. It seemed worth the gamble.

The fact is that the "ammo powder" we feed into SHAKKs is merely a carefully balanced mixture of the chemical elements needed, so that the elemental separator won't have to spend any time or power pulling out the excess of things it doesn't need to make ammunition. But in fact you can load them with anything that will go into the hopper—sand, rocks, bugs, scrap metal, seawater (sea salt, rusty nails, and sawdust works pretty well), hot fudge sundaes. It really doesn't care as long as it gets enough of each element.

If Caesar merely stuffed some miscellaneous junk into the reload slot of each SHAKK, in very little time they'd be as deadly as ever, with thousands of fresh shots in each magazine. This was the last thing I wanted him to know.

It was always possible that he knew already, and this was a trap, in which case I would be executed in about five minutes, tops. I was betting he didn't.

I won my bet. He shrugged. "Well, that's the way of it then. I shall retain the other devices I confiscated, though I don't expect that you or your companions will explain them unless I torture one of you, which would be the end of voluntary cooperation. Since your voluntary cooperation is valuable, and I can probably conquer the whole world without the use of the super-weapons, clearly it is best for me to refrain from such methods . . . though if either of those circumstances should change, well, then that decision would have to be reevaluated, wouldn't it?

"Still, it seems that I ought to provide you with a better weapon, and I note that you do have along one very simple-seeming gadget, something that bears a great similarity to our muskets." He gestured to a slave, who handed me my .45 Colt automatic, plus all the clips of ammunition I had been carrying. "We assumed it was a gun and treated it like one, so it has been kept from moisture, extreme heat, and extreme cold. I hope we have not damaged it."

"They're hard to damage," I said, "and it should be fine. I'll strip and clean it before I go."

"Excellent. Am I right in my surmise that the percussion cap is somehow included in the cartridge, and that the device is set up to cock itself and chamber another round after each shot?"

"That's the basics," I said.

"I shall have my armorers think about these things at some length," Caesar said. "And why are the casings brass, instead of paper, which burns away?"

Sometimes the best way to slow somebody down is to make him conscious of the difficulty of what he's trying to do, so I explained, as casually and accurately as I could manage, "Oh, because if you load at the breech, you need to seal the breech against gas leaks, and that's what the brass does that the paper couldn't do. You have to use a special kind of brass, I don't know exactly how that's made, so that it will expand to seal but still eject easily. Also, to get the very high muzzle velocities these things have—this weapon isn't very accurate but its slugs are deadly at four times the distance your muskets can achieve—you have to seal everything tightly, and right now you aren't making iron good enough for the job." I figured that I didn't really want to tell him about steel, either.

Caesar nodded, turned to a slave who had been standing quietly by, and said, "Repeat that, please." The slave recited exactly what I had said, pauses and all.

I congratulated him on his accuracy, and Caesar said, "It's his accuracy that makes Memorex valuable."

I gaped for a second, and then asked, "How did he get his name?"

"Oddly enough, he was named by your agent, Walks-in-His-Shadow Caldwell. He said it was an honored name in your timeline."

"It certainly is," I hastened to say. No reason to hurt poor Memorex's feelings. I was beginning to really look forward to meeting Walks-in-His-Shadow Caldwell, however; the guy's sense of humor appealed to me, every time I ran into an example of it. "I was just surprised to hear the word here. If I may, then, I'll draw a pack of supplies from one of your quartermasters, take the bicycle I've been using, and be on my way within the hour."

"Excellent," Caesar said. "Oh—an afterthought. It occurs to me that the safest place possible for your two remaining female friends to be is here with my army. That is, it's the safest place for them if you and I truly are the friends I hope we are. If on the other hand, you have any *other* notions about it, from my standpoint, it is also the safest possible place for your two friends to be. So naturally they will be staying here."

That was not an afterthought, as he had said it was. That was the thought he wanted me to leave with. "I expected as much," I said, and smiled in the friendliest way I could manage.

He smiled back at me, and said, "Gods and fates aid your genius, Marcus Fortius."

"Be strong, Caesar," I said. And with that, a slave showed me to the door.

By the time I got back, the others were just getting up. I sent the little British slave to fetch me a packed field kit from the quartermaster, at Caesar's instruction if they asked. That got at least one set of ears out of the tent, and then I sat down and fieldstripped and cleaned the .45 (though in fact they'd done a perfectly fine job of maintaining it), working the slide hard or thumping something on key words so that anyone listening outside the tent would have a hard time hearing.

A few short sentences were enough to explain the basic situation and what I intended to do about it. None of us was happy about leaving Porter here with only one trained person for protection, but none of us had any other ideas; we knew that if Chrys were alive, free, and in the neighborhood, she'd have contacted us by now, and that meant that she was either still captive or a long way away. Probably she was still Pompey's captive, or if she had escaped (which you could never rule out with Chrysamen—she was smart and fast and improvised well), then she was either making her way back here or heading on to Rome, depending on what looked like it would get the mission accomplished fastest.

That other possibility was one I had decided not to think about.

"Basic thing," I said, "Ifway ouyay etgay away ancechay, eakbray ailjay andway eadhay orfay omeray.

Damn, my translator is malfunctioning! Brillig and the slithy toves—mimsey were the borogroves and the mome raths outgrabe."

"I think something is wrong with gamboling on the gumbo with me gambits all a-gear," Paula said.

"Mairzy doats and doazy doats and little lamsy divy," Porter agreed.

"Ixnay, Daddio," I said, and then slid the clip in. My old Model 1911A1 was as good as ever; it felt good in the shoulder holster. "Whoops, that's the problem, when you pull out the hemulator on the gun it jams the fratistat on the translator and we can't understand each other."

Five minutes later, after I'd checked through the pack that the kid had brought me, I was throwing my leg over my bicycle and setting off down the Via Flaminia. It was mostly downhill from here, but not terribly steep; I had only about thirty miles of that downhill to cover, and *I* did not have to go more slowly so that horses could keep up.

The biggest problem with these bikes, which required a little concentration, was that they didn't have any kind of coaster arrangement; the pedals always turned with the wheels. Thus, for control, it was really better to pedal constantly, or on steep down-grades to resist the pedals a little with your feet. That was very tricky compared with the bicycles of my time-line, and it raised my admiration for those adaptable Romans another couple of notches—if they could learn to balance and ride on a bicycle with never-quite-straight wheels, as well as control the bicycle without real brakes, they were pretty amazing guys.

The Via Flaminia was one of those famous cases of all roads leading to Rome, and as I neared the city, the traffic of local merchants and farmers, from the villages and small towns around, got thicker and thicker. I had not overtaken Pompey, but then it was possible that I had passed him—he might have pitched camp somewhere off the road behind me, though in the gently rolling hills it seemed improbable that I wouldn't have seen an army.

Then again, how much army could he have left after yesterday? They could probably all hide in a phone booth, if there were any phone booths.

That was actually a pretty good thought, because while even somebody with Chrys's talent for sneaking around and bare-handed mayhem might have trouble sneaking out of a large Roman army encampment, getting away from twenty guys would only demand somebody's attention wandering for a second or two—the way it might tend to do if the guy had just been on the losing end of a huge battle and run for miles to get away from it.

Then again . . .

I did my best to force the speculations out of my mind. It was a nice, bright, winter day, and since I was bicycling, I was pretty warm and comfortable. After a while I realized that by just blending into the traffic flow and taking my time, I was overhearing a lot of conversation; there were no windows or windshields in the way, and no running engines to fill the air with noise. The loudest thing I passed on the road was one wagonload of ducks and geese. It was enough to give you some doubts about that word "progress."

The road got more and more crowded as I neared Rome, and now I was hearing a lot, but of course people don't talk much about current events, or when they do they assume the other person understands the reference. The one thing I gathered clearly was that there were a lot of live animals and produce going to Rome right now "while the selling is good" and that everyone wanted to get there, sell what they had for gold only—a couple of them said, "Nothing in trade today," very emphatically, as if repeating a slogan—and get back to the farm in a hurry.

Nobody was interested in selling jewelry, but some of them were talking about how much of it they expected to acquire.

Finally I overheard one farmer talking to another, and he said, "So do you believe Pompey is really going to make that last stand he's talking about, on the Palatine Hill, with the special blessing of the gods?"

"I think it sounds good to the Senate, and he wants a few of them to stay there as bait for Caesar," the other said. "And I don't think it will work on any of the smart ones. I just hope there are enough left who will need provisions today, because I'd say it's two days at most till Caesar comes in, and I'd wager he'll be here tomorrow morning."

"I reckon you're right," the other said. "But while he's claiming to make preparations, and working his big magic up on the Palatine, at least a lot of the Senate will stay in the Curia, trying to make up their minds, and there we'll be, right next door in the Forum, with all the things they'll need to run away with right there—for a price."

"Reckon so. I'm thinking besides the jewels and the gold, I might just want to pick up some slaves in trade."

"Bah. Houseworkers from the city. I don't need none of them. They're soft, and if you put 'em to honest work, they'll die."

"Oh, but Quintus, you're a married man. I'm a bachelor. Thought I'd get myself some patrician's bedwarmer and find out what the aristocracy gets—"

"It's all the same, theirs is just better washed."

I passed that wagon, finally, when there was an opening in the traffic stream going the other way. Well, that seemed to answer the mystery. The translator in my head gave me a quick map of Rome; I would be coming in from due north, past Pompey's temple and the main military parade ground (the Campus Martius in those days) and directly into the Forum, so there was no sense taking any of the ring roads around to enter by any other gate; they would all be just as jammed, and I was on a direct route.

It was late afternoon, and I was fairly hot and sweaty, even in the crisp cold of January, by the time I rolled over the Milvian Bridge, a heavy, arched bridge across the Tiber north of the city, and then down through the gate in the Aurelian Wall, the outermost wall of the city.

Rome had grown a lot in the centuries just before, and they had only recently annexed a lot of the "suburbs" by building a city wall that enclosed them; the Aurelian Wall had been a state-of-the-art defensive system when it was built, but now it would be only an hour's work for Caesar's field guns to breach it wherever they wanted.

It was a couple of miles to the old inner wall of the city, the Servian Wall, and the Forum was on the other side of that from where I was. To my right the Campus Martius stretched out, but there was no cutting across—the troops milling about there, survivors of Pompey's legions and raw recruits from the city being formed hastily into centuries, might very well decide I looked like a recruit. On the road I was safe enough, because I looked like a military courier, but let anyone who was able-bodied get too close to the Campus Martius, and he was going to be marching back and forth with a *gladius* and *scutum* in no time.

I really hoped that pathetic excuse for a legion—all that seemed to be assembling there was one scrawny legion—would not be forced to go out and fight Caesar; there was no reason for them to be massacred, except that the patricians who ran the Senate were simply not prepared to face reality in any form.

That last two miles took almost as long as riding into town had, and it was almost fully dark by the time I made my way through the gate in the Servian Wall, now pushing the bike because it was easier than trying to keep my balance in the press of people.

As I passed through the great arched gateway in Rome's inner wall, into the old part of the city, I saw the Forum was lit by torchlight and lanterns at hundreds of stalls, and everywhere, there were long lines of people bargaining for food and for plebeian clothing. As I watched, a couple of stagecoaches rumbled up, lights blazing, and I saw that one of them had Crassus's image on it, clearly stenciled on. Below that it said "Fontes Ultra Ire."

Half a minute later I slapped my forehead; it was another one of Caldwell's pranks. You could translate that as "Wells Far Go."

People were still getting onto the stages in an orderly way, but the line was getting longer and longer. I'd been in a city or two that was about to be attacked or brought under siege, and I knew how fast the lines formed at the train station. I was just glad I wouldn't need to be leaving in a hurry.

As I passed the Forum and the Curia (the building where the Senate met), I looked to my right; there wasn't much light, but I saw something enormous, tall as an eight-story building, up on the Palatine Hill, where the farmers had talked about Pompey making a stand. There had been no building that big there in my timeline—hell, there had been no building that big in Rome—and the shape was odd, too round and too large.

Whatever Pompey was up to, if he had Chrys, he would have her with him up there, and that tall building—lit occasionally by a roaring fire beneath it—would be the first and most logical place to look. Probably the fire that occasionally flared there was for the sacrifices; if Pompey was organizing a sacred band for a last stand, he would be sacrificing a lot of animals.

That made a certain amount of sense, except that I doubted that Pompey was any more superstitious than Caesar was, and if the situation were reversed, Caesar would be headed for Crassus like a bat out of hell, trying to get some kind of deal. Compared to Pompey and Caesar, Crassus was no general, and even Crassus knew it. A talented guy like Pompey—especially since he had a reputation for being good-looking, smooth, and a natural diplomat—would logically be on a stagecoach headed south, or leaving on a ship this minute.

Which meant he was up to something, and that something was probably a technological trick, maybe even something more impressive than the rocket launchers.

Most likely something connected with Chrys.

I took the turn onto Vicus Tuscus, a large street that ran through a patrician neighborhood at the base of the Palatine Hill, and headed that way. When I saw a gate with enough darkness, I ditched the bicycle and most of the pack there; I took a deep draft of water and forced in the last of my hardtack, made sure I had all the money, my distance glasses, and the dagger. I left the *gladius* behind, though it was a good one, because

the last time I had practiced with one had been at Crux
Ops training camp, more than a decade before subjectively, and if I pulled a *gladius* out here, practically
every free adult male would know more about how to
use it on me than I would about how to use it on him.
Besides, I had the .45 and half a dozen clips of ammo,
and I'd take that up against a *gladius* anytime I could
get six feet of clear space.

I ran one last check. I had the works, everything I
was likely to need for whatever came up; was there
anything I could forget? I found the thumbnail atlas
under my fingers and jammed it into my personal
pouch of stuff. Partly that was habit—we weren't supposed to leave bits of high tech lying around for the
natives—and mostly that was because you never know.

Then I realized what was missing.

I spent two long, stupid minutes groping around in
the pack before my fingers closed on my wedding ring.
I had taken it off because it seemed like an invitation to
bandits on the road, and whenever armies start moving
around, there are bandits. I slipped it back on.

It seemed like an omen of some kind; I decided to
believe it was a good one. Of course, the real omen was
that after being around the superstitious Romans for so
long, I was starting to think about omens.

With a shrug, I bent my concentration to the job at
hand; I slipped into the depths of the shadows and
made my way up the Palatine. On the way I passed a
couple of pickpockets, three sentries, and a lady of the
evening. None of them ever knew.

I was in my element—it was dark, and there was a
mystery ahead, one that would require some violence
before it was over.

14

The Palatine Hill was supposedly the first part of Rome ever to be settled, and nowadays it was mostly public buildings—temples and government things—on top, but the patrician families still clung to its sides in huge, well-guarded old houses.

The patricians were the people who claimed to be descended from the gods; considering the behavior of Roman gods (plus the ones the Romans plagiarized from the Greeks), I don't know how that was supposed to be to anyone's credit, but they didn't consult me. For generations, the Roman Republic had been dominated by these people, much more thoroughly than the United States had ever been dominated by its First Families of Virginia, Nob Hill Aristocracy, or Boston Brahmins, even more thoroughly than Britain had been dominated by the old peerage. These people ran the show, were used to running the show, and had no concept that anyone else might have a stake in it.

A century of that arrogance had left them with no

power base on which to stand. One of their own, Caesar, had won the hearts of the people, even though—or perhaps because—he was ruthless and determined to rule as dictator. Pompey, the most talented man on their side, had been hamstrung and pulled down, in part, by his own allies' paranoia and need to throw their weight around; no general could have tried harder or done better, having to carry the Senate on his back. Crassus and the other "new men"— people who had no patrician ancestry and were merely very capable, people who got rich by talent and hard work—no longer had any faith in a system that had nothing for them. In their desire to preserve their power and privileges, the patricians had made it pay to be their enemies; they had made it cost to be their friends; and now they were reaping the consequences of that decision.

The houses on this dark hill might have symbolized it all, that night. Many of them blazed with candlelight and lamplight, for the patrician families who lived there were preparing to run for their lives—but they were planning to run with strongboxes of gold, trunkfuls of fine clothing, everything that might turn into loot. They couldn't possibly pack their own possessions, let alone carry them, and so, though Caesar and his legions might be there early in the morning, though there was no one left to hold the walls of Rome, though the stagecoaches in which they would travel could be easily overtaken by the legions' bicycles—they were still packing, screaming at each other and the servants like cages full of parrots.

Surrounding each shrieking pool of light was a ring of frantically working, terrified slaves, desperately trying to get everything in order for their now-refugee masters, responding to the hysterical orders as best they could. In the outer rooms and dark corners of each villa, there were other slaves, no longer following orders, hiding where they could and stealing what they could; and finally, out in the streets, where I was, there were hundreds of slaves escaping with bits of their masters' property, running away in the hope that with a bit of luck and the jewelry or money they had grabbed, they might win some kind of freedom somewhere.

That made the job a little trickier; I had to swing wide around many houses because so much light was spilling out, and when I crept through the shadows I was constantly coming upon huddled slaves trying to hide, and other slaves moving more or less quietly and carefully. For a while I thought there were a few slaves who were almost as good as I was at creeping through the dark—I was moving along behind one of them and sort of admiring his technique, the way he placed his feet and avoided backlighting.

Then he came up from behind on a small figure, barely perceptible in the dark but revealed by candle-glare reflected off a wall, if you were on the shadow side of him. The one I was following closed in on the other figure, who was carrying a large sack—I guessed it was probably the master's silver service, from the way the figure hefted it.

There was just one flash of the blade, and then the man who had had the sack lay still, and the man with the blade had the sack—and was gone.

I crept forward and confirmed that the slave—an old man, physically weak, with no signs of ever having done any real work—was dead. His face was slack—when you suddenly have your throat opened with one blow, there's no time to form any lasting expression, and whatever he might have looked like in the brief instant he was killed had now disappeared. He looked like he had gone to sleep there in the street—if you could ignore the immense extra mouth leaking blood from under his jaw.

Probably he had been a tutor, or perhaps a butler or head chef. In this neighborhood almost all the pricey slaves would be Greek. Probably he had dreamed about getting back to his home city with a little bit of money from the stolen silver.

Probably he had gotten about three hundred yards.

I slipped on into the night, my dagger already drawn, keeping that additional thought in mind— probably every footpad and lowlife possible was prowling the Palatine tonight, looking for runaway slaves.

I rounded another corner and crept forward. Suddenly light spilled out of the main doorway of a house, and I slipped into a dark alley, low and sideways, to wait out whatever was happening.

I almost laughed out loud. It was somebody fleeing in a litter—four slaves bearing the heavy load down the hill, two others carrying torches in front of it, and a scattering of armed guards around the litter. The litter itself, like most patrician ones, was an object of considerable value, a piece of fine furnituremaking inlaid with gold and silver and decorated with gems.

All it would take, really, would be enough of an attack to convince the slaves that their interests lay elsewhere—and that wouldn't be much—and that expensive litter would spill its expensive and helpless owner into the street like a toy poodle thrown into a kennel of Dobermans.

Undoubtedly the owner thought he or she was "fleeing for my life with just the few things I could carry" and, if by some miracle he or she reached the stagecoach station or the river wharves, would complain bitterly at the crowded and inferior service available.

I reminded myself that though I wasn't much concerned about these voluntarily helpless, spoiled patricians, who had brought it all on themselves, that Rome could easily be burned and looted by Caesar's troops, if something put Caesar into the mood to do it, and it would not be these people, but the ordinary citizens—merchants, artisans, and laborers—who would lose everything they had.

Something moved beside me, and I slipped a bit farther into the shadow. The next moment, something was swinging in at my face—I felt it more than saw it—and I snapped an arm block up, caught the wrist on the little-finger side, drew the arm, and slid my dagger once into an exposed belly, striking upward at the heart and lungs, and then slashed the throat as she screamed.

I knelt and felt the bloody corpse in front of me. Female, as I had thought from the scream, and quite young—her still-warm breasts were small and firm, her hips not yet much widened. Next to her there was a bag of loot, probably not what she had stolen from her own household—probably what she had gotten by knifing people here in this dark corner.

More feeling around revealed three more bodies in the alley—an old woman and two fairly young males. The girl had been pretty talented, but an amateur, and her unwillingness to let go of the bag of loot before attacking me with her knife had made killing her fairly easy.

The litter had passed now, and no one had come in response to the girl's scream. I wiped as much blood as I could off myself, using the bag she had been carrying her loot in, and left the corpses and loot for some other lucky escaped slave. I slipped quietly out of the alley and continued upward.

The distance I had to cover was only eight or nine

city blocks, but in pitch-darkness, trying to move undetected, with the streets full of escaping slaves, muggers, and the occasional litter or patrician family with their torchbearers, it took me the better part of the night to get anywhere near where I had judged the giant building to be.

At least for the last two blocks I was able to go a great deal faster—houses were emptying out all over the Palatine, and everyone was fleeing downhill; thus by the time I reached the uppermost blocks, the bulk of escaping slaves and fleeing patricians was already down the hill, most of the houses were already deserted, and with so little prey around, the two-legged predators too were gone.

Finally, though, I got near enough to the building I was trying to reach to get occasional glimpses of it through the narrow streets, and I was able to see the flickers of light on its sides, and the big yellow letters SPQR on its red surface. I crept closer, until finally I found that I was peering across a torchlit street at a small group of soldiers—real professionals, not just slave bodyguards, to judge by the way they held their *gladii* and the muskets slung over their shoulders.

With a group of professionals on the alert and the light against me, there was no going through by the direct route here; I would have to circle and probe. Depending on how determined you are, and how big the risk you can run is, there's usually a way in.

It didn't take long to establish that these guys were *really* pros. Half an hour of dedicated sneaking and skulking in the perimeter showed me that every post was visible from every other, there were three guards to a post, and they had managed to get enough torches into enough places so that there was no really good band of darkness to crawl through.

Well, that meant taking on a bigger risk, I figured. I could fire a couple of shots somewhere to make a diversion—but here in the dark my muzzle flashes would draw more attention than whatever the shots hit. The opposing roofs were too high to throw a rock onto. Besides, these guys did not seem dumb or naive enough to fall for such a trick. I could wait around and hope, but there were probably just a couple of hours of darkness left, and I had no idea what Pompey was up to in there.

Something startled me, and I looked again, then saw what it was. A ripple had run down the bright red side of the "giant building." Abruptly my brain adjusted to the data, and I knew what I had been looking at, realized I would have recognized it if I had only allowed myself to think without first deciding what it couldn't be. I guess you're never too trained or too experienced to stop making dumb mistakes.

It was a hot-air balloon, a very large one, and undoubtedly the way in which Pompey was planning to escape. Naturally without propane or any other really hot fuel, it was taking a while to get it hot enough, and that was what the big fires burning under it were about. The SPQR on its side probably meant it had originally been a military project funded by the Senate, but I saw now what Pompey was up to; the wind blows west to east, and flying out of Rome, if he kept it aloft long enough, he was bound to come down either in unclaimed territory or at least somewhere Crassus controlled.

It was sort of like a punt in football, except that Pompey was both the punter and the football. Almost anywhere and any situation had to be better than the one he was in; and if he fled on foot, horse, or bicycle, Caesar or his agents had the means to catch him.

It occurred to me that I was one of Caesar's agents, and I was working on the means to catch Pompey. And I didn't have a lot of time left.

I crept forward again and moved around to the place I had picked as the weak spot. There, an alley between two temples opened out toward me, and both guard posts, though able to cover the street, had to move forward to see each other, or the alley between them, because of the way the temples protruded. If Pompey or his legates had had a few extra men, they could have stationed them at the alley mouth and closed the gap completely. The fact that they had not done so meant that their resources were strained, and that reassured me a lot—probably they had few or no patrols inside the perimeter.

The basic problem in coming up with a good diversion is that what you want to do is to pull them off where you're going, ideally without giving them any more idea than they had in the first place that there is anything big to worry about. You don't want them poked up and looking for trouble. That wasn't going to be easy.

The perfect trick would be to land something between one of the guard posts and its neighbor, on the side away from the alley I wanted to get into, so that the alley I was interested in would be unwatched for an instant, and I could slip across. At the time that seemed a bit like saying the perfect way to win a marathon would be to run at twenty miles an hour for one hour and eighteen minutes; the theory was easy, but it neglected the facts.

So I sat down, watched, and hoped for a break. The guard might change, rioting might break out, anything could happen.

But it didn't. The part of my brain that counts

breaths hit six hundred, which meant I had been there two hours. I stretched silently, in place, and was about to start thinking more seriously about taking action, when finally something happened.

A musket volley cut down the farthest guard post I could see, bringing all three men to the ground, and something or someone, bent low, barely illuminated by the lights of the city behind it, ran across into the area Pompey's men had cordoned off. There were blazing flashes as other guard posts fired their muskets, but whoever had just shot his way in was moving too fast for anyone to have time to fire—the figure was gone into the shadows just as the muskets fired—and besides, the things were so inaccurate that with only three muskets in each of the volleys, probably nothing could have found a mark if the intruder had stood still with a fluorescent bull's-eye on his chest.

My Model 1911A1 was in my hand before I even began to think, and my feet were slamming into the pavement. Sure enough, the guard post to my right pulled over to cover the situation, and I ran behind them into the alley; an instant later the guard post to my left had rounded the temple and was racing past the alley entrance. I was in Pompey's compound, at last. I knew nothing of its layout, it sounded as if there were troops running everywhere firing at shadows, and there was at least one trigger-happy force of some kind or other (quite possibly hostile to me as well as to Pompey) present in the compound—but I was inside, and that was a lot farther than I had been seconds before.

I dove into the shadow nearest the exit of the alley. Nothing seemed to be happening in my view, but I heard running feet and gunshots, so I stayed put.

In a few seconds a group of soldiers came into view. "Anything?" barked the centurion in the group.

"Nothing, sir!" they all said.

"Our men are firing at shadows out there, sir," one added. "We've got to get organized, or there's going to be someone shooting a friend."

"Don't I know it," the centurion said, and started bellowing orders.

They assembled in the small square there, beside the big building that I later learned was the Temple of the Great Mother. I had nowhere to go but back—which would get me nothing—or forward, which would get me shot, so I stayed put. The false dawn wasn't far away, and from the sight of the stars overhead, I judged there was going to be a lot of light pretty soon. It didn't look particularly great.

The group of soldiers were doing a fast roll call, and they didn't like what they were finding; mumbles were running through the crowd. Three men dead at the guard post, eight men missing. Some of those were probably guys who had taken a chance to desert and would be making their way to Caesar to sell whatever they knew—but eight was a lot.

A moment later there was a shout—one of the eight coming out of another alley. There was horror in his cry.

The centurion barked, "Rufus! Humilis! Sine-colle! Get over there and help him! All others, load muskets, form a circle, wait for my command!"

Three men sprinted out of the group and the rest rapidly formed their circle. Moments later, there were two more groans in two more voices, and then one of them shouted, "Sir, it's Quintus and Decius. They've both been knifed in the back. Titiculus here just about fell over them."

"Come back *real* slow," the centurion said. "Everyone make sure you know what you're looking at before you pull the trigger!"

"Leave the bodies, sir?"

"We'll have to. They won't care, and you need to get back here. Now *move*."

A few moments later four figures—one of them moving strangely, probably Titiculus—emerged into the dim light of the square and rejoined the group. They formed up quickly, and the centurion said, "Decurion Alba, take your men and reinforce the guard at the platform. Tell the *imperator* that we cannot hold for long, that we are already breached, and he must act quickly if he is to act at all. The rest of you, we're going to sweep the compound and see if we can turn up this mystery enemy. We'll start to the west."

Dead away from me. I all but sighed aloud with relief.

Sure enough, in just seconds, the century was moving away from me, and one little knot of men—a decurion was supposed to command ten men, but in fact the numbers varied between units the size of one of our squads and one of our platoons—moved to the right, then forward.

I nerved myself and dashed to the next shadow, following Decurion Alba and his men. I really did not like this; you shouldn't know too much about your enemy. It occurred to me that this last century, of all of Pompey's legions, was being literally loyal to the death. I revised my estimate that any of the missing men had deserted; probably they were all dead or mortally wounded, somewhere in the cold dark alleys. Whatever was loose in the compound, it was like walking death.

And there had been no collapse of discipline or morale. These men were trained to die in their tracks, and they were doing it as necessary, for the sake of their commander. It wasn't as if their commander were a better man than their enemy; really there wasn't much to choose between any of these guys, so far as I could see.

I came slowly and quietly around the corner to find that Alba and his men had reached their goal; there was the platform, with great roaring fires leading into bent chimneys that then passed into the balloon through the opening at its bottom. The slight smell of roasting rubber told me that the balloon was made of rubberized linen, the same thing the legion ponchos were made of; under it hung—it took me a moment to realize—a stagecoach body, minus the wheels and axles, mounted on a small boat. Clearly landings were something they weren't terribly sure about just yet.

The balloon was tied down by a cable that looped from eyebolts driven into the pavement around it up to the large band that ran horizontally around the circumference of the balloon, through a grommet there, and then back down to another eyebolt, until finally both ends of it were tied together between two eyebolts on the platform. It would take just one stroke of a sharp ax to send the balloon on its way.

Below the boat, hanging from short improvised davits that protruded all over it, were dozens of big sandbags.

On top of the stagecoach was a pile of wood, not yet lit. I realized at once that there was no easy means of controlling that fire in flight, and since it would be the one thing keeping Pompey aloft, he wouldn't light it until he was in the air, or just before; once it burned out, he would be on his way down to the ground.

It was a big payload, which was why the balloon had to be so large and why it was taking so long to get hot enough for takeoff, but it looked very much like Pompey could probably leave now if he had to.

Over the rumble of the fires burning in the three

furnaces heating the balloon, there was a distant boom, and Alba looked around instantly. "Cannon, sir," he called to someone inside the stagecoach body. "From the north, I think; perhaps they're already at the Aurelian Wall, though I can't imagine why anyone would be stupid enough to try to stop them now."

Whatever Pompey said back was lost on me, but all the men laughed, the kind of warm laugh that breaks the tension. I had a sense of just why these men would follow him everywhere.

My problem was that at the current range, with the .45, I could probably take all the men guarding the balloon before anyone could get a shot into me; they'd have to close with cold steel, and I could turn and run if need be, since I was not weighted down by armor as they were. So purely in theory, I should have started shooting, probably Alba first, then a lot of them. The rest might turn and run, and then I could leap up the ladder into the balloon, put a pistol to Pompey's head, and demand to know what he had done with Chrys.

Possibly, I thought, *she's even in there—she'd be valuable enough for him to hold prisoner, surely. He had suffered a great deal because he didn't have an ATN or Closer advisor, as Caesar and Crassus had. He might very well be willing to have even one he had to keep at knifepoint.*

So the plan was pretty simple. Four or six shots— and four or six men dead—would get me into the balloon, and I could work from there.

The only problem was that I had been watching these guys in their very difficult circumstances for the last hour, and I just didn't want to. Alba and his men were a bunch of fine fighters with exceptional loyalty; the centurion was a guy any fighting man would have followed to hell and back. It didn't seem like they had to die for having picked the wrong side.

You see how it is. I like my enemies either deeply personal, like certain Closer bastards or like the one time I fought myself from another timeline, a timeline where I had actually gone to work for them; or if not that, I like them to be completely impersonal—just figures that pop up and shoot at me, and then I shoot back at them, and that's that.

Either way, that's fine. I sleep okay after that. But when you know just enough for them to be human, and all they are is in the wrong place at the wrong time—well, back before I met Chrys, back when I was still an embittered ash of a human soul with no desire other than revenge, I didn't much care. Being in the wrong place at the wrong time was a perfectly valid reason for someone, even someone likable, to die.

Life had changed a lot. Now it wasn't. I kicked myself mentally for a sentimental fool, but I didn't feel like gunning down several good, decent soldiers just doing their jobs, and I couldn't seem to make my hand reach for the automatic. I had not turned pacifist, or anything—if a Closer had popped up, I'd have been firing before thinking—but I had started to think a little too much and feel a bit too much empathy to be the same guy I had been before.

Why is it that changes of spirit never come when it's convenient?

The cannon in the distance were pounding now, and we heard bugles. Caesar's forces were entering the city, an hour before dawn, in a surprise attack that would carry everything before it. Later I learned that they caught practically the whole patrician class at the riverboat docks and the stage stations.

I stood there with that invading army coming in, with Pompey's balloon ready to go at any moment, and unable to move forward because there were a couple of ordinary guys I couldn't quite kill in cold blood. The first gray streaks of light from the false dawn were reaching across the sky, and in a moment or two I would be visible.

The night was suddenly alive with musket fire, volley meeting volley, and light flashed through the alleys in a bewildering pattern, casting long macabre shadows across the courtyard toward the platform, like dark demons leaping toward the balloon. Alba stepped down and looked around for an instant, clearly unsure what to do; then Pompey leaned out and shouted something, and Alba picked up the ax to cut the lines.

It tipped the balance; if Pompey took off without my getting hold of him, I would lose any chance of finding out where Chrys was. The .45 in my hand barked, and Alba fell dead; I fired double-handed, in the approved police style, and took down two other men.

They shot back, but that ragged volley from men scattered that widely could have hit something only by chance, and they were firing into the dark.

There was another roar of musketry. Clearly an advance guard of Caesar's had arrived and was trying to fight its way to the balloon. Inexperienced as they all were with the effects of musketry at close range, probably what was happening was that two centuries were slaughtering each other, leaving no one able to do anything more than keep firing.

The men who had just fired at me hesitated, moving back and forth as they reloaded. I shot another, and that decided about half of them—they ran to join the others. The rest pointed their muskets, half-blinded probably by their own muzzle flashes before, not able to see where I was.

A voice shouted from the stagecoach, and they

turned and ran to join the rest of their century. The stagecoach door popped open as I ran toward it, and a horse pistol pointed out—I fired a shot, but an upward shot at such a small target, especially while I was running, was hopeless. Still, the hand jerked in for an instant, and that gave me time enough to reach the ladder and scale it, leaping up it several rungs at a time, .45 gripped in my teeth.

The pistol boomed above me, a great spray of red, and nothing happened—he was shooting out into space as far as I could tell, not down the ladder. Then another pistol boomed, and I heard the long hiss of the cable running through its eyebolts and grommets—Pompey had managed to sever the cable, and if you broke it in any one place, it released the balloon.

The ladder, propped against the side of the boat, began to go over, and I flung myself forward off it. I was fifteen feet above the ground, and even as I did it I thought I might well hit the pavement or the hot side of one of the furnaces, but my hands found the knot at the top of a sandbag.

My body swung forward and smashed into the bag, and the pistol in my teeth slammed further in, but I managed to keep my grip. We lurched up into the air, me hanging on to the sandbag by wrapping my legs all the way around it and keeping my hands locked on the knot.

We rose rapidly, the sandbags clearing the top of the three-story-high Temple of the Great Mother by about fifteen feet. If I had let go about then, I might have had a fifty-fifty chance of survival—but that wasn't what I was after.

There was a roar down below; they were trying to bring us down with musket fire, but even at our altitude of less than a hundred feet, the muskets didn't have the *oomph* to get anything up here at any dangerous velocity. For one instant, a lead ball hung in the air, a bit below me and ten feet out in front; then it fell back to earth.

We drifted out over the city; the light was getting brighter by the moment, a pale pink spreading across the deep blue behind us as we drifted westward over the city. I could see the alleys of the city filling with marching troops and bicycles—Caesar had indeed arrived in force. Probably even as I floated upward then, Cicero was hiding under the docks, and Cato Uticensis was being beaten to death by Caesar's legionaries in front of his family, but I knew none of that at the time—all that I saw were the great columns of troops pouring into the city.

There was a little flicking of gunfire from the Servian Wall—probably some of those hastily organized volunteers hadn't quite had the sense to desert. A field gun roared in the dark Via Nomentana ahead and to my left, sending a streak of red fire against the wall. Two more bellowed, and then there was flame and smoke from the Porta Collina; the inner city had fallen already, but Caesar's forces were destroying resistance wherever they found it, rather than bypassing it to give a chance for surrender.

It was thorough and brutal—he was making sure that anyone with the means and the courage to resist did so now, and was killed or captured doing it, so that there would be no nucleus around which to form an opposition. The whole thing was perfectly Caesar—it solved all his political problems efficiently, and in its willingness to slaughter a lot of untrained draftees, it was cruel enough to frighten his enemies into quiescence.

As I had been watching the invasion roll in, we had

passed on from the top of the Palatine Hill, and since it's steep, this meant we were now a few hundred feet in the air.

I was still hanging on to that huge sandbag, my legs wrapped around it, my hands on the knot, the pistol in my jaws. I cautiously let loose with one hand, took the .45 in hand, and carefully tucked it into the shoulder holster, fastening it closed. At least I didn't have to worry about breaking my teeth.

One of the hardest things to get used to about ballooning is how silent it all is, and how still, especially in a balloon like this, with no burner going. Thus when I heard the general's boots on the boat over my head, they boomed distinctly in the morning air, and I breathed very slowly and cautiously, hoping not to be detected.

There was a scraping noise—it sounded like he was climbing around on the lines—and then the *whump!* of a fire starting. He had ignited the additional burner; we would be going up and staying up a lot longer. The balloon rocked gently at the pressure on the various lines as he clambered back down into the boat body.

I was still working on a way to get over the gunwale and into the main body without being detected. The davit stuck out from the side of the boat about two feet over my head; the sandbag between my legs was about the size and shape of a boxer's heavy bag, and not at all easy to climb.

Cautiously, I humped upward once, hard, and got my hands a few inches from the davit. The clump of Pompey's boots was over on the other end of the boat, as best I could tell, and I reached up to grip the line well above the knot.

I tried not to look down at all, or to think about just how far down it was or how long I could fall before I hit.

I pulled myself up on the rope, cautiously unwrapping and rewrapping my legs, getting ready for the hard push up to the davit, still six feet overhead. Another hard pull should bring me to the point where my feet rested on the bag—

With a sickening lurch, the balloon shot upward, rocking hard. I hung on as long as I could, and despite my own advice to myself, I looked down.

A sandbag, like the one on which my feet rested, was tumbling away in the bright morning sun, no doubt to terrify everyone wherever it might crash into the city. Pompey was dropping ballast; now that I listened, I could hear his knife sawing another line; I dared not let go of my grip, for when that line parted—

There was a noise a bit like a pistol shot as the line went. Another sandbag plunged down through the cold morning air. Another line dangled empty from another davit. I realized, suddenly, that given the way this balloon worked, and that he was trying for the maximum possible distance, he had every good reason to get rid of most of the sandbags as soon as possible.

I heard him sawing again, and I threw myself up the line, getting my feet on the sandbag this time and taking a hard grip. Once again the balloon lurched upward as another bag went, and my feet swung off the swinging bag below; I hung by my hands fifteen hundred feet above the ground.

Pompey's footsteps were now coming toward the stern of the boat, where my sandbag hung; probably he was about to balance the load. Even as I thought that, I heard the sawing, closer than ever, and saw the sandbag directly across from mine begin to vibrate. Mine would be next.

15

Climbing up hand over hand, not using your feet, is one of those things you do so endlessly in ATN Training School that it's second nature, and I was climbing as hard as I could before I even had put my situation into words. Still, I had never done it when it was quite so far to the ground, nor when at any moment there might be another hard yank.

Just as I reached for the davit, the jerk came, another sandbag plunging away. I was ready for it, but it did make me swing backward and forward alarmingly before I got a hand on the davit.

A shadow fell across me, and before I could think—and a good thing, too, thinking is way too slow at a time like that—I had kept my grip on the davit, let go of the line, and yanked the .45 out, pointing it upward into Pompey's surprised face as he was about to slash my hand, which would have severed the tendons and sent me plunging.

"Don't even think it," I said.

He leaped back out of sight, and I started to work on swinging up onto the davit, using just one hand. I couldn't holster the gun without the risk that he would be back to cut my hand, and I had only one hand to hang on with, so I was trying to get my legs up and around the davit, which was taking a lot of swinging.

It didn't get easier when, with a bang, he used one of his horse pistols to cut another sandbag free, and yet another. The jerks made my swinging wilder and uncontrolled, and for one god-awful second all the pressure of my weight was on my wrist, torqued as far as it would go, with all the city of Rome and the land around it spread out far below me, and my body swung far out away from the hull of the boat, feet pointing into empty sky.

But that gave me the momentum I needed, and he was reloading, so I whipped forward, kipped up, and got my legs around that davit. My thighs locked, and now at least I would be harder to get rid of.

Two more bangs dropped two more sandbags—now only the one below me was left—but I no longer cared much, securely locked on as I was; I sat up hard, caught the gunwale with my left hand, levered myself into position, and came up pointing the Model 1911A1. Pompey crouched in the bow, his horse pistol braced and leveled, about fifteen feet from me.

"You've got about a 50 percent chance of hitting me, maybe, if you're really good with that thing," I said, "and I suspect you know that."

"Granted," Pompey said.

"Watch this," I said, and fired two rounds out to the side. "I've got three left. If we start shooting, figure the odds are overwhelming you're dead."

"Very obviously true," he said, and sat down, keeping the horse pistol level at me. "Depending on just what you intend to do to me, however, it might be better to take your chances. I assume I am in the presence of Marcus Fortius, the ATN agent?"

"You are. And I believe you sent me a note implying that you were holding Chrysamen ja N'wook prisoner. Do you have her with you?"

What he did next I could never have anticipated.

He burst out laughing. There was a strange quality to it, because he seemed not quite able to stop, and he kept right on laughing till tears ran down his face, and he got quite red in the face.

He had been a handsome man in his youth, with curly hair, a firm chin, flashing eyes, and high cheekbones—he could have been a film star in my timeline, kind of a squared-off Kirk Douglas. Now, he was close to sixty and running to flesh, a baggy second chin hanging in and his jowls a little too prominent. The laughter brought so much color to his face that I could see a few little broken veins in his nose, probably not so much from drinking as from having been out in the weather too much.

It was the kind of laugh that makes you think of every really sick joke you know, the kind that you laugh at because they are so nakedly horrible in their implications that it's the only way the mind can defend itself. And at the same time, there was something brave in it—a little touch of courage, like the kid who whistles when he goes by the cemetery, but goes by it anyway.

At last he stopped, and said, "Thank you for not shooting me for a madman, sir. Well. The gods have often had their way with me. The Judeans claim that this is because I invaded their Holy of Holies and saw their Ark of the Covenant, which they say contains the tablets on which their god wrote down some wholesome advice for them. Perhaps they are right, for ever since I returned from the East, there has been one catastrophe after another, whether I tried to act nobly for the common good or merely to look after my own interests. And so often it has been just this sort of bizarre prank of the gods. It is said my *genius* is somehow bound up with Mercury, who is the god of transformations and changes, and moreover is reputed to have a dreadful sense of humor."

"Our *genii* probably know each other," I said. "Suppose you tell me the joke, so we can both laugh."

He sighed. "It was a bluff, you see. I had almost caught her, but she turned out to have some unexpected skills, and, well, she escaped from several of my best men, leaving a couple of them dead, if that's of interest, even while I was drafting the message. Suddenly all I had of her was a few curls from her head. So I enclosed those in the letter, and I calculated that if she got back to you soon enough, the only harm done was that Caesar would know I was willing to lie to him—which he surely knew already. But in a war zone, many things can happen, and besides, ATN has a program of its own that might send her in another direction. If she didn't make her way back to Caesar, I might get him and you to expend valuable effort in finding her. So now I find that all that I did was very nearly ruin my escape . . . or perhaps it's already ruined. Well, you may keep me at gunpoint as much as you choose, and you can trust me or not, but I know that ATN has no preferences about who wins this struggle, so I shall put this thing away"—he tucked the horse pistol back into its scabbard—"and now, if you're willing, we can wait out the journey. There's more than enough food and water on board for two."

I thought for a long while. "You have no idea what direction she escaped in?"

Pompey sighed. "Alas, no information I can trade with. She escaped from us near the Via Flaminia, when we stopped to eat and rest, about ten miles outside the city. That is all I can tell you. Whether she went forward toward Rome or back toward Caesar, I couldn't say."

I figured Chrys must have gone forward toward the city, because if she'd headed back toward Caesar, I'd have met her on the road early that morning, or she'd have even arrived in camp. Which meant I'd probably been pretty close before, and I was getting farther away all the time.

On the other hand, now that I knew she was alive and free, in the city, able to go to Caesar if she needed to, I was a lot less worried.

"Sure," I said. "Why don't we get something to eat, and then see if there's anything to talk about? If you don't mind, though, I'm going to keep this thing trained on you."

"Understood, as I said before. I suppose we should retain that last sandbag in case we need it for landing—or do you perhaps have a sentimental attachment to it?" His mouth curled puckishly.

"Oh, there was a time when I couldn't have parted with it, but I feel different now," I said.

There was clearly no hope of talking him into landing soon—that would amount to a death sentence for him—and for that matter it would have been pretty tough to bring the balloon down even if we had been trying. And now that I suspected Chrys was probably okay, the major worry was Paula and Porter, for whom I could do little even if I were right there in Caesar's camp.

There are times when there's nothing to do but drift and enjoy the scenery. The biggest problem was with staying awake; I had been up all night, but I had a feeling that if I fell asleep and left Pompey on guard, I would be apt to wake up without the .45 and tied up—unless he had decided that I was just a complete liability, in which case I would probably wake up somewhere in the sky, with the ground spread out far below me, coming up faster and faster until a last instant of oblivion.

Pompey undoubtedly had a similar feeling about me. The trouble was that neither of us *knew* about any good reason the other might have for killing him or tying him up; but we also didn't know of any good reason the other might have *not* to, and we also had no way to evaluate how many other deals the other person might have going. Clearly we were on our way to join Crassus, where either of us might expect a warm welcome—or not.

So instead we sat and ate; one advantage of the abundance of slaves (as long as you got to be a master) was that a lot of things were first-rate. He had a bunch of hampers packed with all kinds of goodies, and we ate one of the two hot ones first while it was still hot. Italy rolled by underneath us—we seemed to be being pushed along by a front line from an incoming winter storm, moving steadily to the southwest.

Italy itself runs to the southwest, so we were very slowly drifting down the spine of the Apennines, passing mostly over uninhabited country, edging slowly over to the western side of the peninsula. I got out my thumbnail atlas, which could call up a navigation unit that ATN had implanted on the moon when we first got here, and we determined that we would probably head to the west of the Gulf of Tarentum (or Taranto, in the modern spelling) and pass out over the bootheel someplace. It at least gave us a fighting chance to come down in Macedonia or Greece—Roman territory where the garrisons would still be sympathetic to Pompey.

It occurred to me that the situation now was that each member of the Triumvirate had an advisor from ATN, assuming that Walks-in-His-Shadow Caldwell was still with Crassus, and that his "disappearance" there had been temporary.

"I would assume so," Pompey said. "He does tend to take off for long periods of time. He might have been needed at that western colony, Terra Elastica, or possibly down in Africa Australis, the new colony that he had launched far down Africa. Of course in these days anyone can have bad luck with a knife or a cup of poison, you know, but he had very few real enemies, despite having a very odd sense of humor."

"You've noted that, too?" I asked.

"Do you know him?"

"Haven't met him yet. He's done a fine job here, by the way," I said, "though I'm sure it doesn't seem that way to you. Most timelines that we try to advance don't move nearly this fast or well. Partly it's a matter of this historical period and place being such a good one for it, but it's also Caldwell's effort."

"He's a tall, thin man," Pompey said. "His skin's a sort of brownish shade, roughly the same color, I'm told, as the inhabitants of Terra Elastica. Likes to talk and laugh. Sort of a deep spirit of fun about him. I'm afraid Crassus was the most natural one of the Triumvirate for him to end up with—both men seem to have *genii* that love the mundane and the small details. I have some knack that way myself, as you might have noticed with my use of the rockets—all we Romans do—but Crassus could never look at a thing without

thinking of three ways to make it better and six ways to
sell it. Not a general at all, poor fool, and of course
hopelessly without grace or breeding, but his practical
gifts are remarkable, and that seemed to mesh naturally
with your man Caldwell."

I nodded. There was no particular reason to try to
persuade Pompey that it was his attitude, and those of
the other patricians, that had blinded him to why people like Crassus were bound to take power, eventually
must take power.

We passed a pleasant enough afternoon, watching
Italy roll slowly and all but silently by beneath us.
Pompey was an educated, cultured man, in many ways
like Caesar but with much more personal charm, a
livelier sense of humor, and a keen feeling for irony
that his last few years of disappointments had given
him.

We talked about books and poets, Greek literature
mainly since it was the same for both of us (though of
course much more of it still existed in his timeline). We
discussed the battles that had been fought at dozens of
places we passed over, for it had taken the city of Rome
centuries just to conquer the peninsula, Italy itself had
been invaded a number of times, and more than once
the parts of Italy that were supposed to be Roman allies
had risen to throw off the yoke, causing yet more wars
to blaze back and forth. Pompey seemed a little sad at
all that, finally commenting only that although muskets demanded courage and presence of mind, they
would never require the ability to "look a man in the
eye, shove a bar of iron into his guts, and wrench it
around as he dies before you—and it's that spirit that
makes our fighting men invincible, at least in even
numbers on level ground."

We even managed to talk a little politics; he was

fascinated with the setup of the United States, though I'm afraid he perceived all the checks and balances of the Constitution as a way for rich people to keep their money, and things like the space program, the interstates, and the national parks as ways to buy off the populace to avoid revolt, those being the only purposes of government he could really comprehend.

We were a lot lower than most airplanes commonly go, and the wind was moving us along at not more than about thirty miles per hour, so it was almost sundown when we first sighted the sea ahead of us. It would still be at least an hour until we crossed the coastline, and it was beginning to get cold in the boat, so we decided to dine inside for our next meal, the second hot hamper (or as hot as the straw it was packed in could keep it, anyway).

"This is a very civilized way to travel," Pompey said as he finished the last of his meal, "as long as you don't have much concern about where you're going or when you get there." It was now fully dark outside.

"One of my favorite books when I was a child made that point," I said, polishing off something that could easily have passed for baklava at any deli in New York. Then a thought struck me. "I think we're in trouble."

Pompey was instantly alert. "Explain," he said; it was as if the mask of command had simply dropped across his face.

"It's a cold clear January day out there, and we're at probably ten thousand feet. We should have been freezing our asses off. In fact it was freezing cold when I was first working my way aboard, right?"

"True—*Jupiter!*"

"Yep," I said. "The metal bottom of the burner has been acting as a space heater outside, which is why it was so pleasant and warm all day—and that burner is what was keeping us up. It must have burned out much faster than you had planned on."

We burst out the door; it was dark, and we saw at once that we really were in just that kind of trouble; the underside of the balloon reflected only the faint red glare of a few coals. The fire would surely be out within the hour.

We were just passing over the coast. "That's Barium below," Pompey said, pointing to the faint grid made by the white-stone streets in the dim moonlight. "I recognize it by the plan. Well, we have at least seventy miles to go, a hundred if we're swept farther south. How fast are we going down and how fast are we moving?"

I got out the thumbnail atlas and called in a request; the atlas included a clock, so I then waited five minutes and called in again. Then I worked the calculator; saw the result, worked through it again. "Uh-oh," I said. "We were at 11,604 feet five minutes ago. Now we're at 11,501. And in that time we've covered 1.9 miles. If you project that out, unless the wind picks up, we're going into the drink 50 miles from here. Not far enough."

"Well, first measures first," Pompey said. "Let's see what we've got around that will burn—we need to lose weight, and we need to warm the air."

There wasn't much to start with. The picnic hampers were the biggest single item; we decided we'd want to hang on to a couple of blankets, the rope, the oars, and the maps (Pompey insisted on that last—he clearly had a healthy distrust of technology). It took a little climbing, and there is something about being up in the rigging of a balloon, even in fairly calm air, at night that is tough on the nerves, but we managed to get them thrown into the hopper, where after a minute or two they blazed up.

"What next?" I said. "We don't need the sandbag davits, and that's a few substantial sticks of wood."

We broke them off, and I started to climb up to pitch them in, except for the one that still held our sandbag—we wanted some control on landing if we could manage it—and one other davit, after Pompey suddenly said, authoritatively, "Save that one out."

I set it down in the bottom of the boat, put the tied-together davits into a pack on my back, and worked my way up the lines again until I was over the brazier. The hampers, straw, and spare blankets had mostly burned out already, but when I tossed the davits in among them there was a brief flare-up. I just hoped it was hot enough to get the davits going.

When I got back down, Pompey handed me a large piece of wood, and said, "If you don't mind climbing, I'll be happy to keep handing you wood. I'd like to get that fire built up before it has a chance to go out completely—I don't relish the thought of climbing into the brazier with flint and steel."

"My thoughts exactly," I said, and climbed back up. There was a hole in the chunk of wood, so I put my arm through that, and it was fairly easy climbing.

The problem was that the lines had to run away from the brazier to avoid getting burned, and the most natural and easy way to climb on a rope that goes up at an angle is with your body underneath it. That meant by the time you were even with the brazier, you were too far away from it to throw anything in; you then had to climb back along the lines that ran to the bottom hole of the balloon. Thus you were at least twenty feet up from the boat, and ten feet above the metal brazier, before you could drop a load in.

At least it was easy this time. I dropped in the chunk of wood, right on top of where a few of the davits had begun to burn, and climbed back down. There were several boards tied together waiting for me; Pompey shouted that he thought he had gotten all the nails, but I should be careful. I slung it up, climbed up again, saw that the first piece of wood had caught, and tossed in the bundle. There was a great crash, and sparks flew up into the balloon; I hoped that whatever fireproofing there was continued to work.

When I climbed back down, there was still more wood, including a piece like the first one. It finally occurred to me to ask, "Where are you getting this?"

"I'm taking the stagecoach cabin apart, of course," Pompey said. "The balloon is secured to the boat, not to the cabin, and I'd rather be cold and land in Macedonia than settle comfortably onto the sea."

"Agreed," I said, and set off back up the lines. This was turning into a lot of exercise, so it was warming me up considerably, and the wood in the brazier was beginning to catch as well, so it was getting warmer still. Moreover, as the fire got bigger there, it wasn't quite so necessary to climb all the way out over the brazier in order to hit the fire exactly with each addition of fuel, so the job went faster. After perhaps forty minutes of dedicated work, we had put the whole cabin into the brazier, and it was blazing brightly. The balloon over our heads glowed yellow and red with reflected light, and the bottom of the brazier was hot enough to warm the boat pleasantly.

We helped ourselves to some wine from the supplies, and assisted the balloon further by pitching the empty bottles over the side. Then I got out the thumbnail atlas, and said, "All right, now let's see what effect we're having."

We were back up at twelve thousand feet, and holding steady, now moving at just over two miles in five minutes. "If that fire lasts another hour," I said, "we should make it easily. And with probably only a couple of hours of being unpleasantly out in the weather."

Pompey made a grunt of satisfaction. "After it burns out, you'll see why we saved the entrenching tool. I plan to climb up there and shovel out the dead ashes as well. That should amount to at least half as much as the sandbag."

Another hour went by; on the course that the wind was taking us, we should be coming down in Macedonia in just about three and a half hours—if the fire kept burning long enough.

It actually went a little longer. We had no objections. "We'll actually get there before midnight," I said. "Depending on where we come down, we may not even have to camp out."

We had another bottle of wine—there would be nothing that required us to be sober for at least two hours, and it seemed like a pleasant way to pass the time. Pompey taught me a couple of the basic dirty songs of the legions, and I gave him a couple from ATN training camp. We were delighted to discover a couple that seemed to overlap between the two sets; apparently people who do violence for a living have very similar tastes down through the centuries.

Even through the mild buzz of alcohol, I was still forming my basic assessment, and it was this: Pompey was a brilliant man, and much the more likable guy as opposed to Caesar. You could trust Pompey in a way that you could never trust Caesar.

But Caesar had more brains and more imagination. I hated noticing that, because of what it foreboded, but there you had it; in any kind of contest between the two of them, I would bet on Pompey to put up a brave, honorable, and intelligent fight, and then to lose.

For the hell of it, I asked Pompey how he felt about Caesar's proclivity for raping younger slaves.

"Oh, hell, yes," Pompey said. "Want another glass?"

"Sure," I said. "No point pouring it over the side without straining it through us first."

"By Castor, that's true," Pompey said. He seemed pretty fond of the bottle, I noted, and he was drinking about two to my one. Well, people said he looked a lot like Alexander the Great, who also had a booze problem; and in Pompey's case, given his generally successful career, I wasn't sure it was really a problem. A man can adore getting drunk and still not be an alcoholic.

The thought brought a need to both our consciousnesses, so we both lurched to our feet, grabbed a line, raised our tunics, and lightened the balloon some more. "Hope there are no fishermen down there," I said, joking.

"Ah, fuck 'em. That's what plebeians are for," Pompey said, laughing.

As we sat down, it occurred to me that though we both found that funny, Pompey meant it. But I kept the thought to myself.

As we settled back, Pompey handed me my glass, and said, "Now, where were we? Oh, yeah, Gaius and raping slaves. Well, god knows we've all done that, when we were teenagers; something about the way a slave boy or girl will scream and cry, because of course they're afraid to strike us or really stop us, you know, gets the blood pumping. But most of us find out very quickly that a hurt slave is a bad slave, and that it's far better to treat them with kindness and gentleness so that they'll want to be in your bed, they'll be jealous of whoever else is, and determined to please, and so forth.

"But for Gaius it's just . . . well, he loves power. He's also about as sex-mad as any man I've ever known—

even his best pal and favorite catamite, Marcus Antonius, says that Gaius is 'a woman to every man and a man to every woman.' There are those of us who think that that shows, well, a lack of control at the least.

"And then, finally, there's the matter of . . . now this is talking out of school, you know, but the truth is, Marce, I've gotten to like you. You're a good man for an emergency like this, and I'd rather trust you than not, so if you're plotting to kill me, be quick and give me no warning."

"I'm not," I said, and shuddered, for it echoed what Hasmonea had said a little too closely for my liking.

"I didn't think you were, since you so easily could have," Pompey said. "Anyway, as I said, it's not utterly unknown, there are rumors, but as you probably know, Caesar was my father-in-law for a long time."

I remembered that detail; Caesar was a few years younger than Pompey, and his daughter would have been a whole generation younger, but it was not uncommon for political marriages to have big age gaps in those days. Hell, if you looked at some wives of senators and governors, it wasn't all that uncommon where I came from. "Yes, I remember—her name was—"

"Julia, of course. The family name becomes the praenomen when a woman marries. Well, not to make the story too long, apparently most of the dark rumors are true, and even his daughters knew about it when they were quite young; some of them had slave playmates who were badly hurt by Caesar on his little forays. Now don't misunderstand me—it's a master's right to do whatever he likes with his slaves—but still and all, a man who can't control himself and puts his household into that kind of uproar—well, I think Julia was very happy to be with me, because I certainly run a quieter and kinder house than that. Indeed it was one of the better political marriages I've ever seen, if I do say so myself. And at least this way there's an heir out there descended from both Caesar and me. That might help, someday, in patching all this back together."

We drifted on; I stopped drinking soon enough to be sure of sobering up. As it began to get cold again, I checked our position and rate of descent; if the wind held, we would make Macedonia with twenty miles to spare, so we decided it wouldn't be necessary for the two of us—just a bit alcohol-impaired if the truth be known—to make the dangerous climb up into the brazier and shovel out ashes. We pulled blankets over ourselves and sat idly chatting and eating some hardtack and fish paste; if I was short on sleep, at least I was well fed.

An hour later we had descended to an altitude of only about a mile, and I put on the distance goggles and set them for infrared. Sure enough, there was a swath of coast to the east; though the moon had set and it was too dark to see, especially through the winter fogbanks, the distance glasses showed it thoroughly.

"Piece of cake," I said.

Pompey seemed a bit baffled, and explaining it didn't help much, but really explaining it was just a way to pass the time while we waited out the last hour before landfall in Macedonia. Unless he had a balloon himself, it would take Caesar weeks to get this far; we were perfectly safe. I just hoped that the same was true for Chrysamen, and for Paula and Porter.

After half an hour I got impatient and decided to check again, so I put on the distance glasses and looked.

The coastline was gone; there was nothing but water as far as I could see.

I grabbed the thumbnail atlas, and the way I did

must have tipped Pompey that something was wrong; he was instantly wide-awake and cold sober, and he said, "Are we off course?"

"It looks like—"

Then the image flashed up on the map, showing our course for the last hour and a half. We had come within three miles of the Macedonian coast.

And then we had made a neat little buttonhook, and headed back out to sea. You can't feel a change of direction in a balloon; since you move with the air, there's no wind to go by, and the accelerations are usually very gentle. Thus there had been nothing to alert us to the reversal of our course. Not that we could have done much if there had been; we had no means of spilling warm air from the balloon.

We were now only a thousand feet above the waves, and we were about fifteen miles out to sea, moving farther away from land every minute. "We forgot about the land breeze," I said, suddenly realizing. "At low altitudes, the wind blows strongly away from land during the first few hours of the night."

"*You* forgot," Pompey said cheerfully. "I never knew. Well, I'm glad we saved the oars, and I'm glad you still have your wonderful little navigation gadget. I predict we will have no trouble at all keeping warm tonight."

16

Fortunately for us the sea was reasonably calm, which doesn't happen often in those waters, and most especially not in January. The balloon settled gracefully, and the one sandbag still dangling turned out to be invaluable, for when it hit the water it took on seawater and sank, pulling us down instead of leaving us bouncing. We rose and fell ever so slightly on the sea, the balloon still holding its lines taut above us.

We waited five minutes, to let the balloon cool further, and then cut the sandbag free, sending it to the bottom. The boat stopped listing and righted itself; we began to saw through the lines on the bag of the balloon itself. We didn't want to run the risk of capsizing, so we cut them in pairs, diagonally, one of us on each side of the boat, until finally we severed the last pair of lines and the gasbag rose slowly and majestically above us, drifting off downwind at a few miles per hour.

We turned from watching it go to getting out the oars; the thumbnail atlas could be used to hold us on a

course, so we plotted the shortest one to the coast—
it was all stony beaches along there anyway, and it
wouldn't much matter where we came in, we'd be
walking for quite a while—and started pulling away.
I was in pretty good shape, though tired, and Pompey
seemed to be up to the job as well despite his overweight. Though the wind was against us, it was close to
low tide now, and in another hour would be running
in our favor; unfortunately, tides in the Med don't
amount to much, but we'd take anything we could get.

Rowing is not a real efficient way to get anywhere;
that's part of why it's such good exercise. After a long
hour and a half, we took a break for some cold food,
and to work a little congealed bacon grease into our
hands. By now we were in fairly thick fog, and all the
more grateful for the thumbnail atlas. We seemed to be
drifting a little toward the coast at this point, probably
on some local current, and I figured we might as well
take advantage of it.

We had just finished the meal—and it was occurring
to me that I had been up for almost thirty straight
hours and that getting us navigated to the coast was
about as much as I could do before I would have to
sleep, whether I really trusted Pompey or not—when
we heard a strange sound; a splashing that sounded
like a big rock with water running against it, or
maybe—

The prow of the ship reared out of the fog like a dark
avenging god. There was no time to do anything before
it was upon us; we weren't hit right on the prow, but
slapped hard to the side, hard enough to capsize the
boat and hurl us both into the water.

The black waters of the Adriatic closed over me and
instantly I was chilled to the bone, colder than I had
ever been before. I came up for air with the lookout's

cry ringing in my ears, and something splashed next to me; instinctively I grabbed it and felt it drag me forward in the water. Stupid, half-frozen, and still exhausted by my lack of sleep, I took long seconds to realize they had thrown me a log with a rope tied to it, and were dragging me in.

Minutes later I was alongside, bumping the side of the ship, and they were shouting for me to hold on tight. A few quick heaves brought me out of the water and sprawling on the deck. I looked to my left and saw Pompey, gasping and blowing like a fish.

There were shouts and cries all over the sea, I realized, many of them from the ship we had been brought into. We were not merely in a passing freighter, but in some kind of a fleet.

They rolled us unceremoniously onto stretchers and carried us downstairs. I felt sailors' hands searching around on my body but couldn't seem to move my arms to stop them, not even when they began to pull my clothes off; then I heard some exclamations.

Suddenly there was a blinding glare; I blinked indignantly, as I had been almost asleep, and then saw two men bending over us. "Well, we know who this one is," the older man was saying, looking down at Pompey. He was a small, plump older man who could easily have played a corrupt city councilman, a rude uncle, or perhaps an unsuccessful car salesman in any Hollywood picture, wearing a lumpy-looking not-quite-straight toga under his cloak. "Though how he got here or what he's doing here is a complete mystery."

The other fellow was tall and thin, and when he looked more closely at me, he said, "Oh, I know who this one is, too."

My blurry eyes focused, and I said, "Caldwell?" He looked just slightly familiar, and I couldn't think why.

"Yep. Looks like somebody decided I needed rescuing, back at ATN's Central Command. And might be they're right."

"How—did—you—know—me?" I said. Plainly the older guy must be Crassus, and we had found what we were looking for; so there couldn't be anything so important that it couldn't wait until I got some sleep.

I was just drifting out when he said, "A few times they had me doubling for you, though god knows we don't look alike. I sure hope you're not mad about the little joke on the airliner, years ago—"

"Small universe," I muttered, and fell asleep.

When I awoke, twelve hours later, Pompey was already up and about. My clothes had been wrung out and mostly dried and were sitting at the foot of the bed. I figured I wasn't a prisoner, since my thumbnail atlas, spare clips for the .45, and distance glasses were on top of the pile, along with the .45 itself, still in its shoulder holster. I got up and went up on deck, to find it was another warm, sunny day. I borrowed some olive oil from the cook (it's not gun oil by any means, but it beats the hell out of saltwater), went and found the others, and sat stripping, cleaning, wiping, and reassembling my weapon while I got caught up on what was going on.

Once I heard it, it all fell into place. Walks-in-His-Shadow Caldwell (he was a Mandan, from a timeline where they had been much more successful in dealing with the white man and had a state of their own in the High Plains) had been over in Persia and India, getting his innovations introduced among the Bactrian Greeks that Alexander had scattered through that area two hundred years before, and creating a new trade network, one of many, for Crassus's banks and trading companies to control. "Give it a hundred years,"

Caldwell said, "and I think we'll have Roman roads from Lisbon to Saigon, carrying trade in quantity both ways. And probably railroads as well, if I can ever get us off the jam point with making good quality iron, which is turning out tougher than I expected.

"But anyway, when I got back and heard that Caesar hadn't been kept in line with Crassus's cash, like we were hoping he could, then it was obvious the Civil War was going to break out after all, and right on schedule. That's an obvious catastrophe—I mean, look at what happened even in the unaltered timeline, the Romans lost two whole generations of young men and had huge numbers of foreigners to demob from the legions and settle into Roman society. This could be a lot worse—what you saw at the Battle of Falerii was an example. Neither side really understands in the gut just how much muskets, horse pistols, field artillery, and for that matter plain old stirrups will add to the slaughter."

"Oh, I'm getting an idea of it," Pompey said, a little impatiently. "Yes, I realize neither Caesar nor I had ever fought against an army equipped with firearms, and we had no idea how much damage could be done to our own forces. The butchery was dreadful, and there isn't really time to retrain, either, so I imagine the next battle will be just as bad."

Crassus nodded; he was swaddled up in six blankets and looked like he should be playing some role written for Rodney Dangerfield as he sat there, sipping spiced wine from a cup. "For that reason, Cnaeus, I was delighted to pass my *imperium* to you. I'm not so stupid as to have any trouble telling who the real general is here. Do you see no way of minimizing the slaughter?"

Pompey spread his hands. "I don't, and I doubt that Caesar does. If only we could trust him—but his *genius* is so influenced by Mercury, you know, and by Venus.

He *might* decide to offer honorable terms and then abide by them. Now that he has wiped out the Senate, for every practical purpose, there is no longer a Roman Republic—there is only Rome and its territories. There's no reason why the Triumvirate could not be put back together, perhaps some kind of new Senate created, and our offspring intermarried enough to create a workable ruling house and line of succession, as long as we avoid that explosive word 'king.' I have a son who is Caesar's grandson, you know, and if you have a suitable granddaughter, Marce—"

"This is all in anticipation," Crassus said firmly. "Even if he makes us a decent offer, it will be hard to know whether or not he will keep his word. He has generally been an honorable man—but there's his treatment of the Gauls to be considered, and I find that I feel that if a man keeps his word only when it's not too inconvenient, you might as well just say he doesn't keep his word, and have done with it. I think if he beats us, he will want to consolidate his power, and therefore will be generous—perhaps astonishingly generous—in peace, hoping to make allies of us. By the same token, if we win, and we are generous . . . well, Caesar was always a man who was either at your throat or at your feet. I am afraid we cannot treat him in the way he would treat us."

By the time we finished our conversation, we were coming into the harbor at Barium, which Pompey and I had passed over the night before. The night's fog was gone, and I could see that there were hundreds of ships following Crassus's lead vessel; they had made an unprecedented night crossing, taking advantage of the sea breeze at night in Greece and the land breeze in the morning off Italy, because Caldwell also had a thumbnail atlas.

Nobody would have expected them anytime so soon, and with luck they would be one full day's travel on their way to Rome before Caesar's agents alerted him.

Moreover, Caldwell had come up with a secret weapon—the rubber-coated horseshoe. Apparently in his timeline the horse had lasted a little longer in competition with the automobile, and it was discovered that horses' feet, like anyone else's, preferred "sneakers" for walking on hard pavement. The Romans didn't even shoe their horses, so what Caldwell's newest innovation meant was that Crassus and Pompey could bring a much larger force of cavalry onto the field. Further, he had duplicated Caesar's field artillery, though he didn't have quite so much of it, and the armorers even now were looking at Pompey's multiple-rocket launcher.

Of course, Caesar might have a trick or two of his own.

Pompey had stolen the horse pistols, hoping to have them duplicated for the next time he commanded cavalry, but oddly enough it didn't matter that they had gone to the bottom of the Adriatic. Crassus had brought something better than the pistol; he had Parthian cavalry.

The Parthians were a tough bunch of nomads who had been running Persia and most of Mesopotamia before Crassus turned up with muskets. (In my timeline, or for that matter in Caldwell's or Chrys's, Crassus and a Roman army had been wiped out by the Parthian cavalry at Carrhae in 53 B.C. I thought it wouldn't be discreet to mention that.) The secret of their success was a short, powerful bow and ages and ages of practice at firing it from horseback.

Caldwell had given them stirrups, for a more stable

platform, and the compound recurve bow—which meant that they had three or four times the rate of fire, accurately and at longer range, than Caesar's Gauls did. Plus, if we met somewhere in the middle of Italy, as was expected, Caesar's cavalry would have many more horses unfit for service, due to fast marches on winter roads, than Pompey, whose Parthian archers would have shod horses.

We had superiority in cavalry. He had superiority in field artillery—Caldwell had only been able to make a few pieces, and his crews had nothing like the experience of Caesar's legions. And naturally infantry would be what would settle it anyway, and that was about even. So at the moment it looked like a toss-up.

They were planning to stay one day at Barium, and Pompey was already trying to figure out how to get kneelers and musket holes on every *scutum,* plus have enough drill time to get everyone acquainted with Street Firing. I told him about the hollow square technique that was used in the eighteenth century of my timeline for a defense against cavalry, and he groaned. "Oh, Jupiter, Marce, not *another* thing for them to learn. These forces are good—no, they're magnificent— but so much to learn in one day, and then to march the next and quite possibly fight within days of then! And if you've got a defense against the kind of cavalry attack that threw my flanks back at Falerii, I *have* to make time to teach it to my men. I can't let them die from being underprepared." He sighed again, turned back to work, and then sent a legate after me to take down notes on everything I remembered about the hollow square, which wasn't nearly enough.

The reason that we had sailed into Barium, instead of other ports like Brundisium or Tarentum, was that it offered the maximum surprise; if we had sailed farther up the coast, the next road suitable for moving legions was at Hadria, hundreds of miles to the north, and we'd have been detected; if we had come in any farther south, we would have had to travel farther by road, giving Caesar more lead time. Barium, located right where the heel joins the Italian boot, was perfect, with a road connection from the Via Minucia to the Via Appia, and thence to Rome. It meant a long hard march for Caesar, no way of sneaking around to get at our backs, and therefore—we hoped!—victory.

Always assuming Caesar didn't think of something even more clever.

Even in winter, the southern parts of Italy are mild, and it was a bright, sunny day in Barium. I enjoyed a day of loafing, went to bed early, and found myself on a bicycle, riding with Caldwell and the generals, very early the next morning. At least this mission was getting my thighs in shape.

We took our time, keeping the army and the horses in peak condition and also giving us more time to drill. We camped that afternoon just twenty miles from Barium and spent several more hours working through everything—Street Firing, hollow squares, firing from behind the *scutum*. The next town of any size was Canusium, a bit over twenty miles away, and we rode there the next day and repeated the process. It was deliberately kept pleasant and simple, but discipline was kept tight.

"What I hope," Pompey explained to me, "is that Caesar will note, for example, that Canusium threw open its gates for me. With a bit of luck we can make it appear that the whole south is solidly for us, and our slow, steady progress will help put political pressure on

him to beat us before too many territories ally themselves to our cause. Already we've got a dozen garrisons
in the south going over to our side.

"And if he's forced to act quickly, then it is all to our
advantage to keep our marches short. He's going to
have to come to us for his battle, and I want him to
have to come a long way in a hurry."

Before dawn, I was dozing uneasily in the room that
had been found for Caldwell and me in Canusium
when suddenly there was a crash of horns and the
sound of many feet running. I jumped up and was
dressed just an instant before a messenger boy arrived
to tell us that we were needed in Pompey's quarters.

When we got there, the noise and confusion were
overwhelming, but Pompey looked as if he always rose
at this hour and had just gotten out of his morning
bath. "Well," he said, "I have to admire the old bastard.
Caesar not only got here, he found a way to get behind
us, and one that few Romans could resist. He's at
Cannae—the battlefield where Hannibal won his
biggest victory."

I looked at the map spread out before us. Cannae
was almost on the coast, less than ten miles from
Canusium in the valley of the Ofanto. "How did he—"

"A forced night march down an old unpaved military road in the valley, after a forced day march of
more than forty miles. His scouts stalked mine, and his
whole army slipped in between patrols! Magnificent! I
can only hope his men are as tired as they should be
from all that."

Outside, centuries were forming up, and soon the
creak and thud of thousands of wooden bicycles filled
the air. The finest army Rome had ever seen was rolling
out.

The old road down the river valley was not a good

one, but it was adequate for the purpose, and the way it was rutted told us clearly that Caesar had indeed passed this way. The dawn found us forming up on the broad plain of Cannae, where Hannibal had thrashed a Roman army 150 years before, using the same double-bow tactic that Pompey had tried unsuccessfully against Caesar.

Caesar's forces, seen through distance glasses, were unprepossessing; he seemed to have left most of his cavalry and even a great deal of his field artillery behind. If he had hoped to take us from the rear, entirely by surprise, he must have been counting excessively on the power of that surprise, for "I'm not sure there would be enough forces there just to watch us all, even if we were all unarmed prisoners," Pompey said. "I suppose it could be the madness that is supposed to come with power. Or he has a huge reserve somewhere, but my Parthian scouts have not been able to find that, and two of them have circled his whole force looking for some hidden line of communication. It's as if he's daring us to attack. And why no attempt at a last-minute parlay? With the new weapons, even if this is as one-sided as it looks, there will be tens of thousands unnecessarily dead . . . well, gods hear me, on his head be whatever comes."

Strangely, too, Caesar sat there waiting for us. His position was good, and well entrenched—we couldn't take him by surprise with a sudden assault—but he did no probing, did not seem even to be interested in what our scouts were doing around his forces.

"Gods, gods, gods," Pompey muttered. "It's so utterly unnecessary if he's going to do it like this. He didn't bring forces adequate to win, but he brought more than enough to bring the death toll to the highest Rome has ever seen in battle. What can that mad-

man be thinking? And as the weaker party, I would
have expected him to take advantage of the first attack,
but no—he sits and waits." Pompey pushed the map
away and straightened. "We can find no trap. If he
wants to kill himself in such a novel way, I suppose we
shall have to let him."

The forces had been in position for some hours now;
the musket-armed legions mainly in the center, with
wings of Parthian cavalry and Greek and Judean
archers on the near flanks, and the field artillery to the
rear of the flanks, ready either to execute an "end run"
and catch Caesar's army in the cross fire, or to move in
and provide cover for the center.

Normally the battle would have been joined within
an hour of dawn, but Caesar had not cared to attack,
and Pompey had preferred to use the time for thorough
preparation, trying to hold the death toll, at least on
his own side, down. As I looked out over the broad
plain, from where I stood on the hastily erected observation tower with Walks-in-His-Shadow Caldwell, I
finally said, "Pompey is right, you know, Walks. This
whole thing makes no sense at all."

"I don't understand it either," the Time Scout
answered. "And I don't trust anything I don't understand. Not when Caesar is involved. There's something
up his sleeve for sure."

The signal was given, and the standard-bearers
advanced; slowly, deliberately, the legions in the center
of Pompey's line began to advance. Just as slowly,
those from Caesar's line—only about two-thirds as
many—advanced toward us. I put on my distance
glasses and looked; I could see that some of them were
exhausted and stumbling already, and my heart ached
a little for the fact that they had poured their hearts
into getting here for the battle, and now they were not

the least bit fit for it. It appeared Pompey was to preside over a massacre, whether he wanted to or not.

Now the Parthians were in motion, swinging wide, getting ready to shower Caesar's legions with a cross fire of their deadly arrows. The tower under us vibrated so that we could feel it through our feet, and the distant thunder of their hooves put us in awe. In the bright winter sunlight, it was like a scene out of some great epic, the slow-advancing lines in the center led by their eagle standards, and the great sweeps of horsemen on either side.

From the middle of Caesar's forces came a thin, black stream of something into the air—something almost invisible that seemed to scatter. "Walks," I said, "what do you think that is?"

"What do I think *what*—Holy shit."

The Parthians went first, horses slowing to a walk and then stopping, their bewildered riders perhaps kicking them once before falling off them. Then the legions began to fall over, and I realized that "I think he has—"

Suddenly my knees became very warm, soft, and weak, and I sank to the floor of the observation tower. It got really dark, darker than it ever does at night, and I had the most wonderful, happy dreams.

When I woke up, three hours later, I was quite hungry, and there was the pleasant odor of hot beef soup. I opened my eyes to find I was sitting upright, with my feet in leg irons, inside a large tent. Crassus and Pompey sat facing me, and Walks was to my left, and all of them were locked up, too. All of us were just coming awake, Pompey next after me, then Walks, and finally Crassus, who had a joyous, beaming smile on his face until he began to wake.

With all of us awake, none of us could think of anything to say, so we remained silent. I kind of wished I could fall back into my dreams.

The smell of soup got stronger, and the tent flap opened, and in came Gaius Julius Caesar himself, followed by slaves with the hot soup. "Now, gentlemen," he said, "you are supposed to be hungry, so first you will eat and then we will talk."

I was about to say something when a bowl of soup was put in one of my hands, and a spoon in the other; then I was eagerly gobbling it, as was everyone else there. When we had all finished, I said, "You figured out how to use the NIFs. And you must have figured out how to reload them as well, because they don't carry enough rounds to knock out the whole army. You took us all prisoner—"

"Almost all," Caesar said. "I'm afraid there were at least eight broken necks from people who fell unconscious at bad times—snipers dropping out of trees, men whose horses hadn't been knocked out first, that sort of thing. It's odd, but I find I'm made more sad by those deaths than by all the ones my legions ever suffered—perhaps because I know all their names, and saw all their bodies, and I am now writing letters back to their families."

Pompey sighed. "So now you have us utterly in your power. What do you intend to do with us?"

Caesar smiled. "Would you concede that I have the power of the *imperium*? I mean, in all truth, Cnaeus. Does it seem to you that my *genius* has given me that?"

"I suppose I must concede it—I would have to be stupid not to. And I must say that I don't feel very confident that I have any such power anymore."

"Nonsense," Caesar said. "It is only that mine is superior to yours. Is that clear to you?"

"Painfully so."

"And you, Marce," he said to Crassus. (Crassus's name was also Marcus, like mine. The Romans only had fourteen first names, so it was hardly surprising that there were a lot of us.) "Would you, too, bow to my *imperium*—if it were understood that you had an *imperium* of some worth yourself, inferior only to mine, coequal with Pompey's?"

Crassus seemed uncomfortable. "Gaius," he said, "the gods alone can bestow *imperium* or take it away from us; we claim that we have it, but it is up to them to make that true or not. I would not want to tempt divine authority, but, nonetheless, I would say that it is clear your *imperium* supersedes mine, and I bow to your better judgment for the rest."

"One might even argue," Caesar said, "that a better judgment in such matters is very nearly a matter of divinity. But this would be for later."

"You would dare that?" Pompey said. There was no horror in his voice, the way a modern Christian might feel about a man declaring himself to be god; there was only admiration at the audacity, I realized.

"I would," Caesar affirmed. "Though not just immediately. But how is a man to know what he can grasp unless he reaches, eh? Well, then, you see what I offer."

"You would like," Crassus said slowly, "to merge our armies, to re-create the Triumvirate, and then, I should guess, to reconstitute the Republic with your family as the most important, and with ours heavily married into it. You will make great men of us so that you can be the greatest man in history, without rivals."

"Just so."

"I accept," Pompey said at once. "I have battled your *genius* too long, Caesar, and mine is not up to yours."

"And I accept as well," said Crassus. "So far as I am concerned, you are the one true *imperator*."

Imperator, I thought to myself. One who has the power of the *imperium.* In my timeline, that title came down to English as *emperor.*

The Republic had died here, too—five to twenty years early, depending on what you counted as its end—and here, too, the Empire had been born. Brutus and Cassius, along with most of the Senate, were already dead. Julius Caesar was the true first emperor—

"And as for you of ATN," Caesar said. "Hear me. I shall move my timeline forward as fast as I can, and I acknowledge that your enemies, the Closers, are equally my enemies—*any* Roman's enemies in that they are Punics and Moloch-worshipers. I will gratefully accept any assistance you offer. I trust that this is satisfactory?"

Walks-in-His-Shadow glanced at me, and said, "You're the senior ATN officer in this timeline."

"Then it's fine with me," I said. "More than fine. I am delighted that matters have come out in this way."

Inside me there was a sigh of relief; mad as Caesar might be in some ways, and repellent at the personal level, we knew also that he was brilliant, and that in his drive to make Rome great, he would build us a powerful ally. Something somewhere had gone wrong, clearly; perhaps Hasmonea had managed to divert the timeline a little bit. But still, we had given them a huge technical boost, and Walks-in-His-Shadow would have decades more here to move them along. With the Triumvirate intact again, there was also little to fear in the way of a civil war; the battles of Falerii and of Second Cannae would be the whole history of the war.

The new Empire would still have the military genius of Pompey and of Caesar himself, and the business acumen of Crassus, working together in a world that was much larger and much less damaged. Their future, in short, was as bright as it could be, and if Caesar was not a paragon of virtue, he would rule efficiently, intelligently, and humanely, and that's what matters in a ruler.

Then Caesar knelt and unfastened the leg irons on all of us; more than that, he handed me my .45 in its shoulder holster. Clearly he believed that when you trust a man, you should trust him all the way.

I fastened on the holster, knowing now that whatever I had been told, it was wrong. I would never assassinate Caesar; my mission here was accomplished, and no such thing had been necessary. If this was a screwup, I was damned proud of it.

"For the rest," Caesar said, "I regret to say that we haven't found any trace of your wife yet, though I do still have people working on that. We'll provide you every assistance once we get back to Rome, where you can draw on whatever resources you need in your search."

I nodded. "Thank you, *imperator*." The term seemed to come very naturally to the tongue already.

"And also," Caesar said, "there are some people who would like to see you."

Five minutes later I was being hugged as hard as Porter and Paula could manage. I wanted Chrysamen to turn up, and I was worried, but there was a good chance that she had just been lying low in Rome until it became clear which way the wind was blowing. If so, she would probably come out to meet the army as we moved up to Rome. Somehow I felt very sure that I would see her again.

That evening, there was another special event; Porter had been practicing for many hours on the lyre and the Roman flute, having nothing better to do with her time, and she gave a private concert for the Triumvirate and a small circle of invited guests. I sat next to Paula, who said, "I worry a little about her and Caesar."

"Is she, uh, encouraging—"

"God, no, but she still glows with pleasure at the attention from him, and *that* encourages him even though she doesn't mean it to. And besides, she really is fascinated with the Roman instruments, and he really does have a great ear for music."

The music was just beautiful and everyone applauded madly; Porter seemed delighted, and I don't think I've ever heard her play better. During the party afterward, everyone crowded around her to praise her playing, and I could see the kind of glow that Paula was talking about. It did look really good on her.

The celebration of the New Triumvirate and of Caesar's investment as *imperator* was made all the more uproarious by the fact that so many thousands of men who had expected to die, or to see their friends die, were alive and unhurt. The release from the terror of the new weapons seemed to come out in a sort of joyful silliness that veered between an orgy and a really good kids' birthday party.

It was a long party, and it got pretty wild after a while; I noticed Porter had gotten drunk, and in my guardianly role, I had Paula drag her off to bed, not complaining much. Paula had had about two beers, I think (Roman beer was heady stuff but they served it in small cups), and they hadn't affected her at all. I figured Paula was probably glad to go—she must be missing Robbie, the Romans were extremely uptight about the kind of things Paula enjoyed, and besides, some of the men had been leering and making suggestions to her.

They were starting to bring in the slave girls, and being the married kind of stodgy guy I was, I wasn't interested. That reminded me that I still didn't know where Chrys was, let alone know for certain if she was okay, and at that point it became a little too depressing to stay at the party. I made my excuses and staggered back to the small tent I had, next to Caesar's, between his tent and the one Porter and Paula shared.

Where the hell was Chrys? It profits a man nothing if he saves the whole universe and loses his reason to live there . . .

Tired as I was, and even having consumed as much alcohol as I had, I was really having trouble sleeping. I thought I might get up and take a walk through the camp, but then on the other hand, getting dressed seemed like too much work. I let my mind drift to happier times, but all the happier times brought my thoughts back to Chrysamen.

There was a scream; I sat straight up in bed. It was Porter's voice. I had thrown my tunic on over my head before I knew what I was doing, yanked my boots onto my feet, and was racing around to Porter and Paula's tent. The tent suddenly glowed as someone unshuttered the night lantern inside it. Porter screamed again. I rushed harder, for I could see motion that looked like a struggle.

Then I heard Caesar's voice say, "Don't, don't, please"—and then I heard a flat barking shot: Paula's .38 had fired once.

There was a long, frozen silence, before the camp had time to react to the shot. In that dull silence, knowing what I would find, I walked to the lit tent, parted the flap, and silently stepped inside.

17

Porter lay on her bed, yanking her nightclothes back down—Caesar had apparently pulled them all the way up, just taking what he wanted, as he always did. Paula still held the .38 snubnose in her hand, her face a mask of flat, bitter hatred.

I reached and took the gun from her. "You don't want to see what kind of justice they have for women here," I said. I felt curiously numb and dead; it was as if I could see the future.

The future arrived in the form of a muscular centurion who seized the gun and knocked me flat with one blow of his fist. I had an untreated concussion from that and didn't wake up for two days, but that posed no problem to Roman justice; it wasn't at all necessary to have the defendant present at his own trial. If he made it to his punishment, that was plenty.

Paula and Porter weren't called on to testify either. There was this minor problem that I had been a prisoner of Caesar's, and he had never formally manumitted me;

I was therefore his slave. And when slave killed a master, no matter what the provocation, there was exactly one possible penalty. Walks-in-His-Shadow couldn't even get in to talk to Pompey or Crassus about it (they were as adamant as any other Romans), and the deliberation lasted a couple of minutes.

It was a good thing my head was still spinning, and I was still dizzy; I had only about enough concentration to wonder why it was in movies and books that if you got knocked hard on the head, you got up in three hours without even a headache. I had been knocked out once playing football and a few times in martial-arts practice, plus I'd had such concussions here and there as bodyguards and Crux Ops will tend to have.

And never once had I felt just fine afterward. Rather, it usually required days to get over it, and I often wasn't quite myself again for two weeks.

Roman justice was not the kind that waited two weeks. As soon as I was coherent enough, and a squint-eyed legion surgeon who smelled heavily of wine attested that he thought my pupils were the same size, they scheduled the execution for the next day at noon.

At least it was winter; that would make it quick. I found out later that Walks-in-His-Shadow had lost his holy-shit switch somewhere in India, in one of those stupid things that can happen to anyone, and that was why a dozen Crux Ops hadn't shown up to whisk us all away, but it was so foreign to my nature to think about calling for help that I never even wondered why he hadn't. Indeed, that was part of why his had gotten lost, the same reason mine had so often—he didn't think about it much either.

You could call it an exaggerated form of not wanting to stop and ask for directions.

The day came, and I finally got to see Porter and Paula, though I was still too dizzy to sit up, so they had to kind of hug me on the pallet where I was lying. Paula was in worse shape than Porter, but both of them were crying. "Boss, I'm so sorry—even now I could—"

I shook my head emphatically, and whispered back, "Are you crazy? Do you know what impalement involves? Just think about having a stake forced into you till it comes out your mouth, if you get tempted to confess. The only reason you shot the bastard, instead of me, was because you got there with a gun first, that's all. We'd have had to kill him. He'd never have left Porter alone, and he'd never have stopped threatening us, if we had just tried to scare him off with the pistols. So I'm just as guilty as you are, and I get a lighter sentence."

"Crucifixion is a lighter sentence?" Paula demanded, still whispering.

"Comparatively, comparatively. I'm a scholar by trade, you know, we make these fine distinctions." I started to giggle; concussions do strange things to you.

After that little performance, Paula and Porter tried to persuade a couple of surgeons to take a look at me—the universal reaction seemed to be that if I was conscious, I was fit to be crucified. After all, it wasn't as if I were going to be doing any of the work.

At least they didn't put me on the upright cross; that would have been a little tough on a boy who was raised as a good Episcopalian. They used the X-shaped cross that is sometimes called the Cross of St. John or the Cross of St. Andrew; it occurred to me as they were dragging me off the litter that it was probably an honor, among the saints, to get a cross named after you, even if you had to share honors with some other saints, but that what you had to do to get your own cross was pretty tough.

It looked like I might be asking them about it myself in a bit. I wondered in that dizzy kind of way, unable to focus, just how the problem of so many alternate souls was handled in heaven. I mean, what do you do with four thousand Mother Teresas, sixty-seven hundred Francises of Assisi, and so forth? It made me giggle again, which got me slapped hard enough to take out a front tooth. My face was exploding with pain, but I was a little too disconnected to be able to concentrate even on how much my face hurt.

My limbs were limp and heavy after the slap—probably he'd started the bleeding in my brain again—so there was no putting up a fight as they held me down on the rough, X-shaped wood. Since one beam lapped over the other, it meant the whole thing pushed a big, heavy beam directly into the small of my back, with my left arm and right leg jammed a bit back behind me. I could tell that in normal circumstances my back would be getting all my attention, but I was still running my tongue over the broken place where my left front tooth had been, and wondering if what I felt on my upper lip was blood from an abrasion there, or if maybe the guy had ruptured a sinus.

The nails hurt, but they hurt most for the second while they go through. They don't put them in your palms, no matter what the religious paintings have told you, or through your wrists either. Your palms are too frail to carry your weight and would tear through; and a nail among the wrist bones would probably bend, and very likely cut an artery and allow you to expire much too quickly.

They put them into the forearm, well up toward the hand, with your thumb turned slightly back to open the space between the radius and ulna, and they put a couple of them in just to be on the safe side. They do the same number with the tibia and fibula on the lower leg.

It hurts like hell, but flesh is soft and the Roman carpenters were practiced at this—each nail went in in just two or three quick strokes, the first one going all the way through the flesh into the wood, the next usually burying the special broad head into the flesh and taking the nail the rest of the way into the crosspiece.

The first jolt of each nail going through was pretty bad, even through the fog of my brain injuries, and the second and third, as the nail moved through my flesh, wasn't so great either. It sort of gave me perspective on my other injuries and the pain where my back was pinned backward.

Then they set the cross up, and my arms and legs had to take the load. The nails tore the flesh a bit before settling into their new positions, and that hurt quite a lot; I apparently screamed and lost consciousness.

I woke up as they threw a bucket of vinegar over me; the strong smell in my cracked sinuses actually hurt a lot worse than the nails. I hung there, sputtering and gasping, while Pompey and Crassus made speeches that I didn't quite catch the gist of, except that they dwelt at great length on what a bad fellow I was, what a swell guy Caesar had been, and just how much I deserved this.

Already I was beginning to feel a little warmer; I was being crucified naked, and I had been kind of counting on hypothermia to give me some anesthesia.

There was quite a crowd, I realized, and I seemed to be the center of attention. I was vaguely bothered by the fact that I couldn't do anything to cover up. I looked around the crowd for a familiar face, but just the effort of doing that made them swirl and whirl like people had when my brother Jerry, my sister Carrie, and I had ridden the "Tempest" at the county fair, as kids. Jeez, with such a big event, I wished they could be here to give me a little support, they'd never missed my football games—

Holding my head steady gradually stabilized the view, and I began to think a bit more coherently. Very slowly I looked around, noting that my arms and legs already felt dead but very warm. Then I saw a face under a hood and felt my heart leap up for a second with happiness, because on a big day like this, with so many people here, I really wanted—

Something made me rear against the nails, sending agony through my arms as I convulsed savagely several times. I felt myself foaming and my tongue coming out of my mouth; I was vaguely aware of the cries of disgust from the soldiers standing guard around my cross, as I lost bowel and bladder control. I could smell the effect even through the vinegar still burning in my wounded sinuses.

It got really dark, and this time there were nightmares.

"Mark? Are you awake?"

I stretched and found that I could move my arms and legs; this seemed like a good sign. I sighed, let my eyes open, and looked up to see the most beautiful sight in the world—Chrysamen ja N'wook bending over my bed. "Am I at—"

"Hyper Athens, of course. You've been under for a week. The nanos are asking for overtime pay, hubby. When the Romans decide to mess a guy up, they're awfully thorough."

I drew a deep breath. "Porter and Paula—"

"Waiting to go back with us. Porter's getting treated like royalty—apparently some of her later recordings in this timeline are definitive pieces of music for them. Though they're being very careful not to let her hear them—I mean, imagine what could have happened if the young Beethoven had gotten to hear the Ninth Symphony. So she's just playing her early compositions, and some Roman music, and of course some of her piano show-off stuff. Oh, and she's doing a great job of putting off meeting with Thebenides, who's frantic to lobby her for something or other."

"Any girl who can say no to Julius Caesar shouldn't have any trouble fending off a two-bit politician," I said. "How long till they let me get up?"

"About one more day. Meanwhile, at least, they're letting me feed you. Will it be hospital soup, hospital noodles, or hospital hot cereal first?"

It's amazing that a civilization that advanced can't come up with hospital food that tastes any better than ours. I didn't mind, all the same. The company was good.

For some reason it's a big deal to Mark that everything gets recorded. I don't know why he writes these books about our adventures since they can't possibly be published, and Porter and his father and sister all hear the story directly from his own lips anyway. Probably all historians are crazy. But since he asked, and since I have most of today while he's resting, I'm writing this while my memory is fresh.

When Mark ducked into the alley in Falerii, I was going after him until all of a sudden a hand twined in my hair (the damned curls are a little too perfect for being grabbed by). The next thing I knew, I was being pinned by Pompey and two of his centurions—they had gone into the burning city looking for a hostage or for anything that might make them valuable to Crassus, with the army lost. It was the kind of bold maneuver Pompey did without worrying much about the risk, the sort of thing that meant he was never more dangerous than when almost defeated, and this time it paid off.

In the process of getting me tied up, one of them lost an eye, the other one got a broken arm, and I lost a couple of hanks of hair. If Pompey hadn't been there, insisting he wanted me alive and unhurt, I suspect they'd just have stomped me to death there in the alley.

The whole thing took just a few minutes; then they faded into the refugee train that poured out of the city, commandeered a cart, tossed me into it under a load of straw, and carried me off to where Pompey's army was regrouping.

No matter what the incentive, the Romans of that day just could not get it through their heads that a woman might be dangerous, particularly an unarmed woman. And the fact that I was out in public, and not an aristocrat, made them think I must be some kind of camp follower, which is the polite word in the history books for "soldiers' whore." So, sure enough, I got a guard to untie me by promising to show him something he'd never seen before, and then showed him the road to Hades with a quick maneuver that snapped his neck, just when he thought we were about to get to the good part.

I saw Mark ride by on the Via Flaminia, but I was staying off the road for safety's sake. I figured I'd meet up with him in Rome.

After a while I joined a refugee column, stole myself

some rags to make a generic "beggar" disguise, and got into the city that way. I had lost all my gear except the holy-shit switch, so I had no way of locating Mark, but clearly Pompey's balloon was the biggest thing going on at the time, so I figured I needed to penetrate the compound on top of the Palatine Hill. There were so many more muskets than there were men to use them that it was no trouble to steal eight of them from the Campus Martius, and since I figured they were pretty useless singly, with their short range and miserable accuracy, I did a little tinkering, saving only the barrels and lashing those together with the fireholes all facing inward to a single percussion cap, to make sort of a giant shotgun.

Then I mounted it in a window facing a guard post, set a fuse to make it go off, and figured it could serve as my diversion. It worked like a charm—that was the "volley of musket fire" that Mark heard that night.

They were looking for at least ten guys, of course, so a single woman slipping through the shadows could get pretty much what she wanted. The trouble was, it turned out all the action was at the balloon, which was still under heavy guard, and I had no way of fighting my way aboard that. So I kept skulking, and a few times I ran into soldiers in dark alleys. When that happened, I hit hard and silently, generally before they knew they were attacked, and they died right there.

It might not have been sporting, but this was hardly a game. If I were Mark, I guess I'd give you the details of each knifing, but it's the sort of shoptalk that doesn't interest me. Sure, everyone is different on some level, but basically the experience of cutting a man's throat so suddenly that he can't cry out, or of smothering his cry for the critical second while you open his femoral artery and kidneys to knock him unconscious, is alike every time. And, to use a great word I learned from Porter, it's mega-icky.

Anyway, I heard the roar of Mark's .45 and got back to the platform just in time to see him departing, hanging on to the sandbag on Pompey's balloon. I really thought he would try the drop onto the roof of the Temple of the Great Mother—it was a lot better bet than trying to fight his way aboard—but what can I say, we're all individuals. He does things his way, I do them mine.

It seemed to me there was now a good chance that Mark would start working some deal with Pompey, or maybe with Crassus, and since we already had an "in" with Caesar, and were about to have one with the other army, it was probably best to stay loose and see what else I could manage. You never know when the ability to act independently can come in handy.

Naturally I followed Caesar's army south—and that was quite a ride, the worst part of the whole job really, especially since I had to pull over to avoid his rear scouts now and then, and then make up the distance after they'd gone on. I got to Cannae just in time for the aborted battle, and figured I would walk in and say "hi" to Mark the next day, once it was clear that the deal was firm.

Well, as they say, things get in the way. I didn't get a clear shot at helping Mark out of that jam until they actually had him nailed up, so I used my idle days to burgle Caesar's effects and retrieve a bunch of ATN hardware, including the NIFs, which I did some field-programming on so that I could have an effect that looked like "having a major seizure from neural damage and then dying on the cross" and would leave him in a pretty cold coma for a day or so. It worked fine; I gave Mark one shot of that, let them return his body to

Porter and Paula, then slipped into their tent and at last hit the holy-shit switch. ATN grabbed all four of us, neat as you please, and that was the end of that mission.

I suppose Mark will complain that I didn't dwell on things enough, but really, though it was scary at times, it was a pretty standard ATN mission. And don't get me wrong—for all his tendency to overdramatize, my husband is the guy I'd most prefer to have on my side in a fight, anything from a barroom brawl to a duel with atom bombs, anywhere and anytime.

Well, Chrys absolutely refuses to expand that part at all, and since I wasn't there, I can't revise it into anything more interesting. You'll just have to take my word for it that she's terrific and much too modest.

A couple of days later, subjective, we stepped back onto the pavement in a parking lot in Weimar, Germany, in our own timeline, where a battle had just finished the day before. The place was crawling with media—when an internationally renowned child-prodigy pianist disappears in a UFO, and then pops back into existence twenty-four hours later just as was promised, I suppose you have to expect that.

You've all seen the speech she made, and nowadays every grade-school kid sees it, so it's probably time to admit, at least in this book, even if it can never see publication for centuries, that Porter had had weeks to think about what she wanted to say. But the words were her own, and they weren't lies. If you look at the story she told, it wasn't *that* far from the truth. There *are* forces out there greater than we are, and they *do* want us to live at peace with each other—and they *have* left it up to us to find a way to do so.

It helped too that she had never played better than she did that night in the National Theater. There were a lot of ghosts in Weimar that night, I think, and most of them would have been very proud to be present at the first of Porter's dozen Concerts for Peace.

I think that Chrys and I were actually the only people who made it to all of them, even the one in Ulster that was almost canceled because of the threats. It's a pretty strange world when you're sitting there, bursting with pride, because the kid you've tended, worried about, loved as your own for so many years, is working so hard to put you and your wife out of work.

Pretty strange, but you can get to like it.

AFTERWORD

Every so often I take it into my head to rush in where angels fear to tread, and usually the way I do that is to set one of these adventures in a period that's familiar. Hardly any historical period of Western history has received, over the last few centuries, the attention that the collapse of the Roman Republic in the last century before Christ has received. The cast of characters alone is wonderful; the heights of courage and depths of depravity are all there.

As may also be obvious, I am not in sympathy with what has been the most common reading of the period; it seems to me that this was not the time when Roman freedom was lost, but merely an inevitable change of jailers. The Senate had stymied every possible measure to empower the poor and to alleviate their sufferings. It was no surprise, then, that ambitious men made the just demands of the poor into the ladder on which they climbed to power. The tragedy was not that the "Old Romans" fell from power, but that they had ever held it in the first place—and that the ones who toppled them were truly little better, indeed, were men of the same kind.

For those who like a history full of noble Brutuses and wise Ciceros, I remind you only that at that time the Latin word *libertas,* the root of our word "liberty," had nothing to do with what we would think of as civil liberties—and everything to do with preserving the privileges of the few, though it brought the world crashing down around their ears.

But I am forgetting myself; at the end of these, I always remind you that these are works of fiction, and that after all they have nothing to do with our present-day lives, or indeed even with our own real pasts.

And also, I always thank that wonderful gang of picky people, the best players of the game of alternate history I know, the group of writers and historians that meets in the Alternate History category of the Science Fiction Round Table (SFRT1) on the GEnie on-line service. I could have done it without them, I guess, but what fun would that have been?

This time around, though, I guess I should remind you strongly that the ideas here are mine; credit the folks below for anything that's accurate, and for being inspiring people to bounce ideas off of, and throw the errors or the parts you don't like at my door. I'd like to thank: Tony Zbaraschuk, Bill "Sapper" Gross, Tom Holsinger, Robert Brown, Kathy Agel, Steve Stirling, Todd "The Mule" Huff, David Burkhead, Timothy "Squire" O'Brien, Al Nofi, Susan Shwartz, Daniel Dvorkin, William Harris, and Dana Carson.